Knocked-up
CINDERELLA

Knocked-up
CINDERELLA

Julie
Hammerle

Entangled Publishing, LLC
2614 South Timberline Road
Suite 105, PMB 159
Fort Collins, CO 80525
rights@entangledpublishing.com

August is an imprint of Entangled Publishing, LLC.

Edited by Kate Brauning and Stacy Abrams
Cover design by Elizabeth Turner Stokes
Cover photography from Shutterstock

Manufactured in the United States of America

First Edition November 2018

For Indy, who was with me while I wrote this book and remains with me in my heart.

Chapter One

ERIN

I reached under my voluminous tulle skirt and scratched my butt, once, twice, three times—heck, no one was around. I'd been hiding behind a massive topiary in the hallway outside the ballroom of the Evanston Hilton Hotel ever since I'd escaped a herd of drunk second-grade parents and their ten thousand questions about the school's paltry foreign language program. My dress itched. My nylons itched. I was developing a pretty massive blister from the clear plastic stilettos I had borrowed from my friend Natalie. Even my earrings were killing me. They were like glittery boulders dangling from my lobes.

But I'd make it through tonight. Somehow. I had to.

Using my phone's camera as a mirror, I checked my appearance. Back when I taught English to fourth graders, I'd ask the kids to add "sparkle" words, fancy adjectives, to their essays. The "sparkle" words for my current state included "laughable," "absurd," "risible," and "ludicrous." I was a forty-year-old woman—a forty-year-old elementary school *principal*—in a half-baked Cinderella costume. At least it was Halloween and not, like, some random day in March.

Having to show up here tonight was an unexpected "perk" of my new job. I had to stay and ride it out, all while wearing a smile. I had to prove to the parents, alumni, and assorted boosters that I was a team player, that I was game enough to make a fool of myself up on stage with the rest of the single ladies to raise money for the Glenfield Academy Athletics Association.

This bachelorette auction marked the first of many, many planned fund-raisers this school year, including the Wintertime Alley Night (yes, the school had a functioning bowl-a-rama in its basement), the Cupid's Crush Valentine's Day Ball, and the elaborate, black-tie Glenfield Gala to close out the year.

After reapplying my lipstick, I hiked up my skirt and yanked at the waistband of my nylons. If the shoes didn't kill me, these control-top pantyhose would. I stretched the band to the hilt and let it snap, satisfyingly, against my stomach, just like, I'm sure, the real Cinderella did whenever she had a moment alone.

A cough from across the way drowned out my sigh of momentary relief.

Heart ramming against my ribs, I dropped my skirt and peered around the side of my topiary sanctuary. A shock of dark hair peeked over the bush on the other side of the hall. I had been operating under the assumption of solitude. I'd scratched my ass. I'd—oh crap—lifted up my skirt and fixed my nylons. My face right now was an inferno.

"I didn't want to say anything." The lurker stepped out from behind the bushes. This guy had come dressed in a regular old tux in lieu of a costume to an event the planning committee had expressly billed as a "costume party." What a rebel. "You seemed to think no one was around."

"Yeah, I kinda did, dude who leers at unsuspecting women from bushes outside hotel ballrooms." I stayed put behind my little tree, finger poised on my phone's 911 button.

"I swear I wasn't leering." He held up his hands in surrender. From what I could see through the branches, he was not unattractive. But still. He was a lurker. I kept my finger where it was. "I was hiding, too."

"What makes you think I was hiding?" I'd entered interrogation mode. The same skills that made someone a stellar FBI agent made me an excellent teacher and elementary school principal. "You're the one who said 'hiding.' Who were you hiding from?"

"Well, that's personal."

Phone still at the ready, I stepped out into the open. Time to be a grown-up. Time to put on my professional principal persona and take charge, nip this conversation in the bud. Besides, while it was true that this guy could be here to harm me, the more likely scenario was that he was someone important to my career—a parent, a rich alumnus, a reporter. I owed it to myself and my profession to handle this ugly situation with grace—all the while prepared to scream bloody murder if necessary. I held out my right hand, the one I hadn't just used to scratch my butt. "I'm Erin."

His eyes lit up with recognition. "Erin Sharpe!" He grinned and, whoa, it hit me that my earlier assessment of "not unattractive" was a gross understatement. This dude was hot—tall and lean but muscular, in his expertly fitted suit. He'd tousled his cocoa-colored hair in a way that was supposed to look natural but probably took him a half hour to accomplish, and he wore glasses with thick black frames that would've looked nerdy on anyone but him. They made him look like Clark Kent, only minimally masking his Superman persona. Pursuing this guy would stress me out. He was much too cool for me. I bet he stayed up way past ten p.m. and enjoyed "spending quality time together." Definitely not my type.

Besides, he was a tree lurker.

I mean, obviously. I had standards.

Yes, I was dressed like fucking Cinderella at a bachelorette auction, but I had standards.

Also, yes, I was an elementary school principal who used the word "fuck" liberally while not at work. You would, too, if you spent most of your day biting your tongue around surly parents, snippy teachers, and unruly students.

"How do you...?" I asked. Even though I knew how he probably knew me. It had been big news around these parts when I left my job in the Chicago Public Schools to take over as principal at the Glenfield Academy. Chicago was a series of small towns in a big metropolitan area, and I'd come in as quite the curiosity on the North Shore—an outsider from "the city," who had never attended private school before, let alone taught at one.

"You're Dirt's girlfriend," Glasses Dude said.

Thaaaat...was not what I'd expected him to say.

He narrowed his eyes and shook his head slightly, waiting for a hint of recognition from me. "We met at Loyola...?"

Ohhh. Right. The night my ex had dragged me to his twentieth high school reunion so he could show all the guys who'd once shunned him that he still had his hair. "Dirk," I said, though who knew why I bothered to defend him by invoking his real name. Old habits died hard, I guessed. "And we broke up."

Glasses Guy grinned. His teeth were perfect, straight, and white. My dentist dad would probably tell me to lock this dude down now, which, *get out of my head,* Dad. *He's not the one for us.* "You stole the wine," the guy said.

"Say what now?" I knew exactly what he meant but was

shocked he remembered it.

"You stole the wine."

"Yeah, *I* know what I did, but why do you?"

"Because it was the most amazing thing that happened that night. You saved the whole party." He raised his hand and I reached up to high-five him, which was odd, but... okay. I may have noted the size of his hands in the process, not that I looked on purpose. It was just that Dirk's hands had been so small we could've shared gloves. The difference was staggering. Anyone would've noticed. Whoop-de-do, Superman had big hands. It hardly counted as breaking news.

"Dirk didn't think my stealing the wine was so great," I said.

"Dirk's an idiot."

I shrugged. I couldn't argue with that. At least not anymore.

The guy swept his arm in front of him as if preparing to paint me a mental picture. "Our twenty-year high school reunion. Everyone drinking and having fun, so much fun that we ran out of alcohol. And who comes out of the woodwork with a brilliant idea no one else had thought of—to run up to the school library and pilfer the wine from the guys celebrating their thirty-fifth reunion?" He stared right at me. "You."

My face flushed. Dirk had full-on berated me during the car ride home. He'd said I'd embarrassed him by taking the six unopened bottles from upstairs. I shrugged. "I just figured the thirty-fifth reunion was filled with a bunch of straight old guys, and none of them were drinking the sauvignon blanc."

"Like I said, brilliant."

I had not been called "brilliant" by a man who wasn't my boss or professor in about, oh, ten years. It didn't suck. The dude held out his hand again, and I shook it. His hands dwarfed mine. Everything about him dwarfed me, and I was not a tiny lady by any means. Feeling diminutive was a whole new sensation for me, one that I bashfully enjoyed.

"I'm Ian, by the way. Ian Donovan."

"Ian Donovan," I repeated. "So are you a parent or alum?" And, yeah, I checked his finger. No ring.

Ian chuckled. "I am definitely *not* a parent." He looked me up and down, and I self-consciously crossed my arms over my Cinderella dress. "You're in the auction, then?"

"I don't know," I said. "Whatever." I was totally in the auction, but I couldn't admit that to this too-cool guy, who'd called me brilliant. No truly brilliant person had to get up on stage and parade around, begging for someone to bid on her. I felt like an old mutt in a crowded dog shelter.

"Don't be embarrassed," Ian said. "The Halloween auction is a long-standing tradition, and really it only amounts to having to sit next to the person who buys you at dinner. It's fun, and it helps fund the school's basketball teams. No big deal."

"So you've done this a lot?" I asked.

He shook his head. "Never. I come for the spectacle only. No bidding."

"You come to watch the single women get picked over by the kind of guy who needs to buy a date."

"It's not as tragic as you make it out to be. No one expects the date to extend beyond tonight, believe me. My best friend, Scott, buys his mom every year. Seriously. Just think of this as a free meal."

A free meal. That was how Nat had sold the event to me after my first anti-auction tirade, knowing I'd be loath to turn down a dinner. A girl's gotta eat. "Well, I do love Stephanie Izard." The "date" at the end of the auction was dinner at Girl and the Goat. Even if I didn't meet the love of my life tonight, at least I'd be treated to some spicy *hamachi crudo* and green beans that were, in my experience, way better than sex.

The door to the ballroom swung open and the auctioneer's voice boomed. "Our first bachelorette tonight is the lovely and talented travel blogger, Maria Minnesota…"

Game time.

I nodded toward the ballroom. "You coming?"

Ian stared at the door. His face had gone white. "No."

"Suit yourself." I made a move toward the door and nearly ran right into Natalie.

"Erin, I've been looking for y—" Her eyes snapped to Ian. "*You.* You stay away from her." Hands on hips, Nat glared at him. She looked glorious in her Nakia costume from *Black Panther.* No silly petticoats for Nat. She'd gone full badass tonight—form-fitting green dress, hair done in tight knots.

Ian held up his hands in surrender. "How're you doing, Nat? It's been a while."

"Ten years," she said. "Not long enough." Nat grabbed my wrist and yanked me toward the party like her disobedient child. "We're going to the auction. *You*"—she sneered over her shoulder at Ian—"can go to hell."

"A little dramatic?" I hissed as she pulled me into the dreaded ballroom. My face had probably turned beet red from embarrassment. "We were just talking."

"Ian Donovan is bad news," Nat said. "A ten-foot pole isn't enough. You don't touch that guy with a fifty-yard steel rod."

"You don't think I know that?" I said. "Give me some credit. He's totally not my type."

"I'm glad you realize that."

"Of course I realize that." I glanced back at Ian, who had already disappeared, and ignored the unexpected pang of disappointment in my gut.

• • •

Ian

"A-*hem*."

I spun around on the sidewalk on Orrington. I'd dashed out of the hotel after Natalie Carter, of all fucking people, had burst in and saved Erin Sharpe from talking to me. My friend Scott stood outside the hotel, chatting up a wispy young blond dude in a waiter's tux, from whose lips dangled a lit cigarette. "This is Travis," Scott said.

"Nice to meet you, Travis." I shoved my hands into my pockets and nodded slightly. Travis was obviously Scott's target for the night. He and I had developed similar philosophies about our love lives—no sleepovers, no second dates, no strings. These rules had been born out of necessity, not frivolity. We owned our own business, which took us all over the globe. Scott and I were too busy with work for relationships. Only three things currently mattered to us: friends, family, and Fumetsu Enterprises—the Japanese tech company we were currently courting. They were gonna be huge...once they perfected their technology.

Scott handed his business card to Travis. "Call me later."

Travis snuffed out his cigarette on the concrete and headed back inside.

I rescued the dead butt from the ground and tossed it into the garbage. "Littering?" I said. "A real winner you found there."

"They can't all be perfect," Scott said. "So where the hell were you running off to?"

"You know where I was going," I said. "Or at least you know why I was running." He'd dragged me to this event tonight, because this was our "tradition" and because Tommy, the third in our BFF trio, had stayed home with his wife and kid, and Scott needed me. I'd agreed to come, even though I knew this year would be different. This year I'd broken my own rules and had gone out with a woman twice. The last text I got from her had hinted that she wanted me to bid on her, but the truth was, I never bid on anyone. I made a sizable donation to the school at the event every year, but I never, ever bid. It had become a hard and fast rule. And I would not break it for a woman I barely knew.

"Maria Minnesota," Scott said.

"I was out in the hall when I heard her name called, and I ran." God, I was an asshole. This was the problem with letting anyone step even an inch inside my fortress of solitude. They developed expectations I couldn't meet, and I, inevitably, ended up looking like a dick. This thing with Maria had been fun, and I'd gone into it thinking we were totally on the same page—no hopes that our non-relationship could ever evolve into something more. She was a travel blogger who spent half her life out of town. I was a venture capitalist who traveled the globe. I could be in Dubai one day and Dover the next. When we met, Maria and I agreed we'd meet up when we were both in Chicago once in a while or whatever, nothing concrete. Then she started calling me every other day and texting me personal questions, and I didn't do personal. I didn't do "getting to know you." We hadn't been on the same page at all. She'd misrepresented herself. And now she stood up there on stage, expecting me to bid on her, even though I'd told her point-blank that I didn't do that sort of thing.

"You're a real prince, you know that." Scott raised an eyebrow.

"Fuck you," I said.

He wrapped an arm around my shoulders. "You know I'm joking."

I leaned my head against my buddy's shoulder. The fabric of his tux tickled my cheek. "This event is so stupid."

"You're just realizing that now?"

I pointed to the street. "Come with me. Let's hop in a cab

and go downtown where we belong."

"Can't. Mom needs me."

I groaned. "Right." Scott's mom was a delightful woman who'd basically raised Tommy and me along with her son. She'd kicked Scott's deadbeat dad out of the house when Scott was ten, and her dutiful son had bid on her in this auction every year since he turned twenty-one.

"And Tommy's not here, so *I* need *you*."

Tommy was home with his wife and new baby. He was our business partner, too, but he'd decided to roll the dice and settle down. I was happy for him, but Scott remained dubious, believing there was no way Tommy wouldn't fuck this up.

Scott jumped away, clapping his hands, as if he'd just stumbled upon a brilliant idea. "You should bid on Mom with me. There's no rule that we can't split the date, is there?"

"Probably?" I said. "I've never read the bylaws for this thing." I stared off in the distance. It was a Saturday night, Halloween weekend. People both in costume and not crowded the sidewalks, headed to restaurants, bars, or the train into the city. They all had the right idea. None of them had gotten dressed to the nines for the express purpose of not bidding on someone at a bachelorette auction.

"What else is going on?" Scott asked. "There's more to this story. It's not just Maria Minnesota." As always, he announced her name like a game-show host.

"You know who I just ran into?" I nodded back toward the hotel.

Scott shook his head.

"Natalie Carter."

Scott's hand went to his mouth. "Fuck. That's a blast from the past."

My mind kept replaying the look on her face when she caught me talking to Erin Sharpe. "She told me to go to hell."

"Well." Scott shrugged. "That sounds about right."

"She treated me like a wad of old gum she'd scraped off her shoe." Natalie had looked at me like Tommy'd been looking at me lately, ever since his kid had made her debut. He'd morphed into one of those "wives and daughters" guys, who'd been fine with my single life before he became a dad but had suddenly developed empathy for women because that could be his little girl someday. Utter bullshit. Besides, I did think about the women's feelings. That was why I always told them upfront: *No strings. No second dates. No, I will not be bidding on you in the goddamn bachelorette auction.*

"You're preaching to the choir," Scott said, stopping my speech with a hand before it began.

"I mean, we don't lead anyone on, you and I. We come right out with it: we like being single. We plan on staying that way." Though I'd never been in a real relationship, Scott had—for four years, bridging his twenties and thirties. When Joe left because of Scott's grueling travel schedule, it wrecked him. He came to the same conclusion I had years before: work trumped romance. "We're busy men who own our own company and travel a lot."

I rubbed my hands together. The temperature had dropped since the sun went down, and my righteous indignation no longer kept me warm. "We have full lives. We take care of our friends and family."

"We donate a shit-ton of money to our alma mater, as well as other charities," Scott agreed.

"We're the good guys." The pressure eased off my chest. The version of me Nat remembered had been kind of a jerk. He'd been a work in progress. Now I was Ian Fucking Donovan 2.0. I'd clearly laid out the parameters for Maria, and she'd tried to escalate things. "I don't owe Natalie anything. Or Maria. I have nothing to prove to anyone inside that hotel."

"Which is why you're going to be an adult, come back inside with me, and face your fears." Scott grabbed my tuxedo jacket as I tried to escape to the curb.

When Scott and I returned to the ballroom, we found the auction in full swing. "I hope Mom hasn't gone yet!" Scott grabbed a program and discovered that, nope, we hadn't missed bidding on his mother.

Heads bowed in conversation, Nat sat with Erin Sharpe at one of the front tables, right near the edge of the stage. A pit formed in my gut. Who knew what bullshit Nat had told her. Not that I cared what Erin thought about me, but I was a businessman. I liked to be liked. My livelihood depended on it. Plus, she was principal of the school where I directed many of my charitable efforts. We were bound to run into each other again, and Erin's two ties to me were the guy I'd picked on in high school and the woman who'd had to deal with the aftermath of my one-night stands for three years.

Fuck. Maybe I was an utter tool.

Erin was one of the last to be auctioned. The way she approached the spotlight reminded me of one of those old gladiator movies. I half expected her to take the mic and announce, "We who are about to die salute you." She'd hardened her face, ready for battle, totally contradicting the Cinderella vibe of the rest of her look, what with the flouncy blue dress and the sparkly headband in her short, punky platinum hair. She personified a chip on one's shoulder, and I liked that about her. She hadn't gone all shy and meek after realizing she'd accidentally shown me her ass tonight.

"Next up," said Jennifer, head of the fund-raising committee, who had agreed to serve as auctioneer tonight, "we have Miss Erin Sharpe."

"Doctor Erin Sharpe," she hissed into the microphone.

I held up my drink in salute, laughing. The balls on Dr. Sharpe. Now this was definitely the same woman who'd stolen all the white wine from a bunch of fifty-three-year-old men. "Good for her. Can you believe Jennifer called her 'Miss'?" I said.

"Classic Jennifer." Scott wasn't paying actual attention. Fielding texts from Travis the waiter had occupied his mind space.

"Sorry," Jennifer said with a sniff. "*Doctor* Erin Sharpe. Dr. Sharpe is the new principal at Glenfield Academy. She likes long walks on the beach—"

Erin glared down at Natalie, who had definitely roped Erin into this nonsense. Natalie taught at the school, but, as an alumna, she still ran with this crowd. She might have dressed like a superhero spy tonight, but her North Shore princess roots ran deep.

"Dr. Sharpe loves reading poetry to her lovers in the moonlight."

"Oh my God. No, I do not." Erin lunged for Jennifer. "Are you reading someone else's card?"

Jennifer jumped back as Erin scanned the index card. She tossed it to the ground. "Well, none of that is right." She wrapped a slender hand around the microphone. "I'm Erin Sharpe. I have a PhD in education. I'm forty, recently dumped by my boyfriend of ten years, and I like crappy television." She raised her arms in surrender. "Have at me, boys."

How had Dirt managed to woo this fireball? What a fucking waste. Well, maybe she'd find someone good tonight, to make up for the lost Dirt years. I glanced around the room, as paddle after paddle flew up. There had to be someone here worthy of Erin Sharpe, someone smart enough, cool enough, kind enough. The kind of guy who'd help her steal wine from another party, not berate her for it. The Anti-Dirt.

Mark Marrs was bidding on her. He was... Well, he had money. But so did everyone in this room. He had the reputation at my country club for being the go-to guy for really rough vintage porn. Out. Sorry, Mark Marrs.

Tim Cleary was okay, but kind of anti-intellectual, to put it mildly. He'd inherited a bunch of money from his mom's family when he turned twenty-one and had basically done nothing since graduating from Harvard, except ride on yachts, complain about the waitstaff at various restaurants, and tell people he'd gone to Harvard. Big old nope.

Bill Lowery could work...maybe... He was nice, at least, but according to Scott, he might not be all that into the ladies. And Scott knew everything when it came to matters of the glass closet.

Then there was Paul Pfister, heir to the Pfister fortune, related, somehow, to the British royal family, or so he liked to say. Greasy-haired, skinny, annoying like a freaking gnat. He was pretentious with a capital *P*. He'd probably be no different than Dirt, really, all told. He was Dirt with money.

And he was about to win Erin.

Ready to collect his prize, Paul basically vibrated in his seat, beaming at his grandmother, his plus-one for the night, while waving his paddle in the air.

"Going once...twice..."

"Fucking Paul Pfister." I reached across the table and plucked my paddle from underneath Scott's napkin. Hell, it was just one dinner, and I'd planned to donate the money anyway. I lofted my bidding paddle high in the air. "I'm in. Forty grand."

Jennifer banged the gavel. "Erin Sharpe to Ian Donovan for forty thousand dollars. The Glenfield Academy basketball teams thank you for your generosity. We'll be able to afford that new floor!"

My eyes swung right to Erin, who stood on stage, her mouth agape. All the color had drained from her face.

I waved my paddle at her sheepishly. So much for never bidding on anyone.

...

ERIN

I had to be physically escorted backstage by some teenage son of a school advisory board member who'd been roped into corralling the bachelorettes for the evening. I couldn't move on my own. I'd spent the night preparing myself for a date with someone completely objectionable, some dude who lived in his parents' basement and hadn't seen daylight in three years. But instead I had been bought by Ian Donovan.

He'd said he wouldn't bid on anyone.

But then he bid on me.

For forty thousand dollars.

Forty. Grand.

The...*fuck*?

Natalie grabbed me as soon as I entered the green room, where the rest of the bachelorettes were waiting to meet up with their dates. "Ian Donovan bought you?" she said. "Ian *Donovan*? Why?" Her long, gold metallic nails dug into my triceps.

I shrugged, and my shoulders froze right next to my ears. *Why, indeed.* A really hot guy, who'd told me point-blank that he never bid on anyone at this thing, had paid forty thousand dollars to have dinner with me. With *me*, the principal in the petticoat.

This was... I didn't know what this was. Mildly upsetting? Kind of exciting? An accident? Maybe that was it. A bug or something had landed on his paddle and he'd waved it at just the wrong moment to shoo it away or whatever. That scenario made the most sense. Serendipity by spider.

Natalie pushed my shoulders down to their normal height and kneaded them gently, bringing me back to reality. "You were talking to him earlier. Do you know him?" Nat asked.

I shook my head. "We met in the hallway tonight, I don't know."

Natalie frowned, glancing at the door. Guys had started to pour in, hunting for their dates, some of whom they'd paid top dollar for—for "just" dinner. Was that even true, though? Did Ian expect more? Did I? God, what a terrifying question.

"He's no good," Natalie said.

"So I've heard." She didn't need to work so hard to sell me on something I already knew.

"When I dated his friend Tommy—well, let's just say, Ian is very charming, and he knows it. He makes a great first impression. But, dude, I can't even tell you how many times I had to clean up his mess the next morning." Natalie's long earrings bumped against her neck as she shook her head. "These, like, twenty-one-year-old girls would wander out alone from his bedroom, crying, and I'd have to break it to them that Ian was a fuckstick who never dated any girl more than once. Tommy and I fought about it constantly throughout our relationship. I'd be all, 'Your friend's an asshole.' And then he'd come in and defend Ian, saying, 'He's always straight with the girls. It's their fault if they don't get the message.'"

"Cool," I said. "Well, I've heard the message, loud and clear."

"Have you, though?" Nat raised an eyebrow at me. "You're not exactly someone who's known for having one-night stands. Ian is all fling, no ring."

"Nat," I said. "We're having dinner so the school can afford to refinish the gym floor. That's literally it." Nat had me pegged. I didn't date casually. I jumped from long relationship to long relationship. Nat and I both did, in fact. But I wasn't a total fool. I understood that Ian was not the one.

She looked me up and down. "Mmm-hmm."

"I swear." I widened my eyes to make her believe me. "Just dinner." Because that had to be what Ian had been thinking. He was the one who'd told me this night ended after dessert for, basically, everyone.

"He's coming in." Natalie stared me straight in the eye. "Be careful tonight."

"Careful's my middle name. You know that."

Nat spun me around, face-to-face with Ian Donovan. His soft, milk-chocolate eyes smiled at me from behind his thick, dark frames. He didn't look so dangerous, but then neither did a Lily of the Valley. It was probably how Ian'd managed to lure in so many unsuspecting victims. They all thought they were going to be The One. The One to tame the wild, rich, beautiful bachelor. Well, not me. I had all the information.

Ian flashed me a toothy grin. "When I saw Paul Pfister basically floating to the ceiling on the high that he was about to win a date with you, I had to shut him down."

I blinked as I waited to hear the rest of his explanation.

"It was a friendly gesture, nothing more." He lowered his voice to a near whisper. "We don't have to actually go on the date tonight, if you don't want to. I didn't bid on you expecting anything. No pressure."

Now my stomach took the elevator down to my feet.

It appeared Nat had nothing to worry about.

We don't have to actually go on the date, was what he'd said. What I'd heard was that I was such a loser Ian didn't even want to break bread with me, that he had forked over forty thousand bucks just to be nice.

Was I that big a charity case?

Apparently.

Ian simply pitied the poor, sad woman who'd gotten dumped by Dirt. He didn't find me attractive. He didn't want to spend time with me. He wanted to get out of this obligation, probably so he could screw some pretty young thing instead, just like Nat had predicted.

"Fine," I said. "Great. No big deal." To hide my disappointed eyes, I spun toward the back exit, through which the rest of the group headed, about to board the party bus and go to the restaurant. They walked two-by-two with their dates. I stood alone. Flying solo. "I'll hang out with my friend and the guy who bought her, and you can write off the donation or whatever."

Goodbye, Ian Donovan. Fuck you very much.

As I stepped toward the door and out of Ian's personal space, someone slid next to me, taking his place. Paul Pfister, one of the other guys who'd almost bought me.

"No Ian?" Paul wore a Dracula costume. I gave him props for that. Good for him, dressing up, being a team player. He hadn't come here tonight to make fun of the auction. He'd come to participate.

"I think Ian has other things to do." This guy was more my speed, anyway. I could hold my own with a Paul Pfister. I had the upper hand with a guy like him. I'd probably break out in cold sweats all evening if I had to talk to Ian Donovan for an extended period of time.

"Good," Paul said. "Then maybe we can talk."

"Absolutely."

Natalie stood way up in front of us, almost on the bus. She'd linked arms with her date—some balding corporate lawyer dressed as Harry Potter. Apparently they were both happy with the sale. She appeared adrift in a love haze. Good for her. Good for us.

I turned toward Paul and grinned at him. We were the same height. We'd both come in costume. We nerdy people of a similar ilk had to stick together. "What about the woman you bid on?" I asked.

"She went home sick."

I grinned at him. "Too bad for her."

Panting, Ian sidled up next to me. "Sorry, Erin, I got stuck back there." He glared at Paul, who had started to back away now that the alpha dog had shown up.

I grabbed Paul's arm and pulled him next to me. "Ian, we're fine. You said you didn't want to go on the date, and that's cool. I'm cool. We're cool."

"Erin—" Ian held out a hand to me, but I waved him off, linking arms with Paul and stepping onto the bus with him. Ian apparently felt like he had to be my protector tonight, my knight in shining armor. I didn't need protection or a pity date. I deserved a prince.

And Paul could literally be a prince. "Have I told you I'm related to the Queen of England?" he said as he slid onto a bench near the front of the bus.

Grinning, I glided in next to him. "That's amazing."

"My second cousin's second cousin is her third cousin once removed, and the last time I visited Great Britain, I had an audience with the queen."

"So cool." I let Paul keep talking, waiting for him to take the opportunity to ask me something. It was the getting-to-know-you dance. I counted to thirty. He kept talking about the queen. And he was still droning on about her after another thirty seconds had passed.

"Are you an alum?" I asked. "I'm really enjoying Glenfield Academy. I've never taught at a private school before." There. I'd given him an opening to ask me about my job.

"I graduated from there in 1992, New Trier in 1996. After that I traveled through Europe for a year, before heading to Yale. I received my law degree from Harvard, passed the bar in both Illinois and Massachusetts. Now I run my grandmother's foundation." He kept going and going and going, reciting his entire résumé. He punctuated it with, "My motto is, 'To thine own self be true.'"

Carl. My high school boyfriend, Carl, had had a Shakespeare quote for every occasion, no matter what. When my grandma'd had him over for her famous Swiss steak dinner, he'd said, "Mine eyes smell onions; I shall weep anon." It had been the first quote of many that evening. After we'd dropped him off at home, my parents lectured me from the front seat that I could do better.

"What do you like to do for fun?" I slid away from him on the bench. "I'm a big fan of cooking shows—*Cook's Country, America's Test Kitchen*—"

"I don't watch TV."

That was so Dirk, who used to call my viewing habits "pedestrian" and "low-brow." He'd lie on the couch across the room while I salivated over images of chorizo tacos and butter cake. When we first started dating, this had been one of my favorite parts of "us." He was the cranky academic and I was the principal who needed to unwind at the end of the day. But one day my sister had come over and asked if Dirk and I ever liked to do anything together. I'd told her, "Of course we do." But then I couldn't think of anything.

"But I do love food," Paul said, "I've been a vegetarian for years, but I might start eating meat again."

"Oh," I said, perking up. "Why?" I could actually sink my teeth into this interesting tidbit about Paul.

He shook his head. "I just think vegetarianism is *over.*"

I recoiled, physically backing away from him as much as I could on that bus bench. I would've climbed over him and out the window if I hadn't been wearing a ball gown. The pretentiousness of that statement: *Vegetarianism is over.* I would've accepted almost any other answer for why Paul had decided to give up not eating meat—health, taste, boredom, a double dog dare from his best friend. But I could not abide this pseudo-hipster bullshit. Not anymore. Not now that I'd freed myself from Dirk.

"Excuse me." I jumped up from my seat and hurled myself into the walkway. Paul was exactly my type, which was the problem. I'd been dating different versions of the same guy for twenty-five years—jumping from one unsatisfying relationship to the next, simply to avoid the awkwardness of being alone.

Maybe alone wasn't so bad.

"Ma'am!" The bus driver glared at me in the rearview mirror. "Take your seat!"

"I am." Clutching the seat backs as I made my way toward the rear of the bus, I slid into the empty spot next to Ian. "Okay," I said. "Just dinner sounds great."

Chapter Two

Ian

When Erin sat next to me, I didn't say anything. I had no idea what to say. I'd stepped in it back at the hotel, but I wasn't sure exactly how.

"I'm not a charity case," Erin said finally, as our bus sailed down Sheridan Road.

Oh, so that was it. "I don't think you're a charity case."

She turned toward me, her blue eyes like lasers. "You paid forty grand because you felt bad for me."

I sighed. "That's not…" I turned my body so we sat face-to-face. "That wasn't why I bid on you. It wasn't a pity thing. It was a respect thing. You didn't deserve the misery of having to deal with Paul or whatever other losers were bidding on you. I was…" I wracked my brain for the right words to get me out of this. I settled for brutal honesty. "I wouldn't have placed that bid for anyone but you."

Her mouth dropped open slightly, and I noted the surprise in her eyes. "Why me?"

My eyes crinkled. I couldn't help smiling around her. Erin and I didn't run in the same circles, really. I'd never go out on Saturday night and run into her at a club in River North or anything. Tonight was an anomaly, because she was only here as an employee of the rich elementary school I'd attended. She really was the Cinderella of the auction. "You're the woman who stole the wine."

"Wow, that's getting me a lot of mileage tonight." Her eyes crinkled as she chuckled. Sitting on the bus with a grown woman in a dorky costume was honestly the most peaceful and real I'd felt in a long time. Erin showed no pretense. She was who she was. I usually hung out with PR reps—they were all PR reps—who, if they bothered to dress up for Halloween, would go as a sexy cat or just, like, a random sexy human. "Natalie told me to watch out for you," Erin said.

"You should probably listen to her," I admitted. "But in my defense, she knew me ten years ago, and I've matured since then."

"No more sad women skulking out of your bedroom at eight in the morning?" she asked.

I winced, thinking of Maria Minnesota. She sat a few rows ahead of us, chatting with the guy who'd bought her, some younger dude I didn't recognize. "I have rules now. No more sleepovers. Tell Natalie that," I added. It didn't matter to me what my best friend's ex thought of me, but, for some reason, I did care about Erin's buddy's opinion.

"Oh, I'm sure she'll be overjoyed to hear the news." Erin narrowed her eyes at me. "What other rules do you have?"

I shrugged. "I don't know."

"Sure you do." She smirked and made grabby hands. "Lay it on me."

I rolled my eyes. This was not a conversation to have with Dr. Erin Sharpe. While I enjoyed my lifestyle, someone like Erin might judge me for it. She was a school principal, after all. "No sleepovers, no second dates, no strings," I said. "That's about it." Before she had a second to call me a pig, I told her, "I make sure to let the woman know early on that I'm not looking for a relationship, or anything remotely resembling a relationship. If we hook up tonight, we hook up tonight…and that's it."

Our bus flew over a bump, and Erin grabbed the seat back in front of her to steady herself. "You turn into a pumpkin post-coitus."

I wrinkled my nose. "Yuck. That phrase is as bad as 'moist.'"

"I went for the alliteration, and I regret it." She chewed on the inside of her cheek as she scanned my face, as if seeking further information. "Why, though?"

"Why what?"

"Why no relationships? Why only one-night stands?"

"I just met you." I raised an eyebrow. This was more of a third-date conversation, and I didn't do third dates. Or deep conversations.

"One thing you should know about me is I have a PhD in education and I'm constantly trying to learn about people, what makes them tick. So, why?" She glanced out the window. "We still have at least twenty minutes before we get to the restaurant. You might as well spill."

Well, there was no way I'd tell her the real reason. Not today, not so she could go blabbing to Natalie about what a wounded little boy I was. Only Scott and Tommy knew the real reason. I gave Erin the version I gave everyone else. "I like my life. I own a business that takes me all over the world at a moment's notice. If I'm beholden to someone, I'll end up hurting her when I'm not able to be there when she needs me. We're all better off not letting it get that far in the first place."

She nodded, satisfied. "Makes sense to me," she said. "I'm also all about not jumping into relationships."

"Oh yeah?"

"Well, it's a new thing for me. I've hopped from long relationship to long relationship for the past one hundred or so years. I need a little time on my own for once."

"Alone time is vastly underrated." I rested my forearm on the windowsill. Our bus cruised down Lake Shore Drive in the dark. The view just beyond the northbound lanes was navy-blue nothingness. "I'll clink glasses with you at the dinner in celebration."

She grinned. "About that, can we just have a fun time tonight, like you promised? No pressure, no drama?"

"Sounds perfect." I hadn't had a no-pressure, no drama Saturday night in a long time. I was either out at a club here, trying to impress people fifteen years younger than me, or in another city or country, trying to impress clients. Tonight I had Erin to impress, with her platinum-blond pixie haircut and Cinderella costume, but only in the most low-key, low-pressure way. Tonight we'd be like two bros hanging out, and truly, now that Tommy had become Mr. Family Man, I could use a new bud.

Erin and I booked it for the bar as soon as we reached Girl and the Goat. "Sauv blanc?" I nudged her in the ribs.

"Scotch, please."

I ordered a double for each of us, and we clinked glasses as we observed the other couples around us.

"So," she said. "Of all these pairs here tonight, which one's going to go the distance?"

I laughed. As far as I knew, the Glenfield Academy bachelorette auction had never produced any long-lasting romances, only championship basketball teams. I pointed to Scott and his mom, who stood over in the far corner, basically moaning over the appetizers they'd just put in their mouths. "Those two," I said.

Erin squinted. "The age difference won't be an issue?"

"Nope. They're mother and son," I said. "That's why they're the safest bet. Though Nat and her guy look pretty close."

Nodding, Erin sipped her drink. "We'll see. Nat's a little like me—or the old me. She's a serial monogamist, who just got out of a five-year relationship"—she checked her watch—"a week ago."

I raised my eyebrows. "Wow. She moves quick."

Erin shook her head, shuddering. "And that could've been me tonight, jumping at the first guy who spoke to me. It was how I landed in my last two relationships, and both of those ended—" She cut herself off.

"Ended how?"

"They ended." And I supposed that was Erin's third-date conversation.

• • •

Ian

Things I learned about Erin at dinner: 1) she could match me drink for drink, and 2) she knew her shit when it came to movies and TV.

People didn't normally think of me as a pop culture guy. I guessed it didn't fit my aloof jet-setter persona, but I spent so much time on planes and in hotel rooms that I saw basically everything. And Erin, who was a homebody, did too.

"Oh my God! You're the only person in my life who watched *Killing Eve*! Can we talk about how everyone on that show makes horrible decisions?" She poured about a cup and a half of champagne into my red wine glass. Between the two of us, we'd already polished off an entire bottle of cabernet—on top of the scotch.

"Terrible decisions." I guzzled the bubbly. "Remember when Bill followed Villanelle into the club?"

"What was his plan there? 'Hey, let me just tail a serial killer with no backup.' Oh my God! So stupid!" She clinked my glass and downed her champagne. "You wanna dance?"

A good three-quarters of the party had crowded onto the makeshift dance floor and currently bopped around to "Shout."

"I hate this song," I admitted. Another one of my rules was "no dancing to crappy wedding music."

But Erin jumped up and pulled me to standing. "I hate it, too, and that's why we need to do this, to make a mockery of it."

I let her pull me onto the dance floor where we proceeded to do the John Travolta/Uma Thurman dance from *Pulp Fiction*. Then we did what Erin called the anti-"YMCA," which was basically dancing like a fiend through the entire song, except the "YMCA" part, during which we stood perfectly still, like statues, while everyone else threw their hands in the air.

I wiped sweat from my brow with my pocket square. This was a harder workout than Crossfit. "We're such rebels." I did not dance. I did not join or revel. I sat on the sidelines with a smirk and a tumbler of scotch.

This was much more fun. At least it was with Erin. I glanced over at Maria, who nuzzled her date's cheek. I couldn't picture dancing with her like this. But then, our thing had only been about sex and impressing each other enough throughout the evening to get to the sex, while Erin and I were just two bros goofing around.

The music switched to something slow, one of those old love songs they play at every single wedding, and the other pairs on the dance floor joined together like magnets. Nat and her date had molded against each other like two amoebae. "You want to dance?" I asked Erin. I said it jokingly, casually, like, "Ha-ha, you want to dance?" and I held my hand out to her.

Grinning, she took it. Her hands were small and alabaster, and I noticed for the first time that her stubby nails had been painted in rainbow colors, and she'd obviously done the manicure herself, which, for some reason, pinged my desire. I shook the fog from my head. Erin was my bud. I would not get turned on by my bud's self-made manicure. Still, I pulled her in close, and she let me.

Oh, the booze was getting to me. I'd been able to disguise that fact while we danced fast to all those cheesy songs. But now with Erin up close and personal, swaying against me to lyrics about "love" and "baby" and "stay," and her hot breath tickling my ear, I didn't hate it. In fact, I kept counting to ten over and over in my head, trying to forget her nails and ignore her breath and convince myself that I did in fact hate all of this. I had to hate all of this. Hating this was the only acceptable answer.

Erin was my bro, the principal of my grade school alma mater. I'd keep running into her at events like this all year. "Casual" didn't exist for us.

"Are we still dancing ironically?" Erin's lips tickled the edge of my ear, and it was like I'd never been this close to a woman before. What was happening to me? I was going soft. Well, most of me was. Other parts…not so much.

"I can't tell," I said.

"Me neither." The night had taken a turn, one I hadn't planned on taking. But Erin and I were both looser than we should have been, thanks to the alcohol, and had started crossing lines. Her hips rested right up against mine, and she could certainly feel how much I enjoyed our proximity.

"This is fun," she whispered.

Oh yes, it was. This was when I'd normally have *The Conversation* with a woman, the pre-sex chat. I wasn't Prince Charming. I was good for one night only. I'd be gone before coffee. But Erin and I had already had the talk, hadn't we? She knew the score.

"I'm having fun," she said again. "Maybe this is what I need instead of another relationship. Fun." She wrapped her arms tighter around my neck. "You're fun. Right, Ian?"

Holy shit. "Too much, sometimes." It was my way of broaching the subject that this night would not stretch into morning. I disappeared at sunup, preferably before.

But then she stood on her tiptoes and pressed her forearms into my shoulders, raising her face to my height. She touched her lips to mine, and, I'm ashamed to say, I melted. Like a dumb-ass fool in a Hallmark movie—not that I ever watched those, *please*. She kissed me, and I parted my lips, letting her deepen the angle, allowing her to take control, if just for a moment, while I attempted to regain my senses. This was dangerous. This was a bad idea. I backed away.

"What are we doing?" I held out an arm to block any further advancement on her part. "I'm very attracted to you, Erin, I am, but..." I had to be the adult here, and I didn't do "adult" in these situations. When presented with sex, I chose sex. "We're going to keep running into each other."

Her blue eyes locked on mine. "That shouldn't be a problem, if we both know the deal." She pressed her body against mine again, and I pulled her in tighter. It was a reflex, triggered by her hair, which smelled like jasmine with a hint of vanilla. That scent was my kryptonite.

My mind kept playing the scene of Erin and Nat at brunch tomorrow, Erin crying, Nat repeating a refrain of *"I told you so."* But the alcohol and my hormones syphoned off any and all reason from my brain. My good sense fought a losing battle against my groin. "Yes," I told her. "Yes. Let's go to your place."

• • •

ERIN

I'd had three boyfriends in my life, *boom, boom, boom,* one right after the other, and I barely had time to breathe between any of them. Before I joined up with my college boyfriend, I did get a tiny little taste of the single life. A minuscule taste. A morsel. But it did happen.

I'd been out with my high school girlfriends while visiting their school during freshman year. At the U of I, we'd been able to get into the local bars at nineteen with driver's licenses. I'd never been to a bar before, and I followed my friends' leads. Guys bought us drinks. I ended up dancing with some dude I claimed looked like Leonardo DiCaprio, but who knew how accurate that was. I'd been wearing beer goggles in the dark at one a.m.

Anyway. Thanks to the alcohol and the atmosphere, I ended up kissing Leo out on that dance floor. No names, no numbers. We went our separate ways at the end of the night, but the experience left me feeling powerful. I'd never done something so spontaneous, so random, without fear of consequences or what came next.

Dancing with Ian brought that nineteen-year-old out in me.

I didn't want another grown-up relationship. I wanted to make a colossal, teenager-y mistake tonight. I'd ditched my control-top pantyhose in the bathroom before dinner, and I was free as a bird.

I stood on my tiptoes—God, Ian was tall; my previous boyfriends had all been basically my height—and kissed his cheek. "Let's get out of here." I nibbled his earlobe. Check me out, taking charge. When Dirk and I dated, I'd always wait for him to tell me what came next—in all aspects of life, really.

Ian, however, seemed content to let me take the reins.

I liked that about him.

"Are you sure about this?" His brows knitted behind his glasses. He'd been a perfect gentleman tonight, not at all the person Natalie had described. I mean, I still had no illusions about where this night was headed. We'd talked about it. He was a hookup-only kind of person, but tonight so was I.

"I'm sure." He had to stop being so worried about my feelings. I was a big girl. I could take care of myself.

I laced my fingers in his and pulled him out of the restaurant, careful to avoid catching Natalie's eye. She'd try to talk me out of this, for sure. But she was busy sucking face with her dude while straddling him on a barstool, so we were all making interesting life choices tonight.

Ian and I hopped into a cab, and I slid into the middle seat, right next to him. I caressed his cheek, and he leaned down and kissed me. Damn, he was good at that. I couldn't tell if it was the newness of his lips against mine or what, but the rush, the anticipation, the forbidden nature of this clandestine tryst was a revelation. This was how kissing was supposed to feel. I'd missed out on a lot these past two decades plus.

"You know," he said, torturing me with his breath against my ear, "this is not why I bought the date with you"

"You made that clear." Crystal clear. *I'm your charity case, Ian, we got it.* Even though he'd insisted that wasn't the situation, I had my doubts. I knew from what Nat had said that I wasn't his type. He was basically slumming it with me tonight.

Well, that was his problem.

I ran my fingers through his messy-styled hair and clutched the back of his head, as he lowered his lips to mine again.

The rest of the cab ride flew by in a blur of kissing and groping. I actually reached down and cupped him—I did that! Me! Dr. Erin Sharpe, elementary school principal!—

and he moaned as he arched toward me. I felt invincible, like Wonder Woman. Was Wonder Woman invincible? Didn't matter. I was on fire.

We kissed all the way up to my condo, stopping on every landing up to the third floor to grind against each other. Ah, dry humping. Truly the unsung hero of foreplay. "Shhh!" I hissed as I unlocked the door. "My sister's probably sleeping."

"You live with your sister?" He looked down at me quizzically. We hadn't exchanged much personal information tonight. We'd only really talked about movies and our rules for dating. This tidbit about having a sister who lived in my apartment was probably the one concrete thing he knew about me beyond the fact that I was a principal who used to date the biggest wad of human garbage from his high school.

I shook my head. "Don't worry about it." Tonight was not about "getting to know you." Tonight was about sneaking into my bedroom with this hot random dude and getting laid. I clutched his upper arms. His biceps—I couldn't get enough of them. They were rock hard. So strong. He could probably lift me up like I weighed nothing. He could probably support me while we screwed against the shower wall. Now there was an idea. I dragged him by the hand toward my bedroom at the back of the condo, careful to tiptoe past my sister's door. Thank goodness she slept like the dead. And she kept a white-noise machine humming all night long.

I shut the door and kicked off my heels. "Do you have a condom?"

"Yeah." He sat down on the edge of my bed.

"Of course you do." I grinned.

"My reputation precedes me." He smiled, too, thank goodness. I didn't want him to think I judged him for his life choices, because I totally didn't. Tonight I worshipped those life choices, and also the way his untied bow tie hung around his neck and he undid his top two buttons with one hand—oh my God.

I reached behind my back and unzipped my dress, letting it fall to the floor in a puddle around my ankles. I hadn't been this naked in front of someone in a while. Actually, the last person who saw me like this was my gynecologist, Dana, a few months ago—when Dirk had promised to meet me there but didn't. Honestly neither of them had ever looked at me the way Ian gazed at me right now, which was probably a good thing for my gynecologist, but a total knock against my ex-boyfriend.

"You're gorgeous, Erin." Ian swallowed. He gawked right at my boobs, so I knew he definitely wasn't kidding. I had great boobs.

I stepped closer to him and hopped onto his lap, straddling him, kissing him, grinding against him. His hands clutched my ass, drawing me closer, the entire length of him tormenting me through my underwear. "Fuck me," I whispered in his ear.

He pulled a condom from his wallet and flipped me onto my back. Then he stepped away from the bed and pulled off his shirt, revealing a toned chest and abs that belied his forty-year-old age.

Ian undid his pants and dropped them next to my discarded dress on the floor. He slipped off his boxer briefs, and I slipped off my Costco value-pack panties, revealing myself to him. He bit his lip and slid on the condom like the pro I knew he was.

Waiting for him agonized me. I mean, *come on, dude.* "Now," I said.

He crawled onto the bed, eyeing me like a tiger the entire way up, up, up, until he entered me and time simply stopped.

• • •

IAN

Fuck.

The pillow, the silky pillow, jolted me awake. I owned flannel sheets. Rugged, manly, too-hot-in-the-summertime sheets. I was not a satin man.

But satin currently tickled my cheek and glided against my naked ass.

I was not in my bed.

Fuck.

I flipped over, waking Erin in the process. Her eyes popped open and she bolted upright, pulling the pink sheets to her neck. She looked just as sexy in the morning, with the sunlight glinting off her platinum hair, which stood up at odd angles all over her head. Her eye makeup had smudged under her eyes, giving her a sultry, punk-rock vibe. I was getting hard just looking at her.

Unacceptable.

This was why I never spent the night anywhere. Spending the night led to morning sex, which led to breakfast, which led to exchanging numbers, which led to calls and texts, which led to making plans, which led to relationships, and I didn't do relationships.

Erin would make some guy—some *other* guy—very happy someday. Believe me. She'd blown my mind last night, and it took a lot to do that. I was usually the one who blew minds.

"So," I said.

"Hey." She winced. Erin didn't seem thrilled about this development, either, so that was a positive. I'd gone and fucked it up by making the rookie mistake of falling asleep and spending the night.

She'd just worn me out, I guess. Plus the alcohol. Plus resting my head against her full, gorgeous chest while she stroked my hair.

What had we even been doing? There never should've been any hair stroking! I should've just thrown my pants on and ducked out, like we'd agreed.

And speaking of pants, mine were still at the foot of the bed. I was naked under these pink satin sheets. I needed to figure out a way to gracefully get out from under the covers and pull my clothes on. I was never this bashful around my one-night stands—probably because I'd usually booked the hell out of there before things had a chance to get awkward—but now I'd become a blushing virgin or something.

Erin, however, did the grown-up thing and glided right out from under the covers—fully naked, beautiful, and unselfconscious. She snapped on her bra and slipped on her underwear. Then she stood in front of me, one hand on a full, shapely hip, her breasts presented to me like the prow of the best ship on the planet. "We're both adults," she said in her Dr. Principal voice.

I wasn't sure about that. I felt like a boy at the moment, like a foolish noob. I should've been the one to hop out from under the covers like it was nothing.

So I did.

I jumped out of bed, trying to ignore the fact that I was sporting a semi (thanks, Erin's boobs). I would not let Erin Sharpe, an elementary school *principal*, think I, Ian Donovan, venture capitalist, was shy.

I watched her watching me as I pulled on my boxer briefs and pants. Ha. She wasn't immune to my presence either. *Way to go, Ian. You've still got it.*

I took my time pulling my undershirt over my head, giving Erin the opportunity to enjoy every last millimeter of my toned abs. "So." The only thing left for me to do was make the walk of shame in my tuxedo from last night. The classiest walk of shame of all.

"So," she repeated. "That was fun." She grabbed a pink cotton T-shirt dress from her closet, probably something she wore all the time, for comfort, and pulled it over her head. Bye, boobs. Nice meeting you. "What's the protocol now?" She ran a hand through her bedhead.

"The protocol?" I scanned the floor for my phone, which had fallen out of my pocket and rolled under her bed. This would not turn into a rom-com where I left anything important behind at her house. I was leaving this place with all my stuff, both shoes, every single piece of lint from my pockets.

"Do...I make you breakfast?"

No, was my first instinct. But since I was already there... maybe a cup of coffee for the road...?

She shook her head. "I'm being stupid. You're probably looking for any excuse to get out of here."

Totally. That was definitely what I was doing. I was for sure not thinking about sharing pancakes and coffee while reading the newspaper across the table from Dr. Erin Sharpe, no sir.

"Well, buddy, you don't need to make an excuse. We hooked up. Good times. Now you can leave." She stood at the door, staring at me, waiting for me to make a move.

"Now?" Oh. She really wanted me to go. I got the sense she wanted me out of here even more than I wanted to leave. Well, that was a new one.

I slowly donned my tuxedo jacket, giving her a little time, one last chance, to change her mind about the pancakes. She, resolute, stayed near the exit. "Well, thanks," I said, officially taking the hint.

As Erin opened the bedroom door, she held up her hand. I high-fived her. I high-fived my one-night stand who was kicking me out of her house faster than I'd ever seen anyone do anything.

Booking it, Erin hustled me into the hall and toward the front door, while I tried to shove my shoes on. Her message blared loud and clear: I had to escape now before she turned the hose on me or called the cops to report me for trespassing.

From the kitchen came a voice, "Erin?"

We both spun around. The roommate sister, apparently, sat at the kitchen table, eating cereal. She gawked at me and dropped her spoon. "Erin?" she said again, her eyes swinging toward her sister.

"This is No One. No One, this is my sister, Katie. No One was just leaving." Erin yanked open the door and pushed me out into the hall. "Thanks." She gave me a thumbs-up before slamming the door in my face.

And suddenly, standing alone in the hall with one shoe on and one dangling from my hand, I felt a whole bunch of empathy for the girls I'd ditched like this.

Chapter Three

"I told you to watch out for him." Natalie sipped her tea and raised an eyebrow at me over the rim of her cup. She seemed a tad judgy this morning for someone who'd just admitted she'd gone to third base with the guy who'd bought her at the bachelorette auction. Apparently her thing was "better" because the two of them had made vague plans to see each other again, while Ian and I had not.

"Yes, you did, and I heeded your warning." Now it was my turn to sip tea as if to prove a point. I'd gone out for brunch with Nat and my sister, Katie, a mere hour after Ian had left my house. Okay, after I'd kicked him out. After I'd literally pushed him into the hall and slammed the door in his face. I shuddered from guilt.

I could've been nicer. I could've offered him coffee. But he wouldn't have accepted, and then I would've been the one who'd tried to keep the night going, and I couldn't be that person. I couldn't. I'd made a promise to myself—one ride and goodbye. (Okay more than one ride. Three rides. Three glorious rides.)

"You slept with him," Nat said.

"I did." I bit my cheek to stifle a creeping grin.

"How does that constitute 'heeding my warning'?"

"Well." I popped a grape into my mouth. "I knew exactly what I was getting into, thanks to you."

"This dude obliterated Dirk in the hotness department." Katie participated in the conversation while tapping away on her phone. My sister was only twenty-five. My parents had adopted her as a baby from Korea back when I was fifteen. I felt more like her aunt than her big sister most of the time. We had zero shared childhood experiences, because we grew up in two totally different generations. She glanced up from her phone, shaking her long, thick curls off her shoulders. "Kudos."

"Thank you." I'd had sex—thrice!—with a random hot dude and the world hadn't stopped turning. In fact, the world looked pretty good right now. Colors seemed brighter. I could pick out subtle notes of caramel and sarsaparilla in my tea. Boning a stranger didn't trump climbing Mount Everest or anything, but I was pretty proud of myself.

Nat narrowed her eyes. "I don't buy it."

"You don't buy what?"

She waved her hand up and down to indicate me. "This. There's no way you're not feeling a little twinge of something—guilt, regret, wistfulness?"

"You want me to feel guilty? What the hell, Nat?" I'd never done anything remotely like this before. I deserved a little credit, not shame.

"I don't want you to feel guilty," she said. "I'm just shocked you're not the teensiest bit regretful. I know you. I know us." She waved a hand to indicate herself, me, and Katie. "We fall in love hard and fast."

Katie, eyes still on her phone, nodded in agreement. She'd just gotten out of her first-ever relationship. She and the guy met the week she moved back to Chicago after college. They'd moved in together by the end of summer, and they were engaged two weeks after that. Now she was a twenty-five-year-old divorcée with no job and no apartment, which was why she currently lived with me.

"I'm trying to break the cycle," I said, about to voice for the first time the decision I'd come to last night. "I'm gonna stay single for a while."

"What's 'a while'?" Nat asked.

"A year. At least." I rapped on the table as punctuation. I'd come up with the goal in the shower. As an administrator, I always encouraged my employees to devise SMART goals—specific, measurable, attainable, relevant, and timely—which I was now doing with my personal life. I hadn't stayed single for more than a month since I was fifteen. For the next year, I'd adopt Ian's rules for love as my own: no sleepovers, no second dates, no strings.

"That's ridiculous," Nat said. "You're forty." She tapped on her watch. Time was ticking.

My eyes stung. Like I didn't fucking know that. Dirk and I had been "trying" to have a baby for years, but I only had one ovary and he had sluggish sperm—plus, we weren't doing it all that much, to be honest. By the time I'd finally convinced him to look into fertility treatments with me, he'd already fallen "in love" with the nurse at my old school. "I don't know if you've noticed, but I don't have the best track record when it comes to guys. My entire life, I've settled for Mr. Right in Front of Me instead of waiting for Mr. Right," I said. "I've dated pompous ass after pompous ass, and I'm done with it. I'm gonna take some time to figure out who I am without a guy."

"But you want to be a mom."

"About that," I said, "I've decided I'm okay either way. I came to terms years ago with the fact that having a baby the 'traditional' way might not happen for me. But now that I'm single and getting my own shit together, the world's my oyster. I could adopt or foster or go to a sperm bank…"

Nat shook her head. "This is the saddest thing I've ever heard."

"It's not sad." I pounded my fist on the table, and my spoon jumped about two inches, startling Katie. "It's great. It's reality. It's me finally being an adult about the fact that I can't count on men for anything." Except maybe the occasional orgasm…or three.

"You can count on me." Katie put her phone down, so I knew she was serious.

"Thank you," I said. "And you can count on me." I'd promised to help her find a job now that she, too, was on her own. "I got you on the list of substitutes at the Academy. And they said you could work as my assistant on the days you're not teaching."

Katie gave me a thumbs-up. "Thanks, sis." Look at us women, working together to better our lives—penis-free! Or, well, relatively penis-free. The penis had now become a bonus, not a necessity.

"And you know what?" I said. "The Ian thing? It was the healthiest thing I'd done in a long time. Last night I proved to myself that not every interaction I have with a guy requires a fairytale ending. Sometimes one night is enough. And if it means I avoid falling for a prince who ends up being a royal asshole, all the better."

"I don't want to spoil the ending for you," Nat said, "but Ian's King of the Assholes. Wait around long enough and you'll see."

"That's the point, though, Nat. I'm not waiting around. Our story is over." I wiped my hands. Finished. "Besides, I think you've grossly overestimated Ian's asshole-ishness. He's not a jerk. He's a guy who knows what he wants, and what he wants is to get laid—no strings. I'm one of the few women who took him at his word, and that's why things ended so well for us this morning. We were on the same page." I tried to scrub the forlorn look on his face as I slammed the door from my mind. I had simply been keeping up my end of the bargain. I did not have to feel bad about that.

"You're absolutely, one hundred percent sure you don't have feelings for him?" Nat said.

I'd been flashing back to my night with Ian all day. The sex was…a revelation. I'd never been so free like that before, so unselfconscious. But I had only been able do that, really let loose, because the situation with Ian was a one-night event. There'd be no tomorrow, no fretting over whether or not he'd call, whether I was too loud or too eager or not eager enough. I'd been able to lay it all on the line because the line had an end point. That was the beauty of the fling. It was what I'd missed out on in all my previous relationships. "I have no feelings for him," I told the girls. "We went into last night in full agreement—no strings, no phone numbers, no expectations. I'm good with that. Really good." I blushed, thinking about his full, sweet lips trailing kisses from my abdomen down, down, down—

"You might want to try a fling, Nat, I mean it." I looked her up and down. Her last relationship hadn't ended in the same hellfire mine had, but tears had flowed. Feelings had been hurt. She had been hoping for a ring, but instead he gave her jumper cables, which cued her to move on. "Or even better, a year of flings."

"I don't think so. I've already met someone who wants what I do. Chris and I are utterly on the same page."

One night and one hand job later, and the two of them were already "Chris and I."

"I'm just saying, maybe give it a shot. See who you are, sans a man. It might open your eyes." After one night, I'd become one of those zealots who'd discovered something new and had to tell everyone about it—like that time three years ago when I did the whole "hug all your belongings and get rid of the ones that don't spark joy." I still lived that tidy life today. It had been one of the best things I'd ever done for myself. And this would be, too.

Katie rested her chin in her hand and gazed into the middle distance. "I think this is good. I'm in."

"You're in?" I asked.

She nodded. "I'm a divorced substitute teacher who lives in her sister's guest room. I need to figure out who I am alone, before I figure out who I am with someone else. A year of no-strings sounds like the right play for me."

I touched my nose. She got it. Good for her, figuring this out in her twenties instead of waiting until forty, like me.

"In fact," she said, "I think we should make a pact to stay single for two years. We could do a year in our sleep."

"Says the twenty-five-year-old." Nat downed her mimosa. "Why not just stay single for the rest of your mortal lives?"

"One is plenty," I said. Nat wasn't wrong. I wasn't getting any younger.

"This is a lot of talk," Nat said, "but neither of you has any skin in the game. What's going to keep you from falling head over heels for the first guy you meet?"

"This isn't about reward or punishment," I said. "It's about bettering our lives, about being okay on our own."

Natalie downed the rest of her tea. "You two will be engaged by January."

I leaned across the table. She looked really smug over there with her tea and her third-base boyfriend. "Let's make it interesting. If I make it the whole year without breaking my rules—no sleepovers, no second dates, no strings—you have to teach that after-school elementary science program I've been begging you to do…for free."

"For *free*?" She scrunched up her nose.

"Out of the goodness of your heart."

"Okay, then. If your new single-and-loving-it life flames out in less than twelve months—as I predict it will—you have to buy me that ginormous interactive SMARTboard for my classroom."

"It costs way too much money. We don't have it in the budget."

"Well, either you'll have to find the money—pilfer some cash from athletics or something—or not fall in love until next November."

Katie set her phone on the table. "What about me? I need some motivation."

Nat scratched her chin. "If you lose, you have to wash my car for a year."

Katie nodded. "I can do that."

"Wax it, undercarriage, the whole thing."

"Got it."

"And if she wins…" I say.

"You pay for my gym membership for an entire year, plus specialty classes, plus three smoothies a week."

"You're on." Nat pulled out her phone and started typing.

"What are you doing?" I asked.

"Just looking up all the cool things I'll be able to do with my new SMARTboard." She glanced up at me and winked.

. . .

IAN

Scott met me at the elevator on Monday. "Prepare yourself." He sipped the beverage from his Starbucks cup. He told everyone he drank black coffee, but only I knew the truth.

Scott, Mr. On-Trend, knocked back white chocolate raspberry mochas on the daily. He started every single morning with a sugar bomb that had been passé, flavor-wise, more than ten years ago. It was the most uncool thing about him, and I adored him for it.

"For what? Why am I preparing myself?" I peered past him toward our office space. Everyone stood huddled in front of the reception desk.

"To vomit." Scott started walking and I fell into step with him. "Tommy's back from paternity leave and he has pictures." Scott rolled his eyes at the word "pictures."

"Babies are cute." I nudged Scott in the side. "As long as they're not mine."

"One benefit of being gay," he said, "is not having to worry about some twenty-two-year-old I met one hot weekend showing up later with a blue stick he peed on."

I patted his shoulder. "You're living the dream."

"You know it."

I sidled up to Tommy, who had captured the full attention of every woman in the office as he proudly flipped through about a million photos on his phone. "Welcome back, man." I clapped him on the back.

"Hey!" Tommy scrolled through his photos and landed on one. He shoved the phone toward me. A picture of an amorphous, bald blob, basically swimming in one of those baby bodysuits, filled the screen. "Here's Maeve in the 'Little Rambler' onesie you gave her."

I nodded. "Nice." Tommy, Scott, and I had been best friends since grade school. After college, we started our little business—buying and selling real estate commodities and investing in small businesses. The details were boring, but the money kicked ass. I pointed to my office and Tommy waved me off as the women huddled around him again, cooing. They used to coo like that around Tommy for a totally different reason.

I found Scott waiting for me in my desk chair. He swiveled around like Dr. Evil, all ten of his fingertips touching. "You got out of there fast."

"Give Tommy a break," I said, dropping my briefcase on my desk. "He's just excited."

"He's so domestic all of a sudden. It won't last. He'll snap sooner or later."

"No, he won't." I motioned for him to vacate my seat, which he did, but not before stealing a pencil from the Holy Cross mug on my desk. I plopped down on my chair. Scott's ass had warmed the leather. Thanks, pal. "What were you expecting? He got married. He had a kid. It happens."

"Not to me. Not to us," Scott said, an almost imperceptible tinge of sadness in his voice. Unlike me, Scott had wanted those things, once upon a time. He stared out the window, which looked down—way down—on Canal Street. Our office sat near the top of the Ogilvie building. My corner space gave me a view of the river, the opera house, and the train tracks headed north. During his down time, Scott liked to hang out in here and watch trains come and go at all hours of the day. "Speaking of..." Scott spun around, a too-big grin on his face. "I had a very fun, unmarried experience this weekend with that waiter from the bachelorette auction."

"Congrats." I flipped through the envelopes in my in-box.

"How about you? Did you visit Minnesota?" He winked.

"You know I didn't." I tossed my mail back onto the desk. This was our usual Monday morning conversation, but I was not in the mood today. "I visited no lands, foreign or domestic, this weekend."

Scott narrowed his eyes. "Bullshit. I can tell you had sex. Who was she? The mayor's daughter? The coat-check girl?" His hand went to his mouth. "Oh my God, did you fuck Dr. Sharpe?! Please tell me you did. Ian banged the school principal!"

Rolling my eyes, I picked up the envelopes I'd just sorted through. I needed time. Scott and I always talked about our weekends. We spared no details. Tommy and I had golf. What bonded Scott and I was recreational sex. But I'd decided to keep all the mortifying Erin-related details to myself. "I didn't bang anyone. I wasn't feeling so hot after dinner and went right home. I think I ate some bad shellfish."

"Really?"

"Really." Guilt pinged in my gut. I never lied to Scott or Tommy. Never, ever, ever.

"You're telling me that you—Ian Donovan—did not get laid over the weekend." Scott stood nose to nose with me now, fingertips planted on top of my desk, trying to suss out the truth. He was pulling a Larry David on *Curb*, staring into my eyes, searching for the lie.

"That's what I'm telling you," I said. "I was sick."

That night with Erin existed just for me and her. That's what I'd decided, at least. It had been a fun night, an amazing night, but it was different from when I hooked up with other girls. I'd slept over. She'd been the one who'd kicked me out, which embarrassed the shit out of me. And I couldn't stop thinking about how she just hopped out of bed naked in the morning like it was no big deal. I hadn't had an experience like that in...well, ever.

I didn't do feelings or emotions. I didn't do the sad walk of shame. But Erin had been the one who slammed the door on me.

And it bummed me the fuck out.

I'd love to pretend it didn't, but it did.

Between her and Maria Minnesota, I was on the verge of becoming a romantic or something. My game had slipped.

I had to pretend the night didn't happen and move on, learn from my mistakes—like I did during a round of golf. If

I bogeyed one hole, I didn't take that disappointment to the next one. I shook it off. And now I was shaking off the most recent mistakes of my sex life. There'd be no more staying overnight, no more second dates, and no expectations. The thing with Erin had been a blip. It had reaffirmed that my original guiding principles were correct. I had put those rules in place for a reason, and I needed to heed them.

I looked up and nodded toward the door. "I've got to check messages."

Scott took the hint and left, and I pressed play on my voicemail. A small, annoying part of me hoped to hear Erin's voice through the speaker, though I had no idea why I would.

No dice.

Which was fine. Which was the point. Erin was living up to her end of our bargain. I didn't want to hear from her or anything. I was done with her, just as she, apparently, was done with me.

All proceeding as planned.

I shook my shoulders, dislodging Erin from my mind.

The first two messages were from my friend Isamu in Tokyo, one of the partners at Fumetsu Enterprises, who'd given me the inside track. His company was in the process of developing a completely indestructible cell phone, among other things, and they were playing really, really hard to get. Something I knew a bit about. I made a note to schedule another trip out there ASAP.

The third had come from some woman named Liz Barton, an alumna from my high school who had started her own VC group in town and wanted to pick my brain. I'd ask my assistant to set something up.

My mom had left the fourth message. "Hi, honey! Just checking in. Call me when you get a chance. If you misplaced my number, it's—"

I deleted the voicemail, like I deleted all my mom's

voicemails. I hadn't spoken to her since, well, probably the holidays last year. She was my cautionary tale, my reason to remain attachment-free, and I'd do well to remember that right now.

I pressed the intercom button on my phone and called Scott's office. "Hey, buddy. You up for going out tonight? I could use some fun."

After work, Scott, Tommy, and I hopped over to The Bizzee Sygnal, which had been Scott's choice. He loved watching the sloppy women from the 'burbs falling all over the guys who'd just gotten off work. We let him pick, even though he'd informed us he wasn't in it for the long haul this evening because he had to go up to Winnetka to visit his mom.

Tommy and I followed Scott downstairs to the "oldies" room, where the DJ played tunes from the '80s and '90s, which never ceased to make me feel like an ancient grandpa. Scott hopped up on stage with some thirtysomething women and started dancing to "Forever Your Girl" by Paula Abdul, while Tommy and I grabbed two seats at the bar and ordered beers.

"You're not dancing?" I asked. Unlike me, Tommy had no qualms about bopping around to cheesy music.

He shook his head. "Maybe later."

I nudged him in the side. "Give me the real scoop, man. How's being a dad?" This whole concept was so foreign to me. I had some friends who were parents, but I barely saw most of them anymore. We lived totally different lives, which in and of itself created distance between us. While I was rolling in from the bar at four in the morning, they were getting up to feed their kid or change its diaper. Tommy was my first ride-or-die to take the parenting plunge. Yeah, part of me worried about how that'd change our relationship, but, really, things had already been different since he and Susie got together and he stopped going out as much. For years now, it had mostly been Scott and me alone on the weekends or after work.

"Being a dad is great." Tommy sipped his beer. "Susie's great. Maeve's great."

He was hiding something. I narrowed my eyes and forced him to look at me. "So everything's perfect?"

"One hundred percent." Now he downed half his drink.

"Bullshit," I said. "You're telling me there's not one negative to taking care of a kid—not the diapers or the crying or having to get out of bed in the middle of the night?"

"My mother-in-law is visiting and she's thinking about moving in with us."

"That's a bingo!" I touched my glass to his.

"It's a good thing. She does so much to help Susie. I'm grateful to have her around." Tommy sounded like a pod person. He gazed around the bar as if seeing it for the first time. My friend had morphed into an alien being.

"You're glad to be out tonight, though?"

He shook his head. "I miss my girls." Again with the alien monotone.

I punched him in the arm. "You sap."

Tommy grinned, but the smile didn't quite reach his eyes. I glanced over at Scott, who'd wrapped his arms around two middle-aged women with big hair. He'd always questioned whether or not Tommy could handle life as a husband and father. This was the first time I'd ever questioned it as well.

"There something else going on?" I asked. "You can tell me anything, bud. You know that." Tommy and I had been through absolutely everything together—his dad dying, my mom leaving, his relationships ending.

He hit me with a watery grin. "Just thinking about old times." Now he smiled with his eyes. I relaxed a bit. Same old Tommy. "Remember when we switched identities?"

I shook my head in disbelief. I'd completely forgotten about that. For some reason we'd decided it would be fun. "Oh my God, that was…why the hell did we do that again?"

"Because we were bored or something." He shook his head. "I really leaned into the whole 'being you' thing that night. I fed the girls all your stories about jet-setting around the globe." Tommy was our CFO, and he mostly stayed in Chicago. He didn't rack up the miles like Scott and I did, which was probably a big part of the reason why he could handle being in a relationship and we couldn't. He raised his eyebrows. "I went home with two women that night."

Chuckling, I patted his hand. "And no one can ever take that memory away from you."

"True." He downed the rest of his drink, as Scott made his way back over to us. "At least I'll always have that."

I was about to ask him to elaborate, to get down to the real reason why he was acting so off tonight, when Scott said, "I've got to hit the road."

Tommy threw a few bills down on the bar. That was it. No more talking. Our guys' night out had ended in a whimper. "Me, too. Can we share a ride to the train station?"

Scott nodded. "You coming, too, Ian?"

I glanced around. The bar had started to fill up. This would be the perfect opportunity for me to reaffirm my guiding principles, maybe use a couple of those traveling-the-globe stories Tommy had mentioned. "I'm going to ride it out here," I said.

After the guys left, I finished my first beer and ordered another, trying to psych myself up to make a move. I was Ian Fucking Donovan—a rich, attractive dude with a good personality. I could get any woman in this club. Heck, I could get two women, if I wanted to.

A group of bubbly twentysomethings had gathered at the end of the bar.

Fish in a barrel.

I pointed to the TV, where the Bulls game had been playing earlier. "Did you see the score?" I asked the woman nearest to me, a blonde. I didn't care about the score. I barely cared about sports, other than golf.

She shook her head. "Sorry."

"I'm Ian." I held out my hand in greeting.

She giggled. "And I'm young enough to be your daughter."

Her friends swarmed around her, laughing, and then a group of guys who were much closer to her age came over and sidled up. I wasn't old enough to be their dad. Their uncle, maybe. Their cool uncle who bought them beer when they were underage. "That's Ian," the girl told her friends, giggling. I was a joke to them, an old man who'd lived past his prime.

One of the other girls, a brunette, pulled away from the group. "Don't listen to them. I'm Paris." Paris grinned—nice smile, white teeth. She sported a dress with a cutout over the stomach. Standard fare these days.

"Want to buy me a drink?" She shook her long brown hair over her shoulders, still flashing me that grin.

"I—" I checked my watch. Still early, but, honestly, the idea of chatting up someone whose name I wouldn't remember in a day or two exhausted me. Tonight, just knowing I could've scored was enough. "You know what? I would, but I've got somewhere to be." I raised my glass to her and downed my beer.

Then I opened my ride app, typed in my own address, and went home alone to watch *Black Mirror*.

Chapter Four

"So, what's going on with you?"

Dana, my gynecologist and good friend since kindergarten, perched on her official doctor's stool, while I sat on the patient's bed. At least she'd let me keep my clothes on today. For now, anyway. No secrets remained between Dana and me, at least on my end, but it was nice once in a while to have a conversation with her without my ass hanging out the back of a flimsy paper gown.

I gazed at the Christmas tree in the far corner of the room that had been decorated with blue lights and tiny menorah ornaments. "I'm feeling a little off." I touched my cheek, which felt clammy. I'd probably caught something from the kids at school. This kind of thing always happened, though usually earlier in the year. In years past, by now, by December, my immunity had kicked back in and my body could ward off any bugs the children tracked into the school.

"You look great," Dana said. "You left urine samples?"

"As always." Dana was my OB/GYN, but I always went to her first whenever I had questions or concerns. She could always talk me down from any of my presumed illnesses. I bet Dana never imagined how much she'd be testing my pee as a grown-up, back when we were giving our Barbie and Jem dolls makeovers in third grade. We never asked the Magic 8 Ball if copious chats about my urinary tract lurked in our future.

"Well, we'll run tests on that. But honestly, you're glowing." Dana checked my chart on her tablet. "Are you eating better? Taking the vitamins I prescribed?"

"Yes and yes." A slow smile crept onto my face. In all the years of me coming to Dana for exams, I never had anything new to report, sex-wise. For the past decade, I'd been with Dirk. She knew all about our sporadic sex life and our troubles getting pregnant. But now I had something to brag about. "Honestly, other than the nausea, I feel like I have a new lease on life."

"And a new wardrobe," she said.

"Thank you for noticing." Today I'd donned a pair of black leggings and a blue velvet tunic that looked way too dressy for a Wednesday afternoon, but it matched the new vibe I'd decided to cultivate. I deserved a new wardrobe to match my new attitude. It was time to be who I wanted to be, and who I wanted to be was one of those old ladies who dressed up all the time—sequins were my new sweats.

"What are you not telling me?" Dana rested her iPad on her lap and flipped her reading glasses to the top of her head.

I waggled my eyebrows. "I had sex. Just once. Well, one night. Three times. With the same guy, but it was great and I'm going to do it again. With other people. I have an active sex life, or, well, I plan on having one. In the near future."

Dana replaced her glasses and noted this new information on her tablet. "Really? And now you're not feeling well?" She frowned.

"Just a little off, nothing big. I haven't gotten my period in a while, but you know me, my period comes when it wants." I scrunched up my face. "Is it menopause?" I voiced the fear that had been haunting me for the past week. "Did random sex kick me into the change of life?" I whispered those last words.

Dana took off her glasses. "Well, you're only forty."

"So…maybe?"

"Maybe." Dana pulled out her phone and sent a text. "I'm sure it's fine." She reached over and patted my knee.

My heart beat in my throat. "Oh God." It was bad. I could tell. Here I'd been all carefree about my night with Ian, a guy who'd probably been with billions of women. Yes, we'd used a condom, but those weren't foolproof, right? I grew up in the '90s. This was one of the hard truths we all knew: sex would kill you, New Coke was one of the biggest mistakes of all time, and up-up-down-down-left-right-left-right-B-A-Select-Start would get you thirty lives in *Contra*. "Is it syphilis?" I said. "Did he give me gonorrhea?" I lay back on the bed and pressed my arm to my forehead, like a swooning antebellum socialite…who'd just found out she had The Clap.

Dana patted my knee. "Don't assume anything. My nurse will be here with the results in two minutes."

"Two minutes?" That was how long I had before I'd find out that I had contracted a sexually transmitted disease from the one fling I'd ever allowed myself. At least I didn't have any other partners to contact with this news. Thank God for small favors.

Exactly two minutes later, the door opened and shut. I scrunched my eyes closed, waiting for Dana to give me the bad news. I didn't have to wait long. A few seconds later, Dana said, "E, you're pregnant."

I bolted upright. My head swirled. "No."

Dana held up the thing her nurse had brought in. It was a regular old pregnancy test, and the stick glowed blue. Bright. Ass. Blue.

"Congratulations?" Dana said.

I held out my hand and she placed the test in my palm. I stared at it, unblinking, barely thinking. I'd taken a bunch of these over the years, even though I'd lost hope long ago that I'd ever get pregnant. I just thought maybe, maybe if I merely peed on the stick a little it'd make me pregnant. I'd never seen any of those tests turn any sort of color. This one was as blue as the ocean. With my mouth wide enough to catch flies, I looked Dana right in the eye.

I was pregnant, something I'd longed to be for years.

I was going to have a baby, but not Dirk's baby.

Ian Donovan's baby. A stranger's baby.

I let out a shaky breath. "Thank you?"

...

ERIN

I arrived at work that morning around eleven. When I showed my ID badge at the front desk, Mabel, the security guard, said, "You look pale, Dr. Sharpe. Are you sick?"

"Little bit," I told her.

It would be lunchtime in an hour. Everyone ate at the same time at Glenfield Academy, and kids were allowed to go home for lunch, if their parents permitted it. This place was like a time warp to the 1950s.

When I got to my office, I shut the door, sank into my desk chair, and sent a text to Nat and Katie. "Come to my office as soon as lunch starts. Do not pass 'Go.' Do not collect two hundred dollars."

I folded my hands on top of my desk and waited, silently watching the hand on my Fox Mulder wall clock until it reached the twelve.

"Erin?" Nat knocked on my door.

"Come on in." My voice came out thin and weak.

Natalie slowly opened my office door, and she and Katie entered.

Katie shut and locked the door. Her hand went to her mouth when she saw my face. "Is it cancer?"

I shook my head and pointed to the seats across the desk from me. Once they had both settled in, I spoke. "I'm pregnant."

Natalie's jaw dropped, and Katie hit the side of her head, like she was trying to clear her ears.

After a moment, Nat said, "You're pregnant?"

"And...?" Katie cocked an ear to me, waiting for more information.

I shrugged. "And..." I blew out a shaky breath. "This was what I wanted, right?"

They both nodded slowly, and I could tell they wanted desperately to say the right thing to the pregnant lady who sat across from them, white as a ghost.

"Is it, though?" Nat narrowed her eyes.

I stood and started pacing, shaking out my hands in front of me. I'd had time to think this morning—on the drive up from the city, and while sitting here staring at my clock, but the shock hadn't worn off yet. I'd gone from thinking I'd never, ever get pregnant to finding out I'd been accidentally knocked up. I tried to keep any worries, fears, or hopes out of this. Finding out I was pregnant was just information. Positive information, if a little ahead of schedule. "Dirk and I had been trying for years...ish. And my whole plan had been to start the process of having a kid on my own after the year of being single ended. This...just speeds up the timeline."

"Where does Ian fit in?" Katie asked.

"He doesn't." I'd barely thought of Ian after leaving

Dana's office. One of his swimmers had busted through the net. So what? We'd said our goodbyes. He wasn't looking to be tied down.

"He's the father," Katie said.

Nat shook her head. "Ian Fucking Donovan is your baby's father. This poor child."

I pointed to her. "Nat gets it. Ian and I agreed 'one night only.' This goes way beyond that. He travels all the time. He's a playboy. God knows what he does on the weekend. He doesn't want this."

"He does not," Nat said.

"You don't know that." Katie had spun her chair around to watch me head-on.

Nat raised her hand. "I do."

"But he deserves to know about the baby. He deserves the option of being part of this kid's life at least." Katie shook her head. "Erin, you know the right thing to do is to tell him."

"But I don't want his help." I touched my heart. "I'm fine on my own, right? Bringing him into this puts me right back to where I don't want to be—counting on a guy to help me out."

"You can do it on your own," Katie said. "Heck, you can even tell him up front that you need nothing from him. But you have to tell him."

I looked at Nat. She knew how much of a cad Ian was, how terrible he'd be at this job he didn't even want. She shook her head. "Katie's right. You have to tell him."

I sighed.

"But just don't expect anything from him," she warned me.

"Believe me, I won't."

• • •

IAN

My phone buzzed, vibrating my whole desk, seizing my attention from the Tokyo-related spreadsheet Tommy'd handed me a half hour ago. Scott and I had plans to head to Japan soon to impress Fumetsu Enterprises with both our knowledge of their business and our innate ability to schmooze. But right now, the numbers part eluded me. The facts and figures had been blurring for the past fifteen minutes.

I squinted at the digits on my phone. They weren't familiar. The message said, *Hey, Ian. It's Erin Sharpe. Can you meet for coffee?*

My eyes refocused and my heart beat a bit faster when I read her name—out of annoyance, I'm sure. She wasn't supposed to be texting me. That hadn't been part of our deal when we had sex a full six weeks ago.

But maybe she wanted another hookup? I could totally go for that. Erin had been so cool the last time, the way she'd kicked me out of her condo like I was nothing. Unlike Maria Minnesota, Erin was exactly the kind of girl with whom I could have a repeat romp. Erin and I were both hit-it-and-quit-it kind of people.

In theory, anyway. I hadn't hit anything that would need to be quit since meeting Erin. I'd been out a bunch of times with Scott, gleefully playing the role of wingman, but I hadn't found anyone I wanted to take home, even for a night.

Maybe one more dalliance with Erin would be just what the doctor ordered. I had to get her out of my system, and then I could move on, go back to the way things were. This time I'd leave first. I'd be the one to utter the *thank you, ma'am,* after the *wham-bam.* She'd turned the tables on me, and I needed to turn them back, to set the universe right.

I texted her back *Coffee?* with a winky face. Coffee was

never just "coffee."

She wrote me back right away. *No. Literally just coffee.*

So much for that theory. Still, I'd meet her. I'd hear her out. And I'd charm the pants off her in the process, hopefully.

I freshened up a bit before heading down to the street, where bells rang and the streets smelled like cinnamon. People from all over Chicagoland taken the train in to stop at the Chriskindlmarket and see the lights and windows on Michigan Avenue. Tourists and revelers crammed the sidewalks. Maybe that was why Erin had come downtown in the middle of a Thursday. She'd probably gotten off school for winter break and was looking for something...or someone... to do. Well, I'd be happy to oblige. Just this one time.

I straightened my glasses and ran my fingers through my hair one last time before pulling open the door to Starbucks just down the block from my building. I scanned the room, hunting for that punky platinum hair, which I found in the far corner, at a small table.

Erin's hair looked sad. It lay flat against her head, not sticking up or styled in any way. She wore a Loyola University sweatshirt and black sweatpants, and she'd draped a big, marshmallow-like parka across the back of her chair. She clutched a steaming mug of something with two hands, while she stared out the window.

Oddly, though she looked like death, my first instinct was not to scurry away. She was still Erin, the woman with whom I'd had a great time dancing ironically (or not). She was still the woman who took the wine, and it crushed me that right now she looked like the entire weight of the world had settled on her back. I actually had to stop myself from running over there and hugging her, to try to make her feel better.

Who the hell was I?

I removed my coat on the way to the table and sat down across from her. "Hi," I said.

She turned her head and looked at me. Dark gray circles had formed under her eyes, which were red and puffy. She'd been crying. "I'm pregnant," she said.

In a split second of utter shock, confusion, and disbelief, I burst out laughing and said, "What?" She had to be joking. And, honestly, kudos to Dr. Sharpe. This was an epic prank, busting my balls with a fake pregnancy, and her playing the part with the tragic clothes and hair and red eyes.

"I'm not joking." Her face revealed no hint of a smile.

"You're not joking." The blood drained from my face, leaving an icy trail from my forehead to my toes.

She stared out the window as she spoke. "I'm having the baby. It's definitely yours. You don't have to be involved." Now she looked at me. The deadness in her eyes chilled me. She didn't appear angry or sad. She seemed numb, and she looked at me like I meant less than nothing to her. "I'm only telling you because I know I should. I don't expect anything from you."

I believed her. She really didn't expect anything from me. Why would she? I was the king of one-night stands. Not exactly responsible father material.

"I can pay—" Having never been in this situation before, at least not that I'd known about, I had no idea what to do with the information she'd just handed me, but I could give her money, at least. Money I had. Time to devote to another person? Emotional stability? Dependability? Those were foreign concepts.

She shook her head. "I don't need money." She reached into her coat pocket and handed me a business card.

I glanced down at it. It was from an OB/GYN office, and someone had scrawled a date and time across the top. This was really, really real. Not that I hadn't believed Erin before, but now I had proof —in black and white ink.

"That's an appointment for my first ultrasound. You

don't have to come."

I might have been new at the whole being-a-father thing, but I certainly wasn't new at recognizing when I wasn't wanted. "Okay," I said. She was the boss.

Erin, still not looking at me, nodded, grabbed her coat, and left the coffee shop without another word.

I chugged the rest of her hot tea, barely registering the burn on the roof of my mouth as I stared at the card she'd given me. *Monday afternoon. December 23rd. Two o'clock. Dr. Dana Costello.* I was free. Or not "free," but I could move things around. Easily.

No. I should respect her wishes. Erin only told me this news out of obligation. She didn't want me there. She had made that abundantly clear.

But maybe I wanted to be there?

Fuck. What was I thinking? Of course I didn't want to go. The last thing I wanted was to be a part of this kid's life, a part of anyone's life. I'd avoided this level of responsibility my entire adult life. I'd only end up hurting my child, not to mention their mother. I was just like my own mom, but, unlike her, I knew my limitations.

However, instead of chucking the business card in the trash and erasing this whole afternoon from my mind, I pulled out my phone and added the time, date, and location to my Google Calendar to buy myself some time to think, just in case. I didn't have to make any bold decisions right this second.

· · ·

IAN

"Who, pray tell, is Dr. Dana Costello? And why are you seeing a gynecologist?"

I nearly dropped my coffee as I stepped into my office the

next morning. I found Scott in my swivel chair, slapping the business card Erin had given me against his palm. I could not get rid of it. Every time I tried chucking it into the garbage, someone—me—snatched it back out.

"I came in here this morning to watch the trains, and, lo and behold, there on your desk sat an OB/GYN's card. Where did you two meet? She sounds fancy."

The air drained from my lungs. Scott thought the two o'clock appointment was a date. I supposed that made more sense than the alternative—that I'd knocked up the one-night stand Scott didn't even know I'd had. "Dana and I met a couple weeks ago. At The Bizzee Sygnal. After you left."

"You met a doctor at The Bizzee Sygnal? Wonders never cease." He handed me the card.

I tossed it into the garbage—for real this time—and paced in front of the floor-to-ceiling windows. Morning rush hour was still a go, and train after train pulled in and out of the station below. "She'd gone to the bar with some college friends. We got to talking." I shrugged, ignoring the sick feeling in my stomach that if I had met a doctor at The Bizzee Sygnal a few weeks ago, I would've made an excuse not to sleep with her. My mojo had disappeared.

"So, bud," Scott said. "I came to tell you something." I noticed then that Scott looked the way I felt—drained and confused.

"You okay?"

Shaking his head, he stood and closed the door. "My mom's sick."

For the second time that week, an iciness snaked down my spine and drifted through my limbs.

On instinct, I stepped over to hug him, but he waved me off. "I know," he said. "I don't want to get all—" He flailed his arms. "I've been dealing with hospitals and tests and what-ifs for the past few weeks. Now we're facing logistics. It's cancer.

Stomach. Doesn't look like it's spread. She's going to have chemo and radiation. She'll be fine." He placed his hands in prayer position and stared at the ceiling for a moment before looking at me again. "But I need to step back a bit, business-wise."

I nodded. "Whatever you need." Scott's mom had cancer. Scott's *mom*. She was Scott's entire life—the only person who trumped either work or friends. If he lost her…

I couldn't think about that.

He said, "I don't want to leave you in the lurch right now with the Tokyo stuff—"

I waved him off. "Man, don't worry about it. I've got it. You know that."

"Thank God for Ian," Scott said. "Mr. No Entanglements."

I chuckled nervously. Heck, I'd just gotten word of a very significant entanglement, if I wanted it to be.

"Fuck cancer," Scott said. "Let's talk about something happy, like you and the lady doctor. Have you two gone out since you met?"

I shook my head. God, how could we pivot to this banality? The word "cancer" still hung in the air like an anvil about to drop on our heads.

"But you're meeting up on Monday?" Scott asked.

I'd play along. If Scott didn't want to talk about it, we wouldn't talk about it. When he felt ready, we would. I'd be there for him, always. "I don't know if I'm gonna show up." Hell, that was the truth.

"You're gonna blow off the doctor? The gynecologist?"

"Maybe." I'd been back and forth about this since Erin told me the news. She didn't want me there. She didn't need me there. I got that. I respected it. But what did I want? I wasn't looking for a romantic relationship, but I had managed to stay close to my childhood friends all my life. Maybe I could make room for a kid.

What the fuck was I thinking? No, I couldn't. I was leaving for Tokyo for two weeks. I'd have to go back there again and again over the next few months. And that wouldn't be the end of it. After we signed that deal, there'd be others—in Australia or South America or wherever.

I didn't have room in my life. For anyone.

"I know what this is," Scott said. "You've been gun-shy ever since Maria Minnesota." Again, as always, he said her name like a game-show host. "Is this Dana woman looking for a commitment from you?"

I shook my head. "No." Erin wanted absolutely nothing from me. She'd said so. Explicitly.

"Did you tell her you don't do relationships?"

I nodded.

"Then I say go for it. Everyone knows the score. It's a date, not a wedding."

Scott got up to leave, and I stopped him. "Buddy, I'm—" The end of that sentence didn't make it out of my throat. My eyes stung with tears.

Blinking hard, he nodded. Then he plucked the appointment reminder from my garbage can and placed it on my desk before leaving my office.

The baby.

Right now this kid existed only in my head. But if I opened up my life, it'd mean opening up everything. I didn't do that. I had no room in my life for anything but work and my friends.

The kid didn't need me. He or she'd have a great mom, and that'd be enough.

I ripped the card to shreds and tossed the pieces back into the garbage.

Chapter Five

Katie placed a hand on my knee, which, yes, had been bobbing up and down like a piston. "You're nervous," she said.

"I'm fine." I nudged her hand off my leg and focused on planting my heel into the carpet to keep my foot from going a mile a minute again. I was fine. I was simply sitting in the waiting room of my gynecologist's office—oh yeah, and *obstetrics*, yikes—waiting to get a first look at this tiny human growing inside me.

And I had to pee something wicked.

I crossed my legs, squeezing tight. "I am a forty-year-old woman with a forty-year-old bladder. They should not make me wait like this." And my lower leg started pumping again, less out of nerves now and more to distract myself from the fact that I had downed four glasses of water in the last hour, and each and every one of them was ready to make a return appearance. I tried to focus on the Christmas music softly wafting through the waiting-room speakers.

"They're not making you wait." Katie picked up a magazine. "Your appointment's not for another five minutes. You should've listened to the nurse's instructions and drunk the water more slowly."

"Yeah, well, what does the nurse know about anything?" I shot an evil eye at the receptionist, who, in all honesty, definitely had exactly zero to do with my current situation. She hadn't told me to drink the water. Heck, she hadn't knocked me up. Really, if anyone was to blame for my current state, it was Ian Donovan. Or the condom company. Maybe I should sue.

"You know," I said, "this probably isn't even a thing, having to drink water before an ultrasound. It's probably just some big joke the doctors cooked up to make us ladies uncomfortable."

Katie flipped through the *Reader's Digest.* "You're totally right, sis. I think you've uncovered the plot. These doctors, who have dedicated their careers to helping women, are really just trying to fuck with you."

"See? You get it."

Katie slammed the magazine shut and tossed it onto the table in front of us. "Okay. Enough about pee and how a vast doctor-driven conspiracy to make you uncomfortable is currently ruining your life. Let's address the elephant in the room. Or, really, the elephant who's not in the room."

I bit my cheek. I did not bring Katie with me to talk. If I'd wanted a lecture, I would've brought Natalie.

Katie's soft brown eyes found mine. She wouldn't berate me. I should've known better. Katie didn't play the blame game. My hormones had me all out of whack. I took a few calming breaths. "This whole situation sucks," she said.

I nodded, my throat closing. It sure did suck. It sucked not being able to drink wine at the Sharpe family pre-Christmas party while everyone cooed over my cousin's pregnant wife. It sucked that I had this secret growing in my womb the whole time, and I couldn't talk to anyone about it, because

I had no idea what to say. *Hey, things are great. I'm single and carrying a stranger's baby, no big deal. Look at how I'm simply crushing life right now!*

"You're sitting in a doctor's waiting room, preparing to see your baby for the first time, and the father isn't here," Katie said.

"The father doesn't exist," I corrected her.

Katie opened her mouth to protest.

But I cut her off. "I know. He exists. He's a living, breathing human being. But for all intents and purposes, he's a ghost." I nodded backward, toward the front door of the doctor's office behind me. "He's not here now. He's not going to be here. It's good for us—all of us—to get used to that." I picked up the *Reader's Digest* Katie had discarded, hoping a page full of inspirational quotes might take some of the focus off my bladder.

"Okay," Katie said. "As long as you're okay with the situ—"

Now it was my turn to toss the magazine to the table. "Dirk and I tried *for years* to have a baby."

"Off and on," Katie reminded me. "And, really, you dodged a bullet."

"Only to be hit by another one." I squeezed my pelvic floor. My God, I'd burst right then and there in the waiting room—death by bladder bomb. "I had a one-night stand—one stupid, regretful night—with Ian and now I'm carrying his baby. A stranger's baby. What are the parents at my school going to say? What do I tell the kids?"

"You tell them nothing." Katie shrugged in her typical way of thinking every situation had a black-and-white answer. Gray areas did not exist for Katie. "It's none of their business. For all they know, you went to a sperm bank because you wanted to have a kid on your own—which you were planning on doing in a year anyway." She shook her head. "But even the truth isn't bad. I mean, when you think about it. You're a successful, strong, intelligent woman who got pregnant and is prepared to raise the kid on her own. You're, like, the model single mom. You've got your shit together."

I blew out a deep breath. "Yeah, my shit's so together that I got knocked up by someone about whom I know exactly two things: one, he's a totally immature playboy who's anti-commitment, and two, he's a really good lay."

"Hey, that's not nothing!" Katie patted my knee again. "This is all very new. You're shocked and scared and probably ready to chuck everything and move to a desert island or something."

"That doesn't sound bad."

"I felt the same way after my divorce."

I wrapped an arm around Katie's shoulders, pulling her in close.

She rested her head on me. "But since then," she said, "I've tried to stay positive, think about what's good in my life now—I'm working out more, trying to better myself, thinking about a career."

"You're getting buff, by the way." I squeezed her biceps and she flexed.

"I know your situation isn't ideal, but I just want to point out that you'd be having the same fears if one of Dirk's probably horribly pretentious sperm had knocked you up. In that *Sliding Doors* scenario, you'd still be a single, unmarried woman, and Dirk would be MIA for all of it. Because Dirk was and is a fucking tool."

"Seconded." A deep voice boomed behind us.

Katie and I spun around. There stood Ian in his work clothes—perfectly tailored pants, shoes with nary a scuff, a supple camel overcoat covering a blue-checked, button-down shirt that contrasted his Hershey's chocolate eyes. A nervous smile flickered under his thick, trendy glasses and his hair stood a bit more on end than usual, like he'd been running his fingers through it all day.

"Hey." I shrugged and faced forward. Whatever. He showed up. Big whoop.

Though try telling that to the butterflies in my stomach.

"Damn," Katie whispered.

I nudged her in the side. She had to get her shit together. So Ian had come to this one appointment. So he looked good doing it. He was still not a person who could be counted on, and that was fine. That was our entire deal. Like Katie said, I was a strong, independent woman, and I was fully capable of doing all of this on my own. I didn't need Ian Donovan. I needed no one.

The nurse opened the door to the office and checked a chart. "Erin Sharpe?" She looked up at us over a pair of reading glasses. I stood, squeezing my legs together. Oh, Jesus, the pee.

"Ready?" I asked Katie. She was the only one here I could count on, really. She was family. She was this baby's actual aunt.

"You two go," Katie said, picking up the *Reader's Digest* again. "You're the parents. I'll stay here and memorize some puns to tell you later."

Ian raised an eyebrow, waiting for me to make the decision, apparently. Well, fine. Whatever. "You're here," I said, heading toward the nurse, not waiting for him to follow. That had to be his decision. "Might as well come in, if you want."

• • •

IAN

This was not like how I'd seen it on TV.

TV had prepared me for clear gel and a wand thing swishing over a swollen, pregnant belly. TV had not prepared me to see my one-night stand with her feet up in stirrups while an attractive, brunette doctor plunged, basically, a dildo inside…well, you know.

Because of one tiny tear in one shitty condom, I was now stuck in a completely foreign kind of relationship with someone I barely knew. We, for better or worse, would be bonded together forever. We were this kid's parents. I, Ian Donovan, was going to be a father.

That was never not going to be weird.

I hovered up near Erin's head, trying to find something to focus on that wasn't the probe inside my fling's snatch or the video monitor displaying the insides of her vag. But landmines lurked all over this room—there was the 3-D model of a woman's reproductive system, the chart with pictures of healthy breasts, and the bottles and bottles of lube. Lube was freaking everywhere.

"Just so everyone knows," Dr. Dana said, "since Erin's forty, she's technically at an advanced maternal age—AMA."

"Geriatric," Erin deadpanned.

"Advanced maternal age," the doctor said. "We don't use 'geriatric' anymore."

"How kind of you."

I could leave. I could actually tap out now, throw my hands up, and walk out the door. Erin wouldn't blame me. It was what she'd wanted in the first place. She'd tossed me that card, but she hadn't actually banked on me showing up. She'd known I wouldn't want to come.

But come I did, and now I was standing in a room full of vaginas and lube, and not in a fun way.

"Usually AMA just means we'll offer you more tests, more ultrasounds. Most of the stuff is voluntary. You know me." The doctor, wand still all up in Erin's business, patted her patient's shin. "I'll let you know what I think is necessary and what isn't."

I mean, but seriously. What was I doing here? I had an out. This kid's mom was fine without me. She was an elementary school principal with a PhD in education. She knew more about children than I'd ever even pretend to know.

I couldn't be the asshole, though. I was already known as the asshole in too many circles, and I couldn't have Erin Sharpe, the woman who stole the wine, the mother of my actual child, thinking about me that same way. I'd see this through. I'd be her rock, whatever she needed. For the next nine months to eighteen years, I'd have to be Ian Donovan: Upstanding Father and All-Around Good Dude.

The doctor looked at me. "I'll give you all the literature," she said. "And I'm happy to explain everything, whatever you two need."

You two? Oh no. Yeah, I'd just been thinking about being a dad, but "you two" was couple talk. The doctor saw Erin and me as a pair, which we most certainly were not. I wanted to shout, "No! We are two singular people who happened to have some bad luck with a condom!"

But I kept my mouth shut.

"Everything looks good," the doctor said, patting Erin's ankle and rising from her stool. She cleaned off the probe and tossed her gloves into the garbage. Then she held out a hand and helped Erin sit up. "You can pee now," she said, laughing.

Erin swung her legs off the side of the table where she'd been lying. "Thank God!"

I chuckled, and Erin glared at me. "What?" she demanded.

I waited until the doctor had closed the door behind her, leaving Erin and me alone with the lube. "Nothing." I hadn't meant to offend her. "Just...nerves." I gestured toward her, perched on the table, her feet in fuzzy socks dangling off the side. "I never thought I'd be...here."

"Yeah, well, me neither." She hopped off the table and took great care wrapping the flimsy paper sheet around her midsection—the complete opposite of how she'd acted the morning after we'd slept together, when she'd hopped out of bed all naked and cavalier.

I laughed again.

And she glared at me again. "Seriously. What?"

"Nothing."

Eyeing me the entire way, she scooted sideways into the attached bathroom, shut the door, and locked it. I sat in the guest chair near the door, a safe, vagina-free spot.

When I'd left work today, Scott had shot me a wink, a pair of waggling eyebrows, and a comment about gynecologists. He assumed I was off to get laid, which was less embarrassing than the truth—that I was going to spend the afternoon standing next to the female stranger carrying my baby while we watched its heartbeat flickering on screen for the first time.

The kid. *Our* kid. The image of that tiny bean on the TV screen had been etched into my brain.

That was my child. My DNA. They were going to be half Ian Donovan. For better or worse, present or absent, I would be a major part of that kid's story. The way I handled this would shape this child for their entire life.

Scott and his mom kept popping into my head, as they had since he told me about the cancer. He could lose his mom. Heck, she could lose him, for that matter. There were no guarantees. Scott and his mom had been there for each other, relied on each other, and now he was looking at, potentially, the rest of his life without her.

My chest ached.

I had been fine, fine on my own, floating in and out of (but mostly out of) other people's lives. People loved me in the short term, for a night or even a weekend. But I was destined to disappoint anyone who put their faith in me, because my life was *my* life, and no one else's. I pulled away from anyone who dared to get close to me. Erin got that. She seemed fine with it. But the kid, the kid would expect me to stick around, and maybe they'd be better off without me right from the start.

Maybe having no father was better than having me as a father.

I grabbed my coat from the rack and slipped it on without a sound, watching the bathroom door, willing Erin to stay inside until I was gone. This was the right thing to do. It had been stupid and reckless to show up here. And even when I met her at the coffee shop, she'd seemed to understand that I was not prepared to be a part of this kid's life—or hers. Erin had been fine with it.

So why wasn't I? Why did I have to go and mess it all up by showing up for this fucking appointment?

I turned the doorknob as quietly as possible, ready to slip out unseen. But I nearly ran into Dr. Dana, about to knock. "Oh," she said, "Hi. Here." She handed me a photo. "Here's your baby," she said with a wink.

Blinking, I stared down at the black-and-white picture. The embryo looked like a grain of rice, if anything. It was a blob. Nothing. A white speck. But it was my baby.

My. Baby.

I clutched the photo to my chest, where my heart slammed against my bones, trying to escape. I sympathized. I needed to escape, too. I waved the picture at the doctor. "I have an appointment." My throat had dried up like a desert, and my words came out in a series of croaks. "Tell Erin—"

The doctor nodded, her eyes narrowing in contempt. Nothing I wasn't used to. I'd returned to my normal, my stasis—women glowering at me with disappointment. "I'll tell her you had to go."

I shoved the ultrasound into my pocket as I ducked my head and hustled out of the building, not even pausing when Erin's sister yelled at me to wait.

Chapter Six

ERIN

Nope. Nope. Nope. *Nope.*

I tossed dress after dress after top after pants from my closet. Then I flopped onto the ground, clutching an ugly pink taffeta party dress that made me look like a swirl of cotton candy. I held it up to show Natalie, who teetered on the edge of my bed, texting. "I guess this is the one."

She glanced up from her phone and recoiled in horror. "That?"

I shrugged. "This is it. The only option. Nothing else fits." Everything I'd bought in my post-sex, pre-pregnancy badass phase no longer fit my growing form. "I may need to go maternity shopping." I let out a dramatic faux sob. At eighteen weeks along, I could no longer pretend I had "burrito bloat."

Nat checked the time on her phone. "But we need to be at the hotel in thirty minutes."

"Maybe I should just not go." I hugged the pink dress to

my chest. If I wore this, I'd look less like Cinderella and more like the pumpkin that turned into her coach. "You can cover for me. I'll play the sick card."

She shook her head. "Can't. You're the draw, my dear—the brilliant new principal with all the fresh ideas. The only way people will pony up money for your new elementary foreign language curriculum is if you're there to sell it to them."

"Shit," I said. "You're right." I'd made this bed. I knew going into this job that schmoozing came with the paycheck.

I hoisted myself up from the floor and Nat held out a hand to help me, but the gesture was too little, too late. "I've got it," I said. "I can get up from the floor, because I can do anything on my own. I'm going to have to, after all."

Nat frowned. "Honey."

I waved her off. "I'm fine, I'm fine. You know that." Pity for me was verboten. We didn't discuss how Ian had left me high and dry after the ultrasound. He was never supposed to be there in the first place.

I let my robe fall off my shoulders and onto the carpet and checked out my growing midsection in the full-length mirror. "Yeesh."

"You look great," Nat said.

"You lie."

"No, I don't." Nat plucked the dress from my hands and held it open as I stepped in. Then she zipped me up and smoothed out the wrinkles. "You know who's probably going to be there tonight?" She held me at arm's length, as if trying to figure out a way to mold me into less of a mess.

"I don't care," I said, shrugging her arms off mine. "This is a work event. Work. I have to be there. He doesn't. And I definitely don't have to speak to him."

"Understood." Nat handed me a pair of peacock-blue earrings that somehow made the pink of my dress look less like bubblegum. Ah, the magic of accessories. "I'm just saying…the last time you and the father of your future child hung out at one of these things…"

"A different era, and well before he walked out on me after our baby's ultrasound. We are done." I wiped my hands together. "Besides we already slept together, and I no longer do repeats—or is this just you working overtime to get that SMARTboard?"

Nat's eyebrows twitched. "Not at all. You and Ian hooked up before we made that deal. I'll let you have him as a freebie."

"You're like a drug pusher offering 'just a little taste,'" I said. "Still. Not gonna happen." I grabbed a pair of emerald-green pumps from my closet. That's how I'd fix my dress situation. I'd go full eccentric. I'd turn my ensemble into some fun, Madonna-esque costume with bright jewelry and lace gloves. I'd have fun with it. I was forty now, after all. And pregnant. A pregnant, single, forty-year-old woman was entitled to wear *whateverthefuck* she wanted. "Tonight is all business. My job is to convince donors that first graders desperately need to learn either French, Spanish, or Latin."

Nat saluted me.

I slipped on three chunky multicolored rings that were like bowling balls on my hands. "I need you to be my support system tonight, talk about how much your students need a daily dose of language."

"And I'll tell them how much I'd love to send the kids away for an extra twenty minutes a day so I can get some planning done."

"Ha-ha." She was joking, but I used to teach, too. Truth lurked under her wit, and I didn't begrudge her that. Teachers often got flack for all their time off, but they worked hard every second of the school day. "Maybe leave out that part."

That night, a few hundred Glenfield Academy boosters crammed into yet another Evanston hotel. I'd worked with

Jennifer, the fund-raising chair, to come up with a menu highlighting France, Italy, and Mexico. On our way in, Nat and I each grabbed a quesadilla appetizer, and she snatched a flute of champagne.

"It's packed," I marveled. When I first started the new job back in August, I fretted that we'd quickly tap out the donors with all the fund-raisers and money drives. But here they all were, ready to hand over buckets of money for a new foreign language endowment.

"Of course it is." Nat patted my hand before wandering off in search of Third-Base Chris, who'd said he'd meet her here.

I busied myself right away—chatting with donors, making sure the food and drink kept flowing, reciting my elevator pitch on the importance of foreign language in elementary schools. I barely had a moment to wonder whether or not Ian would show, but then I accidently caught sight of him hanging out near the bar, a tumbler of scotch in his perfect, strong hand.

Damn.

I'd never considered myself a horny person. But just seeing Ian—the jerk who abandoned me while I relived myself in the bathroom of my doctor's office—across the room in his tux, with his tie slightly crooked like he couldn't be bothered to straighten it—I had to have him. I'd transformed into a Hungry Hippo for him, practically gnashing my teeth in an effort to scoop up all his marbles. And when he took off his glasses and cleaned them with his red pocket square—*his red pocket square!*—I nearly started grinding up against the nearest person—sorry, elderly woman in the rabbit fur coat.

"Dr. Sharpe." The woman in the rabbit fur turned toward me, hand out. "Laetitia Collins. My grandson, Marcus, is a seventh grader."

I shook her hand. "Nice to meet you, Ms. Collins." I

peeked back at the bar, but Ian had disappeared.

Good. Who needed him?

After another half hour of schmoozing and glad-handing, Nat grabbed the mic at the front of the room. "Good evening, everyone!" She grinned at a specific person in the crowd, and I followed her gaze to Third-Base Chris, who double-fisted two drinks as he beamed up at her. "Thank you all for coming here tonight to support our school and its burgeoning foreign language program. I'd like to invite the woman of the hour, Dr. Erin Sharpe, up to the stage."

I set my water on a nearby table and scooted up to the front, where I took the mic from Nat with a hug. A roomful of rich people stared up at me, waiting for me to tell them how to spend their money. A very unusual sensation, indeed, but a perk of my job and a luxury I unfortunately never experienced while teaching in the Chicago public schools. My old school had no money for anything like an elementary school foreign language program, and no hope of raising the funds. These people had no idea how good they had it.

I leaned in to the mic. "Hello. Thank you all for coming tonight. Glenfield Academy has so much to offer its students, but we're always looking for ways to improve, to push the envelope. That's why we're here tonight. In our country, we often start exposing children to foreign languages too late, missing the prime time for language development. With your help, we can implement an exploratory French, Spanish, and Latin program starting in kindergarten." My face burned. Getting up on stage like this tortured me. I was an educator, much more comfortable in front of a bunch of kids than a group of adults hanging on my every word. I spun around and pressed play on the laptop behind me. An image of the school appeared on the large dropdown screen. I'd let the video the fund-raising committee made do the talking for me.

Several kids gave their testimonies about foreign

language, but then a few alumni popped onscreen to offer their thoughts. One of them was Ian Donovan. In a suit. Talking about how his study of language and cultures had helped him in the business world.

I touched the corner of my mouth with my napkin to stem the drool. I had turned into a cartoon wolf. My eyes may have literally bugged out of their sockets.

These pregnancy hormones were no joke.

When the video ended, people clapped, and then they started rushing up to me with questions. And then I spotted Ian again, over in a corner, talking to Jennifer, the head of the fund-raising committee.

He was wearing a suit this time, not a tux. He reached up with one hand and loosened his tie.

Oh. My. God.

My attraction to his tie loosening was nothing more than a Pavlovian response thanks to the last time we had sex. The fact that Ian literally could not be counted on for anything did not change the fact that he was an incredible lay or that I hadn't been with a guy since Halloween.

My body swirled with emotion—desire, anger, hatred, gratitude for his standing up for my foreign language program, confusion.

I grabbed another cheesy canapé from a passing waiter—giving myself a little credit for not grabbing the waiter, too, in my lust haze. Maybe I could feed myself to satisfaction. Maybe food was enough. I mean, back when I was dating Dirk, I'd fill my lonely nights with popcorn and the occasional entire pie. That all worked out very well for me.

As I bit into the cheese puff, I glanced back at Ian. My eyes were simply drawn to him. They would stick on him like glue tonight. The tang of sharp cheddar on my tongue couldn't satiate me. I needed Ian's lips. I needed his hands. I needed him. In me. Like, yesterday.

What. The. Hell. Was wrong with me?

He caught me staring, because, duh, my eyes had been boring holes into him. Instead of running away screaming, he waved. And then he said goodbye to Jennifer and started walking over. Crap. How was I going to have a conversation with this dude without humping his leg? Or smacking him? Or smacking him in the face and then humping his leg? This was seriously a problem I'd never, ever imagined myself encountering. I dumped my cheese puff onto the nearest table and smoothed down my poufy dress as much as possible.

"Hi." Ian kept a safe distance, which was smart. I'm sure he noticed my eyeballs were basically shooting out of my skull and attaching themselves to his ample pectorals.

"Hey." I shook some imaginary hair off my shoulders. That was cool, Erin. Way to be smooth.

"I'm glad you're here. I'd like to talk. To you." He paused. "I want to apologize."

Yes. I was in the mood to "receive" his "apology." Holy shit. I was now in the everything-can-be-a-double-entendre phase. I was a lost cause. *But damn it, no, Erin. He should have to apologize.* I folded my arms. "Fine. Let's hear it."

"I'm really sorry about how I bailed on you. I'm utterly embarrassed." He leaned in closer, and, my God, the scent of him. He was whiskey and leather and some kind of wood. Oak? Pine? Didn't matter. He was *wood*. Ah, *wood*. "I just wanted to say I'm sorry. I don't think I'm cut out to be a *dad*-dad, but I wanted to let you know I'm here if you need anything, like stuff-wise."

Oh, I needed something. A good stuffing.

"I do want to help."

"You want to help?" *Yes, Ian. I am willing to accept your offer. Help me.*

He was about a body's width away from me now. Definitely within grabbing distance. "I'll do anything. Whatever you need."

"Whatever I…" My voice trailed off as I pictured that *whatever* and all its infinite possibilities. My eyes traveled up to his. He was gazing down at me—intense, serious. When Ian'd said *whatever,* I'm sure he meant *building a crib* or *paying for college.* But I didn't need his help with those things. I needed his help in a whole other area. A very specific area. And after walking out on me and our baby in the doctor's office, he definitely owed me one. "Will you have sex with me?" This was an emergency. It was Valentine's Day, and my baby's daddy had offered to help me in any way I needed.

He backed up a few paces. I managed to step outside myself for a second and view the situation as an unbiased observer. I, a four-months-pregnant woman in a Pepto-Bismol pink taffeta dress just asked the hottest man in the room to do her. He'd offered, basically, to help me pick out a baby swing, and I'd asked him for his dick.

Not nutty at all, Erin. Totally within the bounds of rational human behavior.

I backed off. I'd take care of this at home, as I so often did, with my trusty vibrator, Ray Donovan. "I mean. Not. Though. Um. What?" I was just saying random words now.

But a smile had rooted itself on Ian's face. He didn't run away screaming or call in the cops or any other action that would've been fully within his purview. He grinned and leaned in, his brows furrowed in the most delicious, devilish way. "Did you just say what I thought you said?"

Ian stood so close, I could lick him, which was, for some reason, my first instinct. *What have you done to me, fetus? I thought we were friends.* "Yeah," I said. "I'd heard that women can get kind of, you know, amorous while pregnant, and, well, usually they have a partner around to scratch that itch…"

"And you want me to scratch the itch for you?"

Oh, sweet lord. "Well, you are very good at it." Very, very

good.

"And it is partly my fault that you're in this situation."

"Hey, now you're getting it."

He held out a hand, and I laced my fingers between his. Ah, the sweet, sweet friction of skin-to-skin contact. I tugged on his arm and basically dragged him out of the ballroom.

This was an emergency.

• • •

IAN

"There's even a couch in this bathroom," Erin said. "It's almost like they're daring people not to have sex in here."

She perched on the couch, looking cute and sexy and sweet at the same time. She was glowing. I mean, yeah, she was wearing a ridiculous pink dress and a whole bunch of other colors on her feet and fingers, but I wrote that off as part of her job. She was an elementary school principal. She was supposed to dress a little silly. It probably kept the children inspired or something.

I hung just inside the door of the private bathroom for a second, grasping the doorknob for safety. If I hadn't been holding on, I would've run right to her, and the two of us, we needed to talk first.

"Are you sure about this?" I asked. Heck, was *I*?

"Positive."

I hadn't been with anyone since Halloween. That was… almost four months ago. The last time I'd gone that long without having sex, I'd been a fifteen-year-old virgin. I was in a rut. I'd been out a few times while on the road or in town, but I mostly sat alone at the bar watching basketball.

Basketball! Me!

I barely knew myself anymore.

And now the reason for my identity crisis was perched in

front of me, waiting for me to make a move.

"Nothing's changed," she said. "This is a one-time thing. Like last time."

"Though, if we do it tonight, that makes it a two-time thing."

"Dude, you knocked me up."

"If I remember correctly, you had a hand in this situation, so to speak."

"It was your garbage condom." She wasn't mad. At least not about that. Surely, part of her still loathed me for the way I left her at the doctor's office, but right now her face wore a crooked grin, a mischievous grin. A sexy-as-all-hell grin.

I gripped the doorknob tighter. "You were so hot that night, I probably fucked up and put it on wrong."

"So get over here already."

I checked the door again, to make sure it was locked, and then I slowly approached and sat next to her on the couch. I laced my fingers between hers and moved in for a kiss—a chaste little peck. I'd suddenly regressed to being an eighth grader at his first coed party.

Erin playfully shoved my chest. "Lighten up, man. I'm not going to break."

"Are you sure?" My eyes lingered on her abdomen. I knew people had sex while pregnant, obviously. I'm sure Tommy and his wife did, but it just wasn't something we talked about. When a dude got married, or even started to get serious about a girl, the sex talk stopped. Was I going to hurt the baby? Or Erin? Would the baby somehow know what was going on? I mean, I knew *intellectually* that wasn't possible, but still. What if it was? I'd been so worried about scarring this kid after it was born, I never even thought to worry about messing them up before birth.

"I'm sure." Erin pushed me onto my back and crawled on top of me, straddling my hips. She leaned down to kiss me and ground against me. "You're hard," she whispered in my ear.

And now I was a little bit harder. "Well, you're really fucking sexy," I said.

Her knees tightened their grip.

"What do you want?" I asked. "This is all about you. You're the boss."

"I want you inside me. I've wanted you inside me since I saw you at the bar."

This was what I'd been hoping for, right? One last tryst to get Erin out of my system? Well, here she was on top of me, literally grinding against me. I lifted my hips and fished a condom out of my wallet. I held it up to show her. "Is that silly? Do we need one? It's not like you can get more pregnant." I shrugged. This was such an unsexy conversation, but oh well. "I mean." God, I was almost blushing. I hadn't had this conversation with a woman since…college, maybe? "I'm disease free since aught-three." And I hadn't been with anyone since Erin, but I couldn't admit that to her.

She giggled. "Aught-three? Do I even want to know?"

"You do not," I said.

"Well, I know I'm definitely sans STDs. I've just recently been tested for basically every disease or disorder known to humanity, but just to be responsible…" Her sky-blue eyes crinkled at the edges.

I laughed. "We're such Gen X-ers."

Her eyes widened, and she laughed at me. A woman was laughing at me while straddling me, her gorgeous chest bouncing up and down under her strapless dress, and it was totally wonderful.

I didn't want to talk about the other women I'd been with, but whatever. There were no secrets, no boundaries between me and Erin anymore. We were fucking *just one more time* in a public bathroom. She was carrying my child. "…Millennial women don't have the same fears that we were brought up with." I ripped the foil off the condom.

"Oh, that sex will kill you?" She wiggled out of her underwear and tossed it to the ground. We were doing this clothes-on, *wham-bam*. No falling asleep together and accidentally waking up in each other's arms. Erin totally got me.

"Yeah. Sex will kill you, and so will drugs and Halloween candy and Stranger Danger." I rolled the condom on.

"We were raised to think everything would kill us." She eased herself onto my cock with a little moan.

And just like that, the giggles subsided. A wave of calm radiated out from my groin, like my body had just discovered the meaning of life. I placed my hands on Erin's hips as she rocked against me, taking charge.

She leaned down and moaned right in my ear, which got me going, and I bucked up against her.

"Take me from behind," she whispered.

I did what I was told. The lady was in charge. She hopped off my lap and leaned over the couch, clutching the seat back and raising her taffeta-covered ass in the air. I dove right in. It didn't take long after that. For either of us.

When we righted ourselves and I disposed of the pointless condom, I couldn't stop looking at her. I couldn't stop smiling at her. I liked this lady. I was glad she, of all people, would be the mother of my child.

"My ribs hurt." I clutched my side.

"Too old for a bathroom dalliance?" She raised an eyebrow.

"No." I kneaded a knot from my flank. "Too much laughing. That was fun. Fun and hot and all that jazz, but also fun—funny. Glad I could help you out in some small way."

"Nothing small about it." She bit her lower lip.

And all the blood in my body headed south with that look. Goddammit. This was a *one. Time. THING*. My head understood this. When would my dick catch up?

"So." She looked me right in the eye. Her punky hair stuck up all over, and her eye makeup had smudged during our little romp, making her look like the world's sexiest raccoon right now. Again, I couldn't help grinning. She nodded toward the door. "Bye, then."

"Oh, okay." I clutched the door handle for a hot moment, then spun around. "I meant what I said before, if you need anything—"

She shook her head. "You just gave me what I needed. We're done, Ian. We're good." She pulled her underwear up over her legs.

"I'm so embarrassed about how I left you at the doctor's office. I acted like a total chicken." When I'd gotten home, I couldn't stop looking at the ultrasound photo. That was my baby. My child. I was going to be a father—I should've been more mature about the whole situation. I, the kid who'd been bailed on as a fifth grader, had bailed on my own child before the end of the first trimester.

She waved me off. "Ian, seriously. I expect nothing from you. I went into this whole situation assuming you wouldn't want to be involved in any way. Fatherhood, relationships. That's not who you are."

My face flushed. Fuck, that made me sound so shallow. But she was right. She was giving me an out—again. I should probably just take it. "I can't argue with that."

She stood and checked her makeup in the mirror.

Erin was done with me, but I couldn't just leave it alone. "If you want to screw again…at least I know I'm good for that."

She patted my shoulder, like an acquaintance, like someone who barely knew me. "Thanks, but, like I said, one-time thing."

She held out her hand and I shook it, as if we'd just completed a business transaction. Then she opened the door to the bathroom and left without a single glance back.

Chapter Seven

IAN

I barely slept that night. I kept picturing Erin walking out the bathroom door, turning her back on me. She didn't care what happened to me, if she ever saw me again, whether I lived or died. It was, I imagined, the same impression I used to give my own one-night stands—when I was in the habit of having them.

Once again, Erin had flipped the script on me.

I finally hauled myself out of bed at seven, went for a run, picked up some doughnuts at Stan's, and drove them out to Park Ridge to visit Tommy.

As soon as he'd gotten married, Tommy moved out to the suburbs—though he liked to maintain that Park Ridge was *barely* a 'burb. It had great restaurants, mom-and-pop stores, and a train station—not to mention a movie theater! It was walking distance to the city! (Meaning the Edison Park neighborhood, which, if that was "the city," I was father-to-be of the year.) I rapped quietly on the door of his large red brick

Tudor and waited. After a moment, Susie, her long blond hair up in a messy ponytail, yanked open the door, let out a relieved sigh, and said, "Ian. Thank goodness you're here!"

Susie had never, ever looked so happy to see me before.

She ushered me in, plucking the box of doughnuts from my hand. Susie was normally perfectly put together, but this morning she'd thrown on a hole-ridden Marquette T-shirt and a pair of Tommy's boxers. I followed her back to the kitchen/family room, where six-month-old Maeve lolled in her playpen, squirming and complaining.

"Where's Tommy?" My eyes scanned the first floor of their renovated, open-floor-plan home. This place normally smelled like vanilla and oil soap, but a mustiness had set in. Clothes, books, and toys littered every available surface— from the floor to the tables to Susie's rowing machine.

"Who the fuck knows?" She whispered the f-word. "He left this morning to go for a run." Susie rolled her eyes. Tommy was a long-distance runner. He could be gone for hours. "He drove the car to the forest preserve so he could run on the trail up to the Botanic Gardens, but I need to get to the store. Maeve's out of diapers." She shook her head. "All the stores in walking distance are closed right now."

"I can run." I pulled the keys out of my pocket. Erin wouldn't let me do anything for her, but at the very least I could give my best friend's wife a hand. At least that would make me feel a tiny bit more useful.

"No." Susie pulled out her ponytail and fluffed her hair. "I'll go. You stay with the baby."

I tried to protest one last time, but Susie grabbed her coat and car keys and left the house so fast I felt a breeze. I spun around slowly, preparing for...I didn't know what. For the baby to turn into a monster? For her to devour me in one gulp? I had never been alone with a small child before. I had a master's in finance, but I had no idea how to act in the presence of a baby. Maeve lay on her tummy, in cobra pose. "So, you know yoga," I said. "Impressive."

She reached for a rattle at the other end of her pen, and then flipped onto her back.

"Show off," I said.

Maeve grinned and shook her toy.

Quietly, slowly, so as not to disturb anything, I walked backward and perched on the couch. I perused the scattered books on the coffee table. *What to Expect When You're Expecting* hid under one of Maeve's knit caps. I pulled it toward me and flipped to four months. The baby—*my* baby, yeesh—now had fingers and toes. And eyelashes. They were probably able to yawn, make faces, and suck their thumb. Cool. Last time I'd seen the kid, it had looked like a maggot. Now it was doing actual things.

I pulled my phone from my pocket and opened my text conversation with Erin. We'd only messaged each other that one time—when she wanted to meet for coffee to tell me about the kid, and I'd texted her back thinking she meant *"Coffee? ;)"*

What a dumb-ass.

She and I had left things unambiguous last night. Still, there was some niggling part of me that couldn't just let it be. I couldn't sever the tie completely. She was carrying my child. I didn't understand yet what that meant to me, if it meant anything, but I had to keep the door open, at least slightly, until I figured it out. Maybe that wasn't fair to Erin or the baby, but none of this was fair. It wasn't fair that I'd accidentally knocked her up. It wasn't fair that I'd been so hampered psychologically by my mom leaving that I wasn't sure I could handle a life-long emotional entanglement like having a child.

"It was nice seeing you last night," I wrote. Such bullshit. That was the kind of thing you said to an aunt you ran into

at the grocery store, not your baby's mother whom you'd just boned for the last time. I deleted the whole thing and tossed the phone to the coffee table, which startled Maeve, who broke into a wail that her mom probably heard two miles away at Target.

I tiptoed over to the playpen and glanced down. She'd balled her hands into fists, and her face had turned red. "Maeve?" I whispered. "Maevie?"

She kept crying and crying and crying.

Holding my breath, I leaned over the side of her pen and lifted her up, gripping her under her armpits. She looked right at me, scrunched up her face, and squealed, "Waaaaah!"

I laughed. I full-on laughed at a crying baby. More proof of my wanton jackassery. But I hadn't been laughing in a mean way. She just looked so ridiculous and cute and angry. Maeve had to see it for herself. Bouncing her against my chest, I walked her into the powder room, flipped on the lights, and turned her around to see the mirror. "Look at yourself, Maeve. You're a mess."

She stopped crying for a split second to check out her reflection, then started bawling again.

I hugged her against my hip and swayed to and fro, still in front of the mirror. "You remind me of the babe," I sang, and I kept going, performing a one-man rendition of the magic dance song from *Labyrinth*. My voice lulled her to calm. The girl was a David Bowie fan. I knew I liked her for a reason. I walked her back out into the family room and turned on the Bluetooth speaker Tommy kept next to the TV. I searched for "Bowie" on Spotify and pressed shuffle. Maeve and I danced to "Under Pressure" and "Heroes." She had forgotten how upset she was and was now giggling.

I picked up my phone and took a selfie of us, me and my goddaughter. This wasn't so bad, not bad at all. I was actually having fun with a six-month-old. Maybe I could do this, even part-time. I could be a sometime dad, give Erin the night off when she needed one. I'd be a glorified babysitter.

Feeling confident, I composed another text to Erin. *"It was nice seeing you last night. Did you know our baby has fingers now? Isn't that amazing?"*

I pressed send before I could stop myself and started bouncing again with Maeve. This was fun! Being a parent was a breeze. I was already such a pro at it. Look at me absolutely crushing childcare. I was Ian Fucking Donovan: Venture Capitalist and Expert Baby Wrangler.

Then Maeve scrunched up her face again. She turned beet red, but in a different way from when she was crying. Her eyes laser-focused on mine and she looked angry, possessed. For a split-second I considered calling my priest friend to come do an exorcism. But then a sound erupted from her that would haunt me for the rest of my days—a gurgling, bubbling, flatulent noise emanating from her rear end.

Maeve giggled, so I giggled, until I felt a warm wetness creeping under my left hand. "What did you do, Maeve?" I flipped her around. A brownish-yellow stain now covered the entire back of her green turtle-patterned PJs. "Oh, Maeve."

I ran her upstairs to her bedroom and looked around. What was I even supposed to do in this situation? I'd never dealt with anything like this before. I'd left my phone downstairs, so I couldn't exactly Google it. But Tommy was Tommy. He probably had an Echo in every room. I launched the Hail Mary pass. "Alexa, how do you change a diaper?"

From the next room came that gorgeous, life-saving robotic voice, "According to Wikihow..." and I breathed a sigh of relief. Alexa would get me through this. But then she kept going and going and going, step after step. Her instructions were more complicated than changing a tire on a semi. She wanted me to wash my hands and place Maeve on the changing table but keep one hand on her body while grabbing approximately one million tools and articles of clothing. I think Alexa incorrectly assumed I was an octopus. She used the word "genitals." All of it went in one ear and out the other. The only step that truly mattered, I decided, was that I had to remove the loaded diaper and replace it with a clean one. That was the crux of the whole thing. I noticed a diaper holder contraption hanging from Maeve's closet door, and I stuck my hand inside to hunt around. It was empty. No clean diapers. Because that was why Susie had been so eager to get to the store today...

Maeve was a mess. She was literally covered in her own poo. At the very least—for her comfort and my nostrils—I had to clean that up. I pulled a few wipes out of the warming container on the dresser. These flimsy pieces of garbage were not going to cut it. The girl needed a power washing.

We could do that.

From the guest room dresser, I grabbed the bathing suit Tommy kept for me to use in his hot tub. Now, how to put it on? I knew Maeve was just a baby, but she wasn't my baby, and I definitely didn't want to scar her for life. I placed her facedown, poo-up in her crib and shut the door as I pulled off my clothes in the hallway and threw on my bathing suit. There. I'd only left her alone for a total of about ten seconds. How much damage could she have done? I whipped open the door to Maeve's room and found her on her back now, wiggling around, leaving a winding tire-track of crap all over her lime green microfiber sheet.

"We'll leave that for your parents," I said.

After carrying her into the guest bathroom and turning on the shower, I laid her on the bathmat and removed her dirty PJs and diaper, trying to breathe out of my mouth, and only when absolutely necessary. I grabbed whatever bottle of shower gel was available—something rugged and manly and smelling of pine, sorry, Maeve—and carried her into the state-of-the-art, multihead shower. Holding her tight against my chest—I would not drop my goddaughter in this shower—I aimed her backside at the nearest stream. Maeve giggled as the water hit her back and slid down her butt. With a washcloth, I wiped her off, all while singing more David Bowie tunes in her ear.

When she and I were both finally clean, I wrapped myself in a towel and used another one to fashion a sort of makeshift diaper around her bottom half. Cooing more *Labyrinth* music in Maeve's ear, I opened the bathroom door and stepped out into the hall. Tommy stood there, stretching his hamstrings. He straightened up. "What...?" He pulled out his earbuds.

I handed him his baby. "You're out of diapers. And I'm off the clock."

Feeling utterly invincible, I picked up my clothes, changed in the guest room, and went downstairs. I checked my phone. There was no message from Erin, but I texted her anyway. *"I just MacGuyvered a bath towel into a baby diaper. Pretty sure I can do anything now."*

She sent me back a thumbs-up.

· · ·

ERIN

From Ian: *Are you opposed to baseball?*

From Erin: *As a concept?*

From Ian: *As fashion.*

He sent me a picture of a onesie from inside some gift shop somewhere. Denver, I guessed, since this was a Colorado Rockies outfit.

"That's cute." I sent the text quickly and flipped over

my phone as Katie led my one o'clock appointment into my office. Ian had been messaging me regularly for the past two days, since Sunday morning, sharing tidbits about pregnancy and fetal development. Most of which I already knew, but it was kind of sweet—or whatever—that he felt the need to show me his dedication to learning about my pregnancy.

I'd kept the conversations a secret from Katie and Nat, though, because I wasn't naive. I knew these texts could stop at any time, once Ian lost interest in the newness of being a dad-to-be and reverted back to full-time workaholic cad. Composing a message was easy. Actually showing up—and sticking around for the duration of an ultrasound—was hard.

"Erin," Katie said, "this is Maria Minnesota."

Feeling a bit frumpy, I stood and shook hands with the gorgeous tall young woman in front of me. "Nice to meet you," I said. "You and Katie met at the gym?"

"We've been taking this cross-training class together. Your sister is strong!" Maria grinned at Katie, who blushed. That was the best possible compliment Maria could've given her. Katie'd been exercising around the condo for weeks— doing push-ups, lunges, squats, you name it—as her way of dealing with a year of being single. She told anyone who asked that she was in training for the inevitable zombie apocalypse.

"I told Maria where I worked, and she offered her services if we needed any help with fund-raising, so I snatched her up." Katie, notebook in hand, perched on the couch in front of my office window.

I offered Maria a seat in front of my desk and returned to my own chair. "I'm sure you've heard," I said, "our previous fund-raising chair had to step down suddenly after the Valentine's Day party."

Katie made a *doing cocaine* gesture, and then mimed locking her wrists in handcuffs.

"That was a huge shame," Maria said. "Jennifer did a

great job these past few years, but I think we need fresh blood and new ideas. I've run events for charities around Chicago, and I want to make this year's Glenfield Gala the best ever. With my connections from food and travel blogging, we'll be able to bring in huge sponsors, plus get donations and auction items from restaurants all around the city."

"Sounds amazing, and I'm glad to have someone so experienced at the helm." As school principal, I was a de facto member of the fund-raising committee, which was not remotely my bag. I could show up and shake hands, but planning galas and whatnot sat outside my realm of expertise. That was why I made Katie attend this meeting. She'd act as my assistant and run point, bringing me in only when necessary. "You're an alumna, then?" I asked.

"No," Maria said, "but my niece is in third grade here."

"Is Minnesota your real last name?" Katie asked.

I shot her a look. "What do you need from me?" I glanced at my Apple watch, which had buzzed against my wrist. There was another text from Ian. *"Did you know the baby can hear everything? We probably should talk about what music you're playing around the kid."* I wiped the smile from my face and ignored the text. I'd taken to answering only every third message, just to avoid looking like a huge chump when the texts eventually dried up.

"What I need from you is an idea of what exactly you'd like us to raise money for. It always helps to have something concrete to show people—like a STEM lab or a new gym floor."

Katie wrote down a note with a flourish. "STEAM," she said.

"Hmmm?" Maria asked.

"Katie's just repeating my party line," I said. "STEM is great, STEAM is better. STEM leaves out the fine arts."

Maria nodded. "Perfect. That should be our focus,

then—putting the 'A' back in STEAM." She waved a hand in front of her, as if visualizing the poster. "I was a theatre geek, myself. I'd love to see the school raise money for music or the visual arts."

"Or…" I scratched my chin, as both women looked at me. "It occurred to me at the Valentine's Day fund-raiser that we're constantly raising money for our school, to give our kids a leg up."

Katie raised her eyebrows. "Which is the whole point of doing a fund-raiser for your school."

"Yes, but." I stood and started pacing. The people here knew my history when they hired me. I'd told them upfront that I was a bleeding heart who longed to see all children succeed. *All* children. "This school serves a very, very small number of kids in the community. We raise all this money to enhance the education of about five hundred kids."

"That's…kind of what the parents pay the big bucks for," Maria said.

I pointed to her. "But they also pay for us to teach their children how to be good citizens. We throw all these fund-raisers, and I doubt the kids even know what's going on. All they see is that—boom!—they have a new gym floor or—pow!—brand new army of foreign language teachers."

"What are you getting at?" Katie asked.

I stood at the window, gazing out at the parking lot full of nice cars, surrounded by beautiful, timeworn oak trees. At my old school, my office faced a chain link fence, with the alley and a graffiti-covered garage just beyond. No one threw fund-raisers for those kids. No Prince Charming ever showed up to bid forty thousand dollars on a lark for a date with Cinderella. "Let's raise money for the Glenfield Academy arts program, yes, but then I propose that we split any money raised to develop a fine arts program at a CPS school." I turned around, shrugging. "My old CPS school."

"People won't go for that," Katie said.

"Yes, they will. Like you said, they know who they hired." Maria rose from her seat. "Maybe they've never raised money for an inner-city school because no one's ever told them they could or should. And I say we don't limit it to the Gala, either. Let's get the kids involved—selling candy, holding car washes. They should take some ownership of this project."

"I love it," I said.

"I'll get in touch with Katie, and we'll work out the details," Maria said.

We all shook hands. After Maria left, Katie stepped over to my desk and flipped over my phone. "Yup," she said. "I thought so. You've been texting Ian. You're not…feeling relationshippy about him, are you?"

I rolled my eyes. "No. He texts me once in a while about baby stuff. That's it. I never text him back. Totally innocent."

Katie raised an eyebrow. "Never, or hardly ever?" She stepped forward and started doing stationary lunges, a somewhat endearing habit she'd developed.

"Hardly ever." I sat in my chair and straightened papers. My watch buzzed with another text from Ian. I flipped the phone over before Katie could see. She missed it on account of all the lunges.

"I thought you were doing this on your own." She dipped down and up, down and up.

"I am," I said. "But I'm also not going to cut off communication with my child's father just because of some proclamation about staying single for a year."

"This isn't about that." Katie straightened up and stretched at her waist. "It's about you. I don't want you to get hurt. Ian's married to his job, that's it. He walked out on you after the ultrasound."

I shook my head. "I am totally going into this with my eyes wide open. He's showing interest now, which is fine.

But he'll get bored sooner or later, and I'll be back where I started—alone and fine with it."

"As long as you're okay," she said, "and as long as you're not getting attached."

"I am not getting attached," I said.

. . .

ERIN

Being a pregnant principal with a billion social obligations kind of sucked sometimes. There were very few events I could nope out on, even if I wanted to. But I made the executive decision to ditch a Friday night fund-raiser hosted by an alumnus and Republican congressional candidate raising money for a right-to-life organization.

I played the pregnancy card, which meant I was now lying on the couch, curled up with a full vat of buttered popcorn, ready to flip on *America's Sweethearts*. I had decided to start working my way through the entire rom-com genre—from A to Z, and tonight belonged to me, Julia Roberts, John Cusack, and Catherine Zeta-Jones.

Right before I pressed play, my phone buzzed.

It was a message from Ian. *"Did you know about the listeria? Tell me you've been nuking your deli meats for at least two minutes on HIGH."*

I wiped my buttery hands on a paper towel and texted him back, *"I don't even eat deli meat."*

"Good," he said. More little dots appeared on the screen, and I set down the remote. No point in pressing play until he finished telling me everything he needed to tell me. *"So, what are you up to?"* he asked. *"Going to Anti-Choice Jerkstores Present…A Night in Atlantic City?"*

So we were getting all personal now? I thought we were only supposed to talk about whether or not to use cloth diapers. And though I had fun chatting with him, admittedly, I didn't trust him. He was still the guy who left me high and dry in Dana's ultrasound room bathroom. But it wouldn't kill me to engage in polite conversation. I should keep this going for the kid. I sent him back a vomit face emoji.

"Barf because you're sick or barf because that event sounds terrible?"

I giggled. *"The second one. I'm actually having a nice night in with popcorn and rom-coms."* At my current speed, I'd probably finish this bowl of popcorn before the meet cute.

"Sounds nice," he said. *"I could use a night like that."*

"What are you doing?" I asked. *"Skirt chasing?"* It was what I assumed he was doing at all times. I mean, I wasn't delusional. Yes, we'd had two very fun orgasm sessions together, but I wasn't foolish enough to think I was the only one he'd seen naked recently.

"I'm in Kansas City, in a hotel room. I'm supposed to meet clients out for BBQ, but I'm not in the mood."

Mmm...pulled pork. I could go for that right now. I wonder if Smoque delivers? I'd ask Alexa later. *"But BBQ,"* I said. Ian didn't understand how good he had it right now.

"I know," he said. *"But I've been here three days. I'm about to turn into a brisket."*

I pictured him sitting on the edge of his hotel bed, with a barbecued slab of beef as a head. It didn't totally turn me off. *"So, stay in."*

"Maybe I will."

I glanced at the TV, which was stalled on the *America's Sweethearts* Netflix menu page. I was always jonesing for alone time, probably because I was pretty introverted and had to spend my work day dealing with all kinds of people—large and small. Though schmoozing was a part of my job, I loved nights by myself when I could lie on the couch like a slob and eat ridiculous amounts of popcorn without judgment.

But these nights always ended up making me a little sad, a little wistful. Watching bad rom-coms alone was fun, but not as fun as it was with other people. Nat and I used to do this together, when she wasn't out with whomever she was dating at the time. Dirk, if he was around, would sneer at us from his recliner while he read some massive tome about world history or whatever, but Nat and I didn't care. We ignored him and did our thing, laughing and eating and drinking. But tonight she'd gone to the silly Atlantic City event. *"You have Netflix?"* I asked Ian.

"I do."

My fingers faltered as if trying to slow me down. *"If you're serious about staying in, you can watch* America's Sweethearts *with me remotely. We can make fun of how Julia Roberts says 'Kiki.'"* I was half kidding. Ian was probably bullshitting me about wanting to stay in tonight. He wasn't a stay-in guy. He had buxom, brisket-fed Kansas City women to meet.

And...nothing. No response. No little dots. He took my offer seriously, probably thinking this was me trying to trap him into some kind of relationship where we had babies and watched movies together. I'd been hunting for a little company, and, in the process, I'd crossed a line. And not just his. My own line, too. I was supposed to be doing this—all of this—on my own, not chatting up my baby daddy and asking him on a virtual date.

But then the phone rang, and I answered it on the first ring.

"Hi?" I braced myself for the "talk" I knew was coming. Ian was about to tell me that even being texting buddies was too much.

"So what movie is this again?" he asked.

"Um." Were we seriously doing this? Was Ian Donovan opting to stay in on a Friday night to *Mystery Science Theater* our way through a bad rom-com? I spoke slowly, so as not to spook him. "*America's Sweethearts*. Julia Roberts and Catherine Zeta-Jones are sisters. CZJ is a big movie star who's forced to promote a film with her ex-husband, John Cusack."

"That sounds kind of familiar?"

"It's not very good." That was my way of giving him an out.

"Which is the point, right?"

Dude! He got it. Ian Donovan understood the appeal of sitting through a crappy movie you'd already seen. "It's totally the point." I picked up the remote again. "Are we actually doing this?" If he wanted to back out, this was the time.

"We're doing it," he said.

God, this was more stressful than phone sex. Asking him to talk me off would've been way easier. Our relationship was based on orgasms and the ramifications of those orgasms, nothing more. Opening ourselves up to movie-related inside jokes would mean taking our relationship to a whole new level. "When I say go, press play. Are you ready? Are you on the right screen?"

There was a pause. I imagined him in his hotel room, setting up the video. He no longer had brisket head. He was wearing a dress shirt and tie, which he'd definitely loosened using two fingers. "...Ready," he said.

"Go."

The title screen came up. "*America's Sweethearts*," I said, reading the title card. "Or *Billy Crystal Gets His Nuts Licked by a Dog*."

"I wasn't familiar with that alternate title."

"It's like *Dr. Strangelove*," I said.

"Or *How I Learned to Stop Worrying and Love the Bomb*?"

I had learned to stop worrying and was loving this

conversation. Ian was such a movie dork. "You really do know movies, huh?"

"I told you I did. My dad and I used to have movie nights together all the time when I was a kid. He showed me all the classics." There was a pause. I felt every second of it. Talking about our families—this was certainly uncharted territory. "We still do it sometimes."

"That's so cool." I'd never pictured Ian with a dad. His dad was my kid's grandpa. So weird. I wanted to know more. "Like, what? Would you do that when your mom was out of town or something?"

"Or something," he said with a hint of finality, shutting the conversation down.

Well, he gave me something, so I'd give him something. My family was going to be his kid's family, too, after all. "I had to sneak out to my friends' houses to watch movies."

"Really?"

"Yeah. My parents were not screen people. We didn't own a TV. At least not until I was fifteen and they adopted my sister. Then they were like, 'Go ahead, Erin, watch whatever you want.'" That came out harsher than I meant it to. I totally understood what my parents were about. Before Katie, I was their only hope. They parented me like I was their one chance, their one shot. They weren't going to do anything to jeopardize my future or my opportunity for success. Then when Katie came around, they mellowed. They suddenly had another outlet for their attention.

Something stirred in my stomach, and I grabbed my midsection. "Whoa, what?" That came out of nowhere.

"You okay?" Ian asked, his voice rushed.

"I think so." I lifted my shirt, inspecting my abdomen, like there'd be anything to see with the naked eye. "There was just this weird feeling in my belly. Maybe the popcorn isn't sitting well."

"Pain?" he asked. "Are you having contractions?" I heard him flipping through a book on the other end.

"No. It didn't hurt." I searched for the words to describe what I'd just experienced. "It was more like an odd little fluttering."

"Oh my God!" Ian shouted. There was a sound like he'd just chucked the book to the floor.

My heart pounded. "What? Is it bad? Am I dying?" I tried to take a few deep breaths. I knew this was too good to be true. I shouldn't have allowed myself to get attached to any of this. I was losing my baby.

"No!" Ian said. "You're fine! That was the baby. You just felt him…her…our kid move!"

"What?" I clutched my gut, still not believing I was okay.

When Ian spoke again, his voice was calmer. "The baby totally just moved."

I was suddenly slightly less alone in the living room tonight. "No way."

"Yeah. You're almost at twenty weeks now. That's about the time you'd start to feel it." He paused. "Tell me all about it."

I couldn't stop beaming. That little *whoosh* under my flesh was my baby. My baby had made its presence known tonight. He or she was hanging out and watching *America's Sweethearts* with their parents, like a real person. "Not much to tell," I said. "It was literally a little flutter, like a butterfly in my uterus."

"Can I be jealous now? I'm not sad to miss out on actual labor, but this is something a guy will never experience." He paused. "I'm really glad I got to be on the phone, with you, though. For this."

"Me, too." My hand stayed on my gut as I blinked back tears, thanks to all the hormones and emotions. This was our odd little family—me, my one-night stand, and our fetus. This was our first movie together, our first family night in—like Ian used to do with his dad. I wiped my eyes. No use being sentimental over something so silly. Tonight was nothing special. This was no big deal. We weren't a family. We were two strangers having a child together. We'd never have family movie nights together in the future. I'd have movie nights with the kid, and so would Ian, but separately.

"You know," Ian said, "my mom was never around for movie night, but maybe when this kid is born, we can invite you to hang out sometimes, too. That is, if you'd want to."

Oh, and now the tears were streaming. "I would like that," I said. "Very much. And, Ian." I swallowed, taking my time. This was a huge mistake. I should not be doing it. But thanks to the hormones and the baby moving and all of it, I had to take this leap. "Since you've been reading up so much on the baby stuff, you probably know that the twenty-week ultrasound is coming up."

"Yeah." His voice broke a little. "I did know that."

"No pressure," I said, "but if you want to come, I'd be happy to have you there." I told him the date and time.

"I'll be there," he said.

I told him, "Awesome," but my head said *we'll see.*

Chapter Eight

IAN

Scott knocked on my doorjamb. "Where are you going?"

He'd caught me slipping into my jacket, trying to get to Erin's ultrasound on time. We'd agreed to meet outside the doctor's office since we were coming from opposite directions—her from Glenfield Academy, and me from the Loop.

"Nowhere," I said. Good cover, Ian.

"You're all dressed up." Scott's eyes narrowed. "You're wearing a tie." He sniffed the air. "And cologne."

"No, I'm not." I buttoned my coat to cover the tie, which I was definitely wearing.

Scott stepped in and shut the door. Damn. I really had to book it. I did not have time to deal with Scott's sleuthing. I'd already dodged a phone call from that Liz girl who wanted me to mentor her and one from my mom that I'd accidentally answered. She'd said, "Hello?" And I responded, "Gottagobye!"

"I know what this is," Scott said.

"Can we talk later?" I checked my phone—no notifications—and shoved it in my pocket. I had fifteen minutes to get over to Northwestern. *Way to cut it close, Ian.*

"You have a date." Scott plucked a Hershey's kiss from the crystal jar on my desk and painstakingly unwrapped it. This was his version of David Caruso putting on his shades.

"I—" I hesitated. But no. That was the perfect out, wasn't it? A date. "Yes. I have a date."

Satisfied, Scott popped the chocolate into his mouth. "Well, she's gonna have to wait, because I need you to call Isamu. Now. Emergency."

My shoulders slumped. "What?" Isamu was my contact at Fumetsu. Not Scott's.

"He called today, and I picked it up because you seemed busy. He has concerns that we're not going to do right by them, because I slipped and told him about my family stuff—" Scott ran his fingers through his hair, blinking away tears. "I'm sorry, man."

I'd been holding my breath, and I let it out in one big whoosh. I'd spent months—months—tap dancing around Isamu, trying to convince him that we were the right VC firm to launch Fumetsu Enterprises into the stratosphere. Scott had undone all my hard work in the course of one conversation. But that wasn't on him. He'd been trying to help. And if my relationship with Fumetsu was, in fact, that fragile... "Scott. Don't worry. It's fine." I grabbed the phone and dialed. "I'll fix it."

Ten minutes later, having smooth-talked my way back into Isamu's good graces, I jumped into the first cab I saw—beating out another white dude in a suit, so I didn't feel too bad about it. Desperate times, pal. I had five minutes to get to Erin's doctor's office. Five minutes to get across the Loop and over to Streeterville.

I made it in eleven.

Fuck. Shit.

I was so late, Erin had already gone inside.

I dashed up the stairs and into the office, where I found Erin sitting alone in a waiting room chair. Because I was late.

Because I couldn't even do this one simple thing right.

Like a kid about to be scolded by the principal, I trudged over to her. "I'm so sorry," I said. "I got stuck on a call."

"Lucky for you, Dana's running late, too." Erin had come dressed in her work clothes, which were like the toned-down version of the last gala outfit I saw her in. Under a bright pink trench coat, she wore a black A-line dress covered in a pattern of colored chalk. Rubber lobsters dangled from her ears, and she seemed completely unfazed by that fact. She was who she was, full stop. Dr. Sharpe was nothing like the kind of woman I'd meet out at a trendy River North club. In a good way. In the best way.

And I, the jerk, had left her waiting.

I sat next to her, draping my trench coat over my forearm. She flipped through a *Ladies' Home Journal*. "Looking for Bundt recipes?" I asked.

"Slow cooker." She showed me the page she'd stopped on. "Here are the top five set-it-and-forget-it chili recipes." Her eyes crinkled as she smiled up at me.

A drowning sensation washed over me. I couldn't make it to a simple appointment on time—an appointment that meant the world to me. Though I'd been working like a dog to keep the business afloat while Scott took a step back, the Fumetsu deal nearly slipped from my grasp today, the second I turned my back. I'd inadvertently involved myself in a very intricate high-wire act. "I'm really sorry, Erin."

She shook her head, frowning. "It's okay. You're here, right?"

"I wanted to be here on time. Please know I wanted to be

here on time." Though she'd already given it to me, I nearly fell to my knees to grovel for her forgiveness. It was the least I could do.

"It's okay, Ian. We're good." A younger couple on the other side of the room drowned out her words, thanks to their shouting match over how late the dude had stayed out last night. The woman argued that she had to stay home alone and pregnant with all the indigestion, while the guy could waltz in at four a.m. reeking of booze and cheap perfume.

"Yikes." My body cringed with secondhand embarrassment. That was not a conversation to have in front of other people.

"Girl has a point." Erin nudged my ribs. "But at least you and I will never have that fight."

My eyes traveled to her. She still gazed across the room at the fighting couple. "Right," I said.

"You could stay out all night, and I'd never know about it."

I needed her to know that I wasn't this dude across the room. I was the responsible adult human who'd knocked her up, who, damn it, tried to arrive on time for her appointment today. "I haven't been out much since I found out about the baby," I said. "I've become a homebody."

"I never asked you to do that." Her eyes darkened as she turned to me.

"I know… It's just…maybe I'm maturing?" That had to be it. It wasn't like I could keep up my bachelor-in-paradise pace forever. Though I hadn't noticed it at the time, all the drinking and partying had taken a toll. Now that I'd started staying home more, I'd been sleeping better, eating better, feeling better.

She raised an eyebrow. "Way to go on the whole being-a-grown-up thing! You're only forty, after all."

We'd returned to joking, which was quickly becoming my

favorite part of being around her. "Or maybe I'm having, like, sympathy nesting. Is that a thing?"

"Could be," she said.

"I tried going out a few nights ago, but I was just like, ugh, give me Netflix and a blanket."

Erin giggled, and the sound filled the entire room. It resonated against my bones. I silently vowed to do everything in my power to keep that laughter in my life—I'd toe the line, leave thirty minutes early for appointments, be on-call for her twenty-four-seven, whatever she needed. "If that's maturity, then I've been old for fifteen years."

"It's not a bad life," I said in utter honesty. *Who the fuck was I?*

"Not bad at all. So," she said, "what do your friends think of the whole baby thing?"

"Oh. I haven't told them yet." Scott had too much going on in his own life right now to worry about mine, and, well, I couldn't tell Tommy and not Scott. We three shared everything.

Erin's eyes widened.

"It's not that I don't want to tell them; I just don't know what to say." The hurt look on her face forced me to keep going. "I *will* tell them. I will. I kind of just wanted to get through today first." I'd almost told my dad the last time I saw him, but I caved. What was I supposed to do? Tell him that maybe he was going to be a grandfather, if I could avoid fucking this up?

"Have you not told them because you're worried you could bolt at any minute?" she asked.

I couldn't tell if she was joking or not. I bet on the latter. "No..."

"Yeah." She raised her eyebrows at me.

"Yeah." That was definitely part of it.

"It's okay," she told me. "I get it, and I appreciate you

being straight with me. We're both going into this with our eyes wide open—honest and realistic. Like I said before, I expect nothing from you, but having you here is nice." She flipped through *Ladies' Home Journal.*

Her words ripped a hole in my heart. I was still No-Expectations Ian to her. Maybe that's who I'd always be. "You should expect things from me," I said. "I...want you to be able to expect things from me."

She hit me with a wan smile. She didn't believe me, and I couldn't blame her.

The nurse opened the door, called us in, and set Erin up on the table in the exam room—fully clothed. No vagina probes this time. Today I'd get to see the regular old TV-type ultrasound, with the belly wand.

I took my seat near the door, in the safe spot that was clear of lube and model uteruses. "So," I said, folding my hands in my lap.

"So." Erin cleared her throat. "Um...now, I could've found this out ages ago thanks to all the tests and whatnot that I've had to endure thanks to my AMA—"

"Advanced Maternal Age." I'd done my homework.

"But," she said, hesitating, "well, where do you stand on finding out the sex of this baby?"

My heart sped up. "Oh." Since I could no doubt run the table on a *Jeopardy!* category about human gestation, I knew that the twenty-week ultrasound was usually when people found out what they were going to have, if they wanted to know ahead of time. I've always been on Team Find Out. But—"I don't know," I said. "What do you think?" Deferring to the mother. Always a smart play.

"I'd kind of like to have something to call the kid."

"Fair enough," I said. "You have names on your list?"

"I want to hear yours first. If you have them."

I smelled a trap. "You want to hear mine first?"

"Yeah," she said. "Lay them on me."

I'd thought about names a lot, actually, while waiting for a flight at the airport, when noticing my barista's nametag at the coffee shop, while falling asleep alone at night. I'd had a lot of time to think lately. "Well, as far as girls' names go, I've been having a hard time deciding what to do."

"As I assumed you would." Erin's eyes twinkled. "Do we have to go old school, like popular names from the Stone Age, to find the name of a woman you haven't been with?"

"Hey!" I clutched my heart, faux-wounded as my cheeks flushed in embarrassment. That hadn't even occurred to me, because there was really only one girls' name that made sense. Once it popped into my head, I called off the search. "No. The thing is, I spent a lot of time with my dad's mom growing up and I'd love to name the baby after her. But her name was Lois. Can we name a baby Lois, though? I mean... Lois Lane..."

"There are worse things to be called than Lois Lane." Erin's eyes traveled to the ceiling. "Lois," she repeated. "Lois...I like it. And I haven't had any jackass students with that name, either. Always a concern."

"Perfect." I prepared to drop the bigger bombshell on her. "But I know the boy's name for sure."

"You do?" She turned her head toward me.

I nodded. *Please say yes.* She had to say yes.

"Me, too." Her eyes narrowed.

"Uh-oh." Well, I'd lose this battle for sure. She was the mom, the one hauling this kid around for nine months. If she wanted to name him Rutherford, we'd name him Rutherford. Maybe we'd use my pick as the middle name.

"On three?" she said.

"Okay." I braced myself for the worst. "On three. One... two...three..."

We both blurted out, "James," and immediately started

laughing.

"It's my dad's name." My body flooded with relief. Our kid would not be named Rutherford.

"Mine, too."

"Wow. I guess we're decided." I stood, about to run over and hug her or something, maybe just give her a fist bump, but Dr. Dana opened the door before I could get to Erin, She strolled in wielding an iPad. "How's it going, E?" Dana glanced up from her tablet and startled. "Oh, Ian. Good to see you again." She raised an eyebrow at Erin.

"Ian's taking his baby daddy job very seriously." Erin patted her stomach.

"I am," I said. "I've even become a sympathy couch potato."

Erin grinned at me. Over the past two weeks, we'd become something resembling a team. A team that still needed a lot of work, granted, but still. A team.

Dana checked the chart on her tablet. "So far, so good. Tests are all normal. You're feeling fine?"

Erin nodded.

"Well, let's get a look at this baby." She lowered the table so Erin was lying down.

Erin motioned for me to come over. I stood at her side, hands clutched behind my back, as Dana slicked the wand over Erin's abdomen.

"This kid looks good," Dana said.

I couldn't tell a foot from the kid's nose. Really, from what I could tell, the baby looked like Mr. Burns. I readjusted my expectations for this child accordingly.

Dana, eyes on the screen, asked, "Do you want to know the sex?"

I caught Erin's eye. We hadn't landed on a decision. I shrugged. "It's up to you." Though I definitely did want to know, I'd defer to her. There was something kind of fun and

Christmas-morning-esque about not knowing, sure, but I never avoided instant gratification.

Erin smiled nervously. "Let's do it."

My heart racing, I turned to Dana. "Let's do it." This was a big moment, especially now that Erin and I had settled on names. We'd find out today if we were having a "Lois" or a "James." Ever since I'd found out about Erin's pregnancy, I'd been thinking of this kid as an amorphous blob. Finding out its sex would be the first concrete bit of information we'd get.

"Well." Dana pointed to something on screen. I nodded, pretending I totally knew what was going on and that the splotch did not look like a slice of deep dish pizza. "It's a boy!"

A boy. "James," I blurted. I grabbed Erin's hand and squeezed. She didn't pull away. She actually squeezed back. An unwelcome tear escaped my eye and I wiped it away quickly, before Erin or Dr. Dana could see. A boy. I was having a son. We were. Erin and I were going to have a son. All these emotions swirled through me—excitement, dread, joy, terror. "Cool," I said. "Cool, cool, cool." I dropped Erin's hand and shrugged, like all of this was the opposite of a big deal.

· · ·

ERIN

As soon as my feet hit the pavement outside the doctor's office, I started bawling. I couldn't control it. I'd bottled up my emotions through the ultrasound, and now they erupted from my body—through my eyes and nose. I devolved into a blubbering mess.

Ian, who'd been a few paces ahead of me, spun around. "Are you okay?" He dashed back toward the office building, to where I'd hunched over, hands on knees, crying. "What's wrong?"

I shook my head as I gathered my wits. "I'm okay." From my pocket, I extracted a pink handkerchief that had probably been in there since February and blew my nose. So classy. So chic. "Really. I'm fine." I focused my leaky eyes on Ian. "It's just...today was a lot."

He furrowed his brow and nodded. "A lot of good."

"Yeah," I agreed. "A lot of good. But also just a *lot*." I opened my arms to show him how much.

"We're having a James." Ian smiled.

And that nearly set off my waterworks again. I couldn't put my finger on why—why I was crying about having a boy, why I was getting so emotional over Ian being there. Of course he was there. He was the kid's father. He was supposed to be there. Being there was the bare minimum. "Yeah." I started walking down the block, just for something to do. "It's awesome we're having a James. He almost feels real now."

Ian jogged to catch up with me. "Do you ever feel like he's a two-thousand-piece jigsaw puzzle we're never going to complete?"

I spun around. Now I grinned through my tears. I could picture it—this pile of puzzle pieces, scattered across the kitchen table. "That's the perfect way to put it." I touched my midsection. "He's like a tiny stranger."

"And today we found the corner pieces. He's going to be a boy."

"Well." Hand on hip, I launched into my righteous-principal-lecture mode. "They're going to be assigned male at birth, but whether or not they identify as male is yet to be determined."

"True." Ian was practically laughing at me now, which I found both frustrating and cute. How dare he laugh at me for making a salient point and look so adorable doing it! "But can we at least agree there's a fairly good chance that he's going to end up being a dude? Statistically."

"I suppose that's fair." I drew in a deep breath and exhaled.

"What else?" he asked.

"What else?"

He mimicked my exaggerated sigh. "There's something else going on." He made a *come on* sign with his arms. "Give it to me. I'm here to listen."

Where to even begin? My emotions had jumbled into such a mess I could hardly make sense of them. "Okay, well, I've been thinking about that couple in the waiting room and how she was all worried about him coming home late at night. I'm never going to have to worry about you like that." A sob escaped my mouth again. WTF? *Come on, hormones, give me a break*.

"Do you *want* to worry about my whereabouts?" Ian asked.

I dug my fingernails into my palm to stop the flow of tears. "But shouldn't I? Isn't that what I'm supposed to want to do? You're my kid's father."

Ian stepped closer and massaged my shoulders with his big, strong hands. I felt small whenever I was around him. Tiny, even. Petite. Everything about Ian was so large and imposing, in a good way. He made me feel safe. None of my previous boyfriends had ever made me feel that way before—not that I wanted Ian to be my boyfriend or anything—but it was nice for once not to be the one who'd probably have to step up and kill a spider. "What you and I have is better than what those people in the waiting room have," he said.

"How so?"

"We have no reason to lie to each other. We don't have to play the stupid relationship games. From day one, you and I have practiced brutal honesty." His eyes twinkled.

My emotions had shifted wildly from despair to desire, thanks to his powerful hands massaging my shoulders. If there was one thing the couple in the waiting room had that we didn't, it was easy access to sex. That was built into the relationship, but Ian and I... I released an involuntary moan, as he hit just the right spot on my neck.

"Feel better?" he asked.

"Much." I gazed up at him as he stared down at me with those big chocolate eyes under the glasses and the messy hair. This man was my sexuality. I was an Ian Donovan-sexual. "We can't have sex again."

He backed off, holding his hands up in surrender. "I wasn't—"

"I know." I touched the back of my neck where his hands just left. "I was telling myself as much as I was telling you. I... made a bet?"

His eyes narrowed into a question.

My shoulders slumped. "I made a bet with Nat that I'd follow your rules for a year—no sleepovers, no second times, no strings."

His eyes bugged. "But we—Valentine's Day."

"Our first time didn't count for the contest, since my thing with Nat came after the fact." I blushed at the word "came."

He furrowed his brow. "And what happens if you break the rules?"

"I have to scrounge up money for a ridiculous SMARTboard she 'needs' for her classroom."

Ian laughed at me, and, yeah, maybe it was kind of ridiculous, a grown woman making bets with her friends about her love life. "Why?" he asked. "Why are you doing this?"

"To prove I can." I sighed. "To break old habits. I have a tendency to pick guys who don't deserve me, and I'm breaking the cycle. I'm going to stay single until I meet someone who's worth it. Who's worth *me*."

Ian gazed past me toward the street. "I get it," he said. "I get the whole wanting a reset thing. You're not the only one with baggage."

"You have baggage? Ian Donovan? King of No Strings?"

"Heh," he said. "I'm the king of all baggage. My mom left when I was eleven. She moved to Hawaii with her boyfriend, Blake, abandoning me and my dad. I worry I'm going to end up like her. That's why I threw myself into work—I chose that over rolling the dice with emotional entanglements."

"Relationships are not for us," I said.

He looked deep into my eyes. "I'd only disappoint you."

"And I'd grow so aloof that you'd start to think I didn't care."

"We're doing the right thing," he said. "Open and honest communication, friendship, and respect."

I couldn't hide my grin at the bizarre notion that I now had a "friend" who looked like Ian Donovan.

He pulled out his phone. "I'm starved. Want to get food?"

"Food? You and me together? That's not... I'm not hungry." And my stomach growled. *Damn it, baby. Read the room.*

Ian looked pointedly at my growing gut.

I wrapped my arms around my midsection. "Why?"

"Why do I want to get food?"

"Oh. It's just..." What were we doing here? "Dining together..."

"Too much?" he said.

"Too date-like?" I asked.

"You're saying we can screw in a restroom, but we can't watch each other eat soup?" And his stupid eyes twinkled again.

When he put it that way... "Well," I said, trying to

rationalize this in my head. "I suppose it's not the worst idea for us to get to know more about each other—in the name of friendship, respect, and open communication."

"Right, like when James starts talking about his Aunt Wendy, I'll have a frame of reference. That's all."

That *was* all. This conversation would not amount to some big turning point in our non-relationship. It was Ian, trying to get to know his kid's mom a little better. He hadn't been opening a door. He didn't want to change what we had. He was attempting to enhance our friendship, a wee little bit. That I could handle. "Well, first of all, there's no Aunt Wendy, but there is an Aunt Katie. You've met her. At the doctor's office, right before you walked out on me and your son." I winked with a grin.

Our car pulled up to the curb, and Ian held the door open for me. "See? That's what I'm talking about."

. . .

IAN

"Dessert for the lovely couple." The waiter set a piping hot vessel of brioche bread pudding in the center of our table. "On the house."

"Oh, we're not—" I started to say.

Erin waved me off. "Hush, Ian. If it gets us free dessert, we can pretend we've been married for twenty-five years."

"You're saying we got married at fifteen?" I grinned, and she tucked right into the steamy pudding, licking whipped cream and caramel from her spoon.

"You want some?" she asked.

I shook my head, sipping my espresso. Despite the jolt of caffeine, a calm washed over me. "This was fun," I said. "Really fun."

She set her spoon down and smiled at me. "It was."

I raised my arms in victory. "We can totally eat dinner together and have it not be weird!" "Not weird" was an understatement. This meal had lasted three hours, but had flown by in a blur of steak and potatoes and chats about movies and TV and Glenfield Academy. Erin and I had everything to talk about. I couldn't imagine ever getting sick of being around her, which was great because, for the next eighteen years, we'd be co-parenting. "I hope you don't take this the wrong way, but hanging out with you reminds me of hanging out with my best friends, Scott and Tommy."

Erin raised an eyebrow. "Thanks?" She picked up her spoon again and lifted a scoop of ice cream to her lips, which she licked.

My body temperature rose, a vastly different response than the one I'd have around Scott or Tommy. She caught me staring at her, so I shook my head and averted my eyes. "I just mean because I feel so comfortable around you." I set my cup down and leaned across the table. "But you look better in a dress." I winked.

"I don't know about that," she said. "But I'd be up for doing this again, you know, if you want to."

"I do want to," I answered automatically.

Erin and I said goodbye on the curb of Steak 48. She ordered a Lyft up to Ravenswood, and I grabbed one to my condo on Lake Shore Drive. When her car pulled up, the two of us stared at each other. We hadn't touched all day, except for when she grabbed my hand in the ultrasound room and when I kneaded her shoulders right before she told me we weren't going to have sex again. Right now, saying goodbye, would be a perfectly reasonable time to hug, but I couldn't do it. I couldn't cross even that small line. I'd had a lovely night with Erin in the friend zone. For the good of our child and our relationship, we had to keep it there. I held up my hand and she slapped it. I still got a charge from that brief moment of contact.

Erin was hot. She was smart and funny and cool, and keeping her in my life was of paramount importance. Physical distance was the key to us making this work.

She seemed to agree.

When I got home that night, a wave of empty sadness swept over me, though I normally loved being alone in my condo. I turned on all the lights and asked Alexa to play some Pearl Jam. I changed the screen on my projection window from "the woods" to clear glass. I gazed down at the lake and Lake Shore. Cars below me zoomed up and down the drive, headed to meet people and do things while I sat alone in my condo. I pulled out my phone and sent Scott a text. *"What are you up to?"*

In a matter of seconds, my phone rang.

"Hey," I said. "You're calling me." He never called me.

"I am. I have a favor to ask."

My ribs squeezed my chest as my schedule and to-do list popped into my head. I was already dry-drowning under the weight of my obligations—and here was Scott to give me another one.

"I hate, hate, *hate* to do this to you."

I mentally prepared for whatever this was. I'd been bemoaning my loneliness only a second ago. Maybe another commitment would remedy that. "Dude," I said. "I'm here for you, whatever you need."

"You know I appreciate it. I wouldn't ask unless it was an absolute emergency."

"Stop stalling, Scott." I'd already mentally started filling in my calendar.

"Before all this stuff with Mom, I agreed to chair the finance committee for this year's Glenfield Gala."

I groaned. The Glenfield Gala. Scott was about to rope me into a school fund-raiser, notoriously run inefficiently by people who had no idea what they were doing. Yippee. Good times.

"After Jennifer's whole"—Scott made a sniff-sniff sound over the phone—"getting arrested thing, I figured they'd canceled the event or whatever, but the new chair called me tonight. They want to set up meetings, and I just…can't. I cannot deal with sitting in a room with disorganized people right now."

Join the club, bud. I'd been pulling double duty on the Tokyo deal for months, all while keeping tabs on every other business in my portfolio. Plus, I was the only one in our office traveling anywhere right now. If we needed a presence in Paris or Pittsburgh or Prague, I was the one who had to hop on a plane. And, of course, there was Erin and the baby, and my dad, and my own health and well-being, which had really taken a backseat lately…

"What about Tommy?" I said. "Isn't this more his thing?"

"He promised Susie no non-work-related extracurricular activities. She has him on lockdown."

I needed someone to put me on lockdown.

"If this had come up any other week, I probably would've said yes. But Mom's been having a terrible time with the treatment, and I can't leave her alone. She has no one else." He paused, and a small sob escaped. "I have no one else."

"Scott, dude, you have me." I said it without hesitation, without concern for my own life and schedule, without thinking about Erin or the baby. My issues were inconsequential now. Scott needed me, and so did his mom. I couldn't even tell him about the baby right now either. What a fucking sob story that would be—*"Boo-hoo, Scott. I'm so distracted by the happy news that I'm going to be a father."* Sick mom trumped fetus every single time.

The one positive about chairing the Gala: I'd get to see Erin once in a while, which both elated and relieved me.

Seeing her made me happy, and it also felt like I'd be checking off two boxes with every meeting. Work on the fund-raiser? Check. Visit Erin? Check.

Man, I was such a prince.

"I really appreciate this," Scott said.

"Heck, anything for Glenfield Academy, right?"

"'*Hail to alma mater,*'" Scott sang into the phone.

"By the way." I flipped my picture window back to the video screen, this time projecting a secluded Caribbean beach into my condo. "Who took over for Jennifer?"

"Oh, that," Scott said. "Well, um…remember you already said yes. No backsies."

My head throbbed. I should've gotten this info upfront. Paul Pfister had been angling for Jennifer's position for years. I would not survive being bossed around by his pretentious ass for the next several months. "Just spit it out, Scott."

"The new head of the fund-raising committee is Maria Minnesota." Game-show host voice. "Yay!"

Super. My ex-fling, current baby mama, and I would all be working together on this fund-raiser. It sounded like the start of a really bad joke.

Chapter Nine

From Ian: *So, you're going to work, and I'm just getting home from work.*

From Erin: *Isn't it like 9:30 p.m. in Tokyo right now?*

From Ian: *Exactly. [Exhausted emoji]*

From Erin: *But you like what you do, right?*

From Ian: *I love what I do. I just spent the entire day in a room full of suits talking marketing strategy for Asia and Eastern Europe.*

From Ian: *You still there?*

From Erin: *I was just waiting for the "j/k" or the sarcastic face.*

From Ian: *Nothing sarcastic about it. Investing in a*

new company is invigorating. It's like…what's the best part of your job?

From Erin: *Well, yesterday a girl named Caeli gave me a rose she made out of tissue paper.*

From Ian: *Discussing business strategy is like my tissue-paper flower from a girl named Caeli.*

Natalie knocked on my office door at work. "My classroom. Five minutes."

I glanced up from my computer, where I'd been sifting through a crammed in-box. Parents wanted to meet, the head of the school board had found yet another new initiative based on something he'd read about in the *Tribune* five minutes ago, the boys' bathroom on the second floor might have asbestos tiles… I'd entered my zone—putting out fires, being a boss. "I'm a little busy," I said. "What's this about?"

"A surprise," she said. "Katie's coming, too." Nat waggled her eyebrows at me before running off.

I stood and stretched. Immediately the spot between my groin and my leg started to throb from the godforsaken varicose veins. I couldn't stand for more than a few seconds without wanting to remove the lower half of my body. It wasn't that my gut was so big yet, but damn it, the pain in my legs made me duckwalk. I waddled down the hall and pulled open the door to Nat's nearly empty classroom.

She stood at the front of the room, and Katie sat in one of the desks in the first row. I, knowing full well I wouldn't fit into a first grader's desk, folded my arms and stood off to the side, shifting my weight from left to right to ease pressure on my legs.

"Ladies." Nat held out her left hand, and both Katie and I leaned forward to see. The florescent lights above us glinted off the diamond slab parked on her ring finger. "I'm engaged!" she squealed.

"You're…" I couldn't comprehend the words she was saying.

"To Third-Base Chris?" Katie asked.

"Of course to Chris!" Natalie chuckled like we were silly for asking. Though he and Natalie had been seeing each other fairly regularly since Halloween, Katie and I had never actually met the guy. "He proposed."

My chin had locked in its down position.

Good thing Katie was there to pick up the slack. "I'm sure you know how fast this is," she said, "so I'm not even going to mention it."

"It's not fast, not for us. We're not getting any younger." Natalie's eyes twinkled. She looked happier than I'd seen her in forever. "We saw a movie together on Saturday night, and he told me he couldn't live without me. He buried a ring box at the bottom of my popcorn. It was so sweet!"

Tears streamed down my face, and I barely realized the eye faucets had started. This was a daily occurrence. Everything made me cry. Commercials for reverse mortgages. Dead flowers. Not having enough rice in the pantry.

The emotions involved were usually pretty pedestrian— "We're all getting old," "Life is impermanent," "Damn it I just wanted some rice to go with this sweet and sour chicken"—but I couldn't quite identify why I was crying over Nat's engagement. She seemed happy. Though I agreed with Katie that the engagement had happened fast, Nat was an adult woman making an adult decision.

"Are you okay?" she asked.

Katie spun around in her seat to look at me.

I waved them off and folded my arms again, blinking back more tears. "Pregnancy hormones."

"That's it?" Katie narrowed her eyes.

"What else would it be? And I'm happy for Nat!" I added

quickly. My eyes scanned the colorful alphabet above the white board at the front of the room, as I searched for a distraction. The tears weren't just about joy for my pal. Underneath the happiness lurked jealousy. And guilt because of the jealousy. And sadness and regret and fear and resentment and maybe a modicum of anger, I think.

Plus my stomach had turned on me because it was lunchtime and my belly craved food.

I waddled over to my friend and hugged her. "I seriously am happy for you," I said. "Let's get dinner this week to celebrate. I have to meet Chris!"

She squeezed me back.

"But for now I have to deal with this asbestos thing in the boys' bathroom." I rolled my eyes and left the room. They couldn't argue with asbestos. It was the perfect out.

But Katie caught up to me on my way back to the office. Damn it she was fast now with all the working out. My mallard-like body was no match for her. "You sure you're okay?"

I nodded. I couldn't talk. I'd start crying again.

She fell into step with me. "I'm happy for Nat, too, but I'm a little jealous."

I nodded. But being jealous was silly. I didn't want to be engaged. I'd never been more content on my own, living life on my own terms. No strings, no stress.

"And I don't even have anyone on the horizon," Katie said. "You have Ian."

I stopped walking. "I don't have Ian." I chuckled at the thought. "I have a friend, Ian, and we're on the exact same page about our friendship."

"Right." Concern clouded Katie's face. Concern for her pathetic, knocked-up sister.

"I'm exactly where I want to be right now." The tears stung my eyes again, and I wiped them away in anger. "Ian and I are exactly where we want to be. We're great. We text and talk on the phone and he's one of the funniest, smartest people I've ever met. We are great friends, and that's how we'll stay."

"I know you two have been talking a lot." Of course she did. Katie lived with me. For the past month or so, she'd seen me sneaking peeks at my phone during breakfast and dinner. She knew Ian texted me—whether he was in town or Tokyo or wherever—during the evening while we were watching TV. But there was nothing untoward happening between Ian and me. We were buds. Chatting with my pal and the father of my future child amounted to totally aboveboard behavior. "I'm only wondering if you might want more," she asked.

I shook my head. "No." More was exactly what I didn't want. More would be me falling back into old habits, falling for yet another emotionally unavailable man. What Ian and I had was healthy and honest. We both understood we'd fail at more than friendship, so we vowed to keep things at that level. No matter how much fun we had together, no matter how much I dwelled on the sensation of his hands on me sometimes, no matter how much I pictured the two of us living together happily, it wouldn't last, and therefore it couldn't happen.

"If you're only keeping your distance from Ian because you don't want to buy Nat a SMARTboard…"

"Katie, that is so not it." The SMARTboard was secondary. I had committed to singledom for my own good. I pointed down the hall, back toward Nat's room. "What she and this Chris guy are doing? It's a bit silly. You know this, and I know this. I hope it all works out for her, but past history says it goes down in flames. Ian and I are trying to avoid that."

"If you say so," Katie said.

"I do say so." I booked it down the hall as fast as my

fat little duck legs could carry me. "Asbestos!" I shouted, shaking my head.

. . .

IAN

From Ian: *I'm telling my dad tonight.*

From Ian: *I know I should've told him ages ago, but now I'm like, it's really, really real. He's going to be a grandpa, and I have to tell him.*

From Ian: *What did your parents say when you told them?*

From Erin: *We first told them that Katie had been secretly divorced for six months, so they were cool with their forty-year-old daughter being knocked up.*

From Ian: *Damn it I wish I had a sibling.*

On Wednesday, after I flew in from a business trip in D.C., I hopped right into my car and drove up to Winnetka to visit my dad. He still lived in the house he and my mom bought when they were first married. He was a retired painter and spent most of his time golfing or bowling with his friends. I found him out in the garage, cleaning up and taking inventory for spring. My dad took great pride in his yard. We...didn't have much in common.

"Hey, Dad." I picked up a rogue hammer on the ground and set it on the work bench.

"Ian, what are you doing here?" His whole face lit up, and a pang of guilt hit me. I didn't get up here enough.

"Just came to visit." I grabbed a broom from the corner and started sweeping. I'd start coming here more frequently.

I'd bring the baby here all the time after he was born. Heck, maybe I'd move out to the suburbs like Tommy.

I touched my forehead. Nope. No fever.

"I'm getting as much done here as I can now." My dad had made piles of everything—hoses, bags of mulch, algae killer for the pond. "Your Aunt Pat invited me up to Lake Geneva next weekend." Aunt Pat was my dad's sister. She lived in Barrington but owned a summer house in Wisconsin.

"That'll be fun, Dad." I kept sweeping, growing the pile of dirt higher and higher. I was stalling. I'd come out here for one reason, and I was avoiding the issue. Time to rip off the bandage. I set down the broom. "So, I have some news."

My dad stopped in his tracks. He'd wrapped a green hose around his arm, and he held it there like a security blanket. His face had gone stark and white, because I hadn't specified whether the news I had was good or bad. He was right to be a little concerned.

I immediately regretted not inviting him to sit down for a pop or some coffee or whatever. It was a testament to how inexperienced I was at delivering important, life-changing news that I'd chosen to up and blurt it out in a cold, cluttered garage in the middle of April. "I'm…going to be a dad," I said. "You're going to be a grandpa."

"Wow!" He smiled for a split second and stifled it. My dad was no fool. Though he and I had never spoken outright about my plan to stay single, I was sure he figured that was the case. I'd never brought home a woman for him to meet. Not once. "That's fantastic, right?" He furrowed his brow.

"It is." I beamed big, illustrating to him how fantastic. "I'm happy. It's…it's a boy."

"Wow!" he repeated. Subtext littered that "wow." My dad and I talked golf, food, and real estate. That was it. This personal stuff went way beyond our comfort zone, and I'm sure he had no idea what to ask, how he was supposed to feel about this.

I offered up the goods, the tidbits I knew he'd be wondering about. "The mother and I are not together, but we're friends. She's forty, like me, a school principal." I paused. "She's great, actually. You'd love her." It was the truth.

His grin faltered. "You're not together."

"No, which is good," I added quickly. "We're on the same page. She wants to stay single, and so do I. We don't have to worry about our relationship going sour—"

"That's what's holding you back? The fact that you could possibly break up in the future?" My dad tightened the grip on his garden hose.

"It's more than that," I said. "My life isn't suited for a real relationship. You know that. Work takes up so much of my time. I travel constantly—heck, I just got back from Tokyo an hour ago." I checked my watch. I'd been to Japan twice in the last month, just to prove my dedication to Isamu.

My dad set down his hose. "But you're going to make time for a baby?"

"Yes," I said. "A baby I can make time for. I want to make time for him. Like I make time for my friends and you—"

My dad set down his hose and wiped his hands together. "This is the first time you've been up here since Christmas."

Bam. I racked my brain. That couldn't have been right. I drove up to the North Shore all the time...or so I thought. I'd last come up here in February for the Valentine's Day thing for the Academy, and, nope, I hadn't stopped in to see my dad. But life for the past several months had been crazy. Like I said, I'd just gotten back from Japan. I'd been traveling every week and picking up whatever other slack Tommy and Scott left me. Other than exchanging the occasional texts with Erin, work had taken over my entire life.

But that was temporary. Soon we'd seal the Fumetsu deal, then Scott's mom would get better, and Susie'd loosen the reins on Tommy. When James came, I'd make room for him. At that point, it'd be my turn to take a little break. My partners would start picking up my slack. We were a team, after all. "I've changed," I said, straightening my shoulders.

"You've changed." My dad leaned an elbow on one of his many ladders and folded his arms. "How?"

"I—" How had I changed? I'd let Erin into my life. Kind of. I guess. We were getting food together now. Or, well, we had that the one time after the ultrasound. We were texting and stuff, really regularly...

"Are you traveling less?" Dad asked.

Nope. All told, I'd been traveling a bit more. But that was only because I was in the middle of a huge deal and Scott's mom was going through treatment. Once I closed that deal, though, I'd be home more. Definitely.

"Have you made room in that condo of yours for a child?"

I pictured my living room, full of geometric art pieces and an open-flame fireplace. None of that was baby proof. I hadn't set up a room for the kid yet, but I would. I'd been busy. I'd been in Tokyo. And the baby wouldn't be here for another three months. "Things are being decided," I said. "I'm turning the weight room into a nursery." There. That was a proactive step.

"You have a crib?"

"I have one on order." No, I did not. But I would. By end of day today.

"You've taken down the mirrors and gotten rid of that expensive padded floor you had installed and couldn't stop raving about?"

Shit. I'd forgotten about that. The gym was one of my favorite rooms in the condo. Why hadn't I said the den instead? But whatever. I was making room for this child, and it was going to take some sacrifice. "I'm working on it."

My dad nodded, patronizing me. He didn't buy any of it.

This was the man who raised my ass. He saw through all my bullshit. "Have you really, really thought this through?"

I nodded.

"Really?"

"Yes," I said. "Is it what I planned? No. I always thought I'd stay single and unattached for life. But this just happened, accidentally. And I'm embracing it."

"Your mom never wanted kids," he said.

"I know." That wasn't true. I'd never actually had that information, but I figured it was probably the case.

"We got pregnant with you, and she 'embraced' it." The air quotes were his. My dad stepped over to me and placed a heavy hand on my shoulder. "I know you're not her, and I realize you're a grown-up who can make his own decisions, but really think this through. Your mother, who had never been prepared to have a kid, walked out on you at age eleven. Can you see yourself doing the same thing to your son?"

My throat closed up as I shook my head. "I would never." I had lived my entire adult life promising myself I'd never be my mother. Up until now it hadn't been too hard. This kid was the test. And I would pass. "I'm ready for this responsibility," I said. "I'm ready to make room in my life for this person." For *my son.*

He squeezed my shoulder. "Then, good." He smiled. "I'm happy for you."

. . .

ERIN

"It's so silly," Chris said, "but we truly bonded over our embarrassing love of Taylor Swift."

"That *is* embarrassing." I raised my eyebrows at Natalie over the top of my Sprite. She sat across the table from me and next to Chris. The three of us had gone out to dinner at Uncle

Julio's in Old Orchard after work. The two of them couldn't keep their eyes or their hands off each other. I couldn't tell if this was love or lust or desperation, but, whatever it was, they were both fully invested.

I focused on the chips and guacamole in front of me. I'd honestly never seen Nat like this before. Her previous boyfriend had not been this into her, and it had been like that from the beginning. She and Chris appeared to be on the same page. About everything.

"I put some music on in the car during our first date, and Chris started singing along to 'I Almost Do.' He had memorized every single lyric. I was like, 'Busted!'" Natalie patted his wrist, and he squeezed her hand. "After that, we started texting each other silly Taylor memes and lyrics."

"We crossed over from irony into sincerity pretty quick," Chris said.

"We're dancing to 'Starlight' at our wedding."

My mind drifted infuriatingly to my own wedding—my own nonexistent, never-gonna-happen wedding. Because he was the only single guy I had any contact with, the groom on my dance floor assumed the shape of Ian. Our first dance song was "YMCA," which we boogied to like goofballs, as we had the night we first met. I stifled a grin.

And then I flicked a tear off my cheek.

God. Damn. Hormones.

I, Dr. Erin Sharpe, did not care about weddings or marriage or patriarchal constructs. During my relationship with Dirk, I never went gaga over wedding dresses and veils. I had never once pictured anything at all having to do with my own wedding.

This pregnancy had made me soft.

I wiped my eyes with my napkin, under the guise of having to sneeze. Then I raised my index finger. "Be right back." Before Nat or Chris could say anything, I ducked my head and pushed my way to the bathroom.

Resting my hands on the sink, I checked myself out in the mirror. I was in a fairly cute pregnancy stage right now—all belly and boobs. My legs hadn't started to swell yet. I was a strong, beautiful, intelligent woman, who was fine being single. I did not need a fucking wedding—or a man—to validate my existence.

The bathroom door opened behind me, and Nat came in.

She leaned against the wall next to the sink. "Okay, so this is the second time you've cried in my presence in under a week."

"I'm a ball of hormones," I said. "That's all this is."

"I'm starting to take it personally."

I sighed, pulling the hem of my dress down to straighten it. "I'm serious. I don't know where those tears came from. I'm a stereotypical girl all of a sudden, crying over weddings."

"You were crying because I'm getting married?" She frowned.

"No!" I rolled my eyes. "I was crying because... I don't know why I was crying." The image of Ian and me dancing like fools to "YMCA" would die with my brain. I pointed to my gut. "Baby. He's the one making me cry."

Nat reached over and patted my belly. If anyone else had done that, I would've bitten their head off, but I'd given Nat and Katie full belly touching privileges. "Have I told you how proud I am of you?" she said.

I shook my head, blinking back more tears.

"You're the toughest woman I know. You are in charge of an entire school full of children and teachers. You have to deal, on a daily basis, with asshole parents who think they hung the moon. And you do it all with reason and humor." She held me at arm's length. "I only have to deal with one classroom of asshole parents, and it takes all my strength not to murder them."

I giggled.

"And now you're taking on motherhood all by yourself. I couldn't do that."

"Sure you could." Nat made things happen. She kept her classroom shipshape every single day. While my inbox only seemed to grow, not shrink, Nat kept up with her emails daily. She could do anything she put her mind to.

"I need Chris," she said. "I hate admitting that, but I'm someone who needs to be around people, and I found someone who wants to be with me all the time. Maybe I'm weak like that."

"You're not weak; you're an extrovert," I said.

"True." She laughed. "Imagine you dating someone who needed to be in constant contact with you all the time."

I touched my neck. Would that be so bad?

"You're pulling at your collar," Nat said. "And your face just morphed into this grimace that looked anything but content. Just thinking about being in that kind of relationship is making you claustrophobic. You're right to be focusing on your single life." Nat checked herself in the mirror. "You've never needed anyone, and you still don't. You're going to be fine on your own."

"I hope so." I pictured myself dancing alone in my living room to "YMCA." It bummed me out.

"No hope about it." Nat kneaded my shoulders. "Now I have to get back out there, because I've kept Chris waiting for too long, the poor baby." She held open the door for me.

"I'll be right there."

After Nat left, I flicked a bit of cold water on my face and fixed my hair. When Dirk and I were together, we hardly saw each other. He only moved in with me during the final two years of our relationship. Before that, I was on my own almost every night. And I liked it. I accomplished so much during that time. I got my PhD back then. I hadn't spent every waking moment worrying about when I might get a text or what the other person happened to be up to. It wasn't a bad life. It was a life I was good at, and would keep being good at.

But "YMCA."

I patted my belly. Maybe James would dance with me.

When I'd composed myself enough to return to the table, a text came in from Ian. *"Hey! Want to come over tonight? I have something to show you."*

My heart sped up, and my first instinct was to text him back automatically, because, yeah, I wanted to go to his condo. Too much. The truth was, I had started to look forward to these texts more than I should. I was starting to need Ian, and I didn't believe I could count on him.

It was time to pull back. I'd promised myself I was going to do this alone, and I had to stick to the plan. Occasional texts were fine, expectations and desires were not.

"Sorry!" I told him. *"I have plans. Maybe another time!"*

• • •

IAN

When my plane landed after another long week in Tokyo, I checked my messages, silently hoping for one from Erin. She'd had a doctor's appointment the day before—or this morning; it was hard to keep track with the time change—and she'd promised to let me know how it had gone.

But instead of a message from Erin, I had one from my mom and one from that Liz Bolton woman I still hadn't spoken to. She wanted me to call her when I got back from Tokyo. And I had three texts from Maria Minnesota:

"Hi, Ian. We need to talk about the finance committee."

"Hi, Ian. I have some numbers I want to go over with you."

"Are you around? I'd like to drop off some materials."

I groaned, audibly, while waiting for a car outside the airport. A constant weight sat on my shoulders, and I couldn't shake it, unable to fathom a time when I wouldn't feel overwhelmed. Over the past I-don't-know-how-many months, I'd gone from work to the airport to more work to sleep and back to work. I barely had time to exercise or feed myself. I'd been eating takeout for weeks—three meals a day.

And now the fucking Glenfield Gala, which had always been my favorite fund-raiser of the year—big auction, big ballroom, big money being thrown around. But now I hated it. I'd burn it to the ground, if I could.

Except I'd promised Scott I would help out. And the Gala was in support of my alma mater—Erin's current workplace. My helping with the Gala would improve my child's future. He would benefit from this fine arts center, or whatever they were raising money for, someday.

The words "the greater good" kept spinning through my mind.

"I'm on my way home from the airport," I texted Maria. *"You can leave the stuff with my doorman."*

But when I stepped into the lobby of my building, Maria was there, holding a massive accordion folder full of God-knew-what.

She held up the papers. "I should probably explain some of this. I don't know how much Scott's told you, but we're doing things a bit differently this year."

"Fine. Sure." We'd get the conversation and explanations out of the way, so I could curl up in my own bed and sleep.

"I'm really glad you agreed to help with this, Ian," Maria said.

I narrowed my eyes. What did she mean by that? Did she think something was going to happen here? Probably not. It was the sleep depravation making snap judgments. "I'm a little jet-lagged," I said. "So if we can make this quick."

She cocked her jaw to the side. "It'll be quick."

Okay. Not a seduction. The look on her face could've frightened a shark.

"How have you been?" I tried a friendlier tack as Maria and I sat down in my living room—her on the leather couch, me on the armchair. Maria's eyes bounced around the room like this was her first time seeing the place, which it pretty much was. She'd been here once before, late at night. We had sex, and I told her I had to get up early. I shuddered at my callousness. She was right to hate my guts.

"Good," she said. "Working hard, you know."

"Same." I shrugged. "So...?" No need to drag out these pleasantries.

"Right." Maria, all business, passed a folder of papers across the coffee table to me. "Erin had a brilliant idea to use half the money we raise at the Gala to start a fine arts endowment at an inner city school—her old school."

I nodded, grinning despite myself. Dr. Sharpe using her position at a wealthy school to help the kids in need—something that had never once been suggested at Glenfield Academy before. It was utterly brilliant. Anyone who objected would look like a total asshat. She had them by the balls.

My Erin.

Whoa. Where did that come from?

I coughed and handed the folder back to Maria. "Cool," I said. "The new principal, she's, um—" My face flushed.

Maria's eyes widened. "She's great. She even wants to get the kids in on the act, so it really means something to them that they're raising this money—for both themselves and the other school."

"It's a pretty great idea, and I know I can find some donors who'd be willing to get in on this. Some businesses are leery of giving to private schools, but with the public school angle, I think we can get them." I rubbed my eyes. I needed a shower and a nap, not necessarily in that order.

"You okay?" she asked.

I exhaled. "Just tired. And busy."

Maria stood and held out a hand. I rose and shook it. "Thank you for taking the time to work on this…for the kids."

I nodded. "My pleasure." My eyes traveled to the front door, hopefully giving her a sign.

"Do you mind if I use your restroom before…?"

"No," I said. "Go ahead."

She hesitated, and then it hit me. She had no idea where the bathroom was. I pointed toward the back of the condo. "Down the hall, to your right."

After she left, I picked up the folder again. There was Erin's name—and her phone number—right on the top page. In a kneejerk response, I pulled out my phone and texted her. *"I'm back. You want to come over? Watch a movie?"* Yes, I was beat. But I wasn't too beat to see Erin. If this happened to be the moment when she wanted to come over, she could come over. I'd always welcome her here. With open arms.

Or not open arms—not like that. I'd welcome her with a friendly hug and maybe a small kiss on the cheek. Nothing more.

She texted back. *"Sorry! Can't. Plans with girls."*

Damn it. She had so little time for me she couldn't even text in complete sentences. I sent her back a thumbs-up.

"Um…Ian?"

I spun around. Maria stood in the hallway holding a teddy bear. "What's going on? You're building a crib?"

I started to say something, some excuse, but stifled it. No

more hiding this. "I'm going to be a dad." This was my new reality.

She cocked her head, like she was trying to hear me better. "You're...what?"

"I'm gonna be a dad," I repeated. The more I said it, the easier it got, honestly. I could probably tell Tommy and Scott about this without curling into a ball on my office floor.

"Congratulations?" The smile didn't reach her eyes. "Wow. Ian Donovan a dad. Who's the mother?" She shook her head. "Never mind. Not my business."

"It's Erin," I said. "Sharpe."

"Erin Sharpe?" She narrowed her gaze. "Are you two...?"

Was she...jealous? Was that what this was? I'd assumed she was pissed at me for not bidding on her at the auction. Was she somehow going to take it out on Erin? "It's complicated," I said.

Maria nodded. "I bet it is."

She was being snide, which probably meant I was right. She was jealous. "What's that supposed to mean?" I asked.

"You don't do serious. You don't do complicated." She paused. "You don't do attachments."

"I don't."

"A baby's a pretty big one."

"Yeah, and I'm ready for it." She was the second person I'd told about the baby and the second person who'd questioned my preparedness. I ticked off all the things I'd done in the name of this child. "I've been to ultrasounds. I've learned how to change a diaper. I've read every single book I could find on pregnancy and childbirth. I'm ready."

"Sounds like you're ready to be a birthing coach or maybe a babysitter." She tossed the teddy bear at me, and I caught it. "What about the real stuff, the real decisions you'll have to make—school, religion, diet, childcare, how you'll handle the whole Santa thing?"

"We'll figure it out." All those questions would be answered in time—really, I assumed Erin already knew the answers, and she just had to tell me.

"Ian, you have an infinity fire pit in the middle of your living room."

"Which I'm getting rid of…by the time the kid can crawl."

"Okay." She stepped over and picked up her folder. "Sounds like you have this handled."

"Wait," I said. "Let me show you what I have done."

I led her to my home gym and opened the door. It looked like a bomb had gone off inside. Screws and chips of flooring were everywhere. The slats of the crib had been strewn across the floor. I had to keep starting and stopping this project to catch planes to wherever.

Maria giggled, but not in a light, girlish way. This laugh was basically a snort in my general direction. "Wow."

"It doesn't look like much," I said, "but I'm trying. I'm making a place for him."

"That's great, Ian." She turned to me, eyes laughing. "I truly wish you the best." No, she didn't. That comment dripped with sarcasm.

"You don't think I can do this." I pouted. I was a full-grown man, and I pouted because no one believed I had it in me to be a dad.

"Ian, I barely know you. I have no idea what you can or can't do."

"But you don't think I can do this, be a dad."

She sighed. "I think you'll be fine." She started to walk away.

"You're being really rude," I said. "Look, I'm sorry I didn't bid on you at the auction, but don't take it out on Erin."

Now Maria laughed darkly, like a super-villain, and turned around. "You think I cared for one second that you didn't bid on me, and now I'm going to take it out on the mother of your child? How fucking conceited can one person be?" she said. "I'm a professional, and I'm trying to help your alma mater make a fuck-ton of money. I'm fine, Ian. I'm better than fine. I will continue to be fine. But now you've dragged a baby and Erin Sharpe—who's great, by the way—into your hornet's nest of shit—"

"Hornet's nest of…?"

"—which is not fair to either of them. No, I don't think you can do this whole good-guy-parenting thing, because in the two months we were 'together,' you made time for me twice."

"I've changed." I pointed to my torn-up home gym as proof.

"You bought a cheap crib and started tearing down a physical wall. That's as close as you'll ever allow yourself to get to anybody."

Ouch.

"I understood what you were about when we met. You're too busy to make time for other people because of your precious job. How in the hell do you think you're going make room for a baby when you're flitting off to Vancouver every other day?"

"Tokyo," I said. "And that deal's almost done."

"Well, it's Tokyo now. It'll be something else tomorrow. And the next day. There will always be another deal to pursue, another business opportunity. Your kid is going to learn really fast who comes first in your life."

"Wow," I said.

"Yeah." She pointed to the gym. "And maybe think about hiring someone to deal with this mess, because you suck at this, too."

Chapter Ten

Natalie and I faced off with loaded guns clutched in our hands. "On three," she said. "One..."

I grinned. "Two..."

Katie, tapping away on her phone next to me, rolled her eyes. "Whatever. Three."

Nat and I spun around and started scanning everything in sight with our pricing guns, registering at Target for our wedding and baby, respectively. Since she was getting married only a few weeks after my due date, and we were near the end of the school year, our faculty had decided to throw a joint shower for all the teachers and administrators who were celebrating weddings, babies, or big-deal birthdays over the summer.

"Diaper Genie," I said. "Bam!"

"Faux-artsy framed print of the Chicago skyline," Nat said. "Bam!"

"Bored millennial being dragged into some bullshit by

her older sister and her friend." Katie's eyes were still down on her phone. "Bam."

I scanned a cute pair of sandals in Katie's size. "There," I said. "For you. Thanks for coming with us."

"What are your coworkers at the Academy going to say when they see a pair of size eight bejeweled espadrilles on your registry?" Katie asked.

"My needs are as important as his." I patted my ballooning gut as the kid kicked me, probably to remind me that, nope, for the next eighteen or so years, his needs would trump mine, full stop, and I should probably get used to it.

My watch buzzed, and I peeked at it. There was a message from Ian, reminding me to scan the Beaba food steamer. I shot him a thumbs-up.

"Is that Ian?" Katie's eyes were still on her phone.

"No," I lied.

"Yes, it was. I can tell because you're grinning like a dork."

I leaned over and pushed her phone down. "You haven't looked up from that thing once. How could you possibly know I was smiling?"

"I see all." And she was right back to texting.

"Was it Ian?" Nat asked as she scanned a stainless-steel wastebasket.

"Yeah." I shrugged. "He was just making his opinion known on some of the registry stuff." He'd done all kinds of research on everything from co-sleepers to diaper bags to swaddling apparatuses. He'd apparently also—all on his own—dismantled his home gym and decorated it as a nursery. And he'd even built a crib, and he'd sent me several videos showing him throwing heavy things into it—a weighted vest, a medicine ball, a sack of potatoes—to prove that it was structurally sound. He kept asking me to come see it, and I kept balking.

"They text all the time." Katie shoved her phone into her purse, gleefully outing me to Nat. "Every single night."

Natalie gazed into the middle distance.

"What?" I said.

"Nothing." She grinned at me. "Just imagining everything I'll be able to do in my classroom with that brand new SMARTboard."

I pretended to shoot her with my scanning gun. "I have a friendly relationship with the father of my son. Big whoop."

"Yeah, *you* might, but he totally wants to be more than friends." When she noticed my death stare, Katie added, "I may have peeked over your shoulder—don't judge me; I haven't been out with a guy in months; and, aside from weight training and protein shakes, this soap opera drama between you and Ian is all I have. He's asked you to hang out a bunch of times, and you always say no."

"Uh, yeah." I scanned a box of glass bottles. "Because we agreed to live separate lives, and I'm keeping up my end of the bargain. We're friends. That's it. Not even friends. Friend*ly*." Just because two people, who happened to be attracted to each other, talked on the phone all the time, it didn't have to mean anything. We were two adult humans who could definitely keep things platonic.

"That's good," Nat said. "You have the right idea. Keep Ian at arm's length. You're strong enough to do this on your own, and tigers don't change their stripes."

"Ian and I have been honest with each other from the start. He's married to his job. He's not looking for a relationship. And I've been burned so many times, I'm better off sticking with the one person who won't let me down—myself."

If Ian really did want to be more than friends, it was only because I'd been playing hard to get. I'd become a challenge for him, a challenge that would end the moment we got together. "I have a history of picking the wrong guy."

I scanned a package of cloth diapers. *Bam!* "Ian is the very embodiment of 'the wrong guy.'"

"Maybe, maybe not," Katie said. "He seems to really like you."

"Now," I said. "He likes me now. He'll bolt as soon as I give in to him. There's no way this doesn't end badly."

Katie raised her index finger. "Or, what if it ends with you two desperately in love and staying together forever?"

"You're just hard up for some romance," I told her. "Go watch a rom-com on Netflix or something."

"It's what happened to Nat and Chris," she said.

"But Chris is not Ian Donovan." Natalie scanned a set of bed sheets.

"Bingo." Ian was who he'd always said he was—a workaholic who needed his freedom. I, as I had been since the day we met, was playing the role of "girl who took him at his word."

• • •

IAN

On a Friday night in mid-May, a sulky Tommy walked into my office and flopped down in one of my guest chairs. "Let's go out."

"Really?" I'd just gotten back from another trip to Tokyo. I'd planned on texting Erin tonight to see if she wanted to come over, even though I knew she'd say no. She always said no.

I saw right through her game. She was avoiding me—and doing a good job of it. I hadn't seen her in person since March, since the day of the ultrasound. Yeah, I'd been out of town for a lot of that time, but when I was in town, Erin had made herself utterly unavailable.

If her goal was to drive me mad, it was working.

Maybe I should give her a taste of her own medicine.

I texted Erin in advance of our Friday night non-date. *"I won't be able to chat tonight. Going out with Tommy."*

She sent me a thumbs-up.

I hesitated, finger over the phone. My mind said, "Back away from the cell," but my heart said, "Just send her one more teensy message." My heart won out. *"Call you tomorrow probably?"*

With baited breath I watched the screen, but no little dots appeared. Erin had won yet another round in the battle for the upper hand that existed inside my head.

I had to start taking the hint. Every sign glowed neon bright. Erin wanted nothing to do with me outside of parenting our child. And I'd been using her as an excuse to avoid going out, living my old life. I had to start being old Ian again.

I told Tommy I'd meet him at the bar after I finished up at work. On my way out, I asked Scott to join us, but he had a date—a real date, like with dinner and everything. I begged him for details, but he only blushed and said, "It's new."

In a trance, I wandered over to the bar atop the Chicago Athletic Club. The Ian of a year ago never would've predicted any of this—that Scott would be going on a real date or that I'd be weeks away from meeting my own son. The only constant was Tommy, who'd always longed for a family life.

I found him at the bar, drinking scotch and talking to a woman with blond hair. I groaned inwardly. He was wingmanning for me, finding someone for me to hook up with. The Ian of one year ago would've been grateful. Tonight I wanted two drinks and my own bed.

"Hey, Tom—"

He cut me off. "Shelly, this is my friend Tommy."

My shoulders slumped. What. The. Fuck. "Hey," I deadpanned.

Shelly batted her eyes at Tommy. "Ian's told me so much about you."

He wasn't playing the part of my wingman tonight. I was his. And, what? He just expected me to go along with it, to look the other way while he chatted up other women—using my name—while his wife and daughter sat at home? "Hey, Shelly," I said. "Can you give us a minute? *Ian* and I have some things to discuss."

We watched as Shelly headed over to her friends, a group of women all wearing skinny jeans and Uggs. Ugh. The whole thing was ugh. "Tommy, what the fuck?"

He shrugged, eyes still on Shelly. "I'm just having fun."

"You're using my name. I know what that means. That means you're hoping to hook up tonight." My blood boiled. How dare he put me in this position and expect me to go along with it, no questions asked.

"No, it doesn't." He turned to me, eyes glazed over. Tommy had left work early today, and I guessed he was about four drinks in. "Flirting isn't cheating."

"Sure." I picked up his empty tumbler and shook it, rattling the ice. "But how many of these have you had? How long before you're so fucked up the flirting morphs into cheating?"

"You're not my dad."

"I'm not." I ordered two waters from the bartender. "But I am Maeve's godfather and Susie's friend, and damn it if I'm going to sit here and watch you betray them."

"You don't know what it's like," he said. "You think everything is one way, but then on a dime"—he snapped his fingers—"you don't even recognize your life anymore." He widened his bloodshot eyes and stared at me. "I haven't slept in months. I haven't touched my wife in longer than that. Her mother is living with us now, and I'm not even allowed to hold the baby, except under very specific circumstances. I come home from work, and they just start yelling, telling me everything I'm doing wrong, berating me for doing my job." He ordered yet another drink from the bartender. "All I'm asking for is one night of talking to women who don't look at me like they hate my guts."

"But you and Susie—" They were the perfect couple. They wore matching ugly sweaters to every Christmas party. They had both separately picked out the same china pattern years before they got engaged. There was never any doubt that the two of them would make it to ever after.

"She hates me. She's done a complete one-eighty on me." He downed his second drink. "She used to understand what I was all about. She loved that I worked so hard and fell in love with me because I was successful. I'm still doing the same work—trying to stay successful—and she throws it back in my face. She thinks I'm avoiding responsibilities at home."

"Well, tonight you kind of are," I reminded him.

"If I'm going to be blamed for something either way, I might as well have the fun." Tommy ordered yet another drink, and I motioned to the bartender that we'd like some appetizers. I had to get food in Tommy, STAT.

"Dude," I said, "you don't want to fuck this up. Things are hard right now, but you owe it to yourself and Susie to deal with this together—see a counselor, take a vacation." My parents never talked about shit when they were together, and then one day my mom showed up—packed and ready to move to Hawaii with Blake in his Mazda Miata.

"I'm only blowing off steam," he said. "I'm not going to do anything." Ah, but then he started to pull off his wedding ring.

I shoved it back on his finger. "Fine, Tommy. Do your flirting bullshit, but keep your ring on. I'll keep an eye on you." Lucky me. If anything, this was good practice for after James was born, and I'd have to watch to make sure he kept his fingers out of the electric sockets. Tonight was all about keeping Tommy from putting any of his appendages in dangerous holes.

Tommy bought Shelly and her friends in the corner a round of drinks. The women weren't from around here—the big hair and cheap purses gave them away. I knew their kind well. They'd bus into to the city for a ladies' night out, leaving their boyfriends, husbands, and responsibilities at home.

"Girls." Shelly wrapped an arm around Tommy's shoulders. "This is Ian."

"Hi, Ian!" her friends sang.

"And you are?" The redhead next to me in a sleeveless midriff-baring top nudged me in the side.

"Tommy," I said.

Tommy winked at me over the Irish Car Bomb he held to his lips.

"What's your story, Tommy?" the redhead purred.

"I have a wife and child and I'm very happy in my life thank you."

She backed away.

I sipped my scotch, ignoring the women, keeping one eye on Tommy and one eye on the TV broadcasting the Bulls game. My phone weighed heavy in my pocket. I had to physically keep both hands on my drink to avoid texting Erin. None of these women held a candle to her. They seemed nice enough, but they weren't PhDs, they weren't bleeding hearts for all children, they weren't funny and tough and bold, they weren't the mother of my own kid.

Hand shaking, I lifted the tumbler to my lips and drank. My throat had constricted, as a wave of sadness hit me. This life wasn't enough for me anymore. It might never be enough again.

Tommy rose from his seat, downed another scotch, and turned toward the bathroom. Shelly followed him. Fuck. Shit.

Time for Babysitter Ian to step up. This drunk dillweed was harder to deal with than Maeve with a loaded diaper. "Where are you going, *Ian*?"

He made a point of not looking me in the eye, like a child. Like a lying-ass child. "Bathroom."

I stood. "I'll go with."

Tommy shook his head. "No, no. I'm fine. I'll be right back."

Shelly ran her goddamn fucking talons down his arm. Did she not see the wedding ring on his finger? The two of them took a step together toward the bathrooms. We didn't cheat. Yeah, Tommy, Scott, and I had done our fair share of hooking up, but we drew the line at contributing to the delinquency of anyone in a relationship. Tommy had once faked breaking his arm to keep my drunk ass from leaving with a married woman. It was on me to return the favor tonight.

"I'm gonna be a dad," I shouted.

Tommy spun around. "What?"

Shelly gave one more desperate tug on Tommy's arm.

He brushed her off and stepped toward me. "What did you say?"

"I'm gonna be a dad," I repeated. "In, like"—I checked my watch—"two months."

Tommy stared at me as the news sank in. Then a huge grin took over his face and he lunged for me, wrapping me in a huge hug. "Congratulations," he yelled right at my eardrum.

I pushed him away, rubbing my ear, which was now ringing. "Thank you."

Tommy threw a few bills on the bar. "Let's go get some food."

And that was that. Tommy had transformed back into a family man.

We took a car to Au Cheval, where, miracle of miracles, we got two seats at the bar right away. Okay, maybe no miracles were involved. Tommy knew a guy, who knew a guy. We ordered burgers, beers, and chicken wings. I relaxed immediately. This night had suddenly slowed to more my speed.

"I want to know everything." Tommy tossed a chicken bone to the plate. "What happened? Who is she? All of it."

I grinned. Somehow Tommy, the guy who, a few hours ago, had been ready to throw in the towel on his marriage, was the first person to really show enthusiasm for my impending fatherhood.

"Well, it was an accident, obviously. But we're both really excited." I sipped my beer.

"Who's the 'we'?"

"Erin," I said. "Sharpe?" I wrinkled my nose, waiting for his reaction.

"The principal of Glenfield Academy!" Tommy was having trouble controlling the volume of his voice. "You knocked up the principal?!" The grin on his face reached his ears.

I shushed him. "Yes. I knocked up the principal."

"That is so... Oh my God!" His voice finally lowered. "Honestly, she seems really cool."

I grinned. "She is really cool."

He narrowed his eyes. "Are you two…?"

I shook my head as my eyes stung. "We're just friends."

Tommy nodded as he bit into his cheeseburger. Egg, cheese, and grease dripped onto his plate. "And she's okay with that?"

I laughed. "She's fine with it. She's been super firm on the whole keeping-our-distance thing. I invite her over all the time to hang out, but she says no."

Tommy placed his hand on mine. "Dude, are *you* okay with being just friends?"

My throat had constricted again. "Yes" was the correct

answer. "Yes" was what Erin and I had agreed upon. But I couldn't lie to my best friend. "No." I shook my head. "I'm not okay with it."

"Dude!" Tommy clutched my shoulder and shook it. "You're in love!"

I held up a hand. "I'm not in love. I am...in *like* and *respect* with the woman who is carrying my child. I want to be around for him."

"And her. You love her."

My eyes swept the room. "Shut up with the love stuff," I whispered.

"Ian, being in love is great."

"Says the guy who almost cheated on his wife with a woman wearing Uggs less than an hour ago."

He waved me off. "'Almost' is the operative word. I wasn't going to go through with it."

Sure he wasn't.

"The stuff I said before, that was just me venting." Tommy munched on his pickle. "I love Susie, I do. But it's not easy being in a relationship and having a kid. That's simply the truth. There are good days and bad. You only have to worry when the bad start outpacing the good."

"And you still have more good days than bad?"

He nodded, mouth crammed with cheeseburger. "Susie and I are both so sleep-deprived that we're constantly doing stupid shit. She got a tattoo. Did I tell you that?"

Wide-eyed, I shook my head. Susie had once gone on a tirade about a small shamrock tattoo her little sister had gotten on her ankle.

"Of Frasier." He pointed to the inside of his upper arm. "Because that's what she watches in the middle of the night while nursing Maeve. Now she has Kelsey Grammer's face near her armpit to remind her...forever."

I dragged a fry through my ketchup puddle. "So...are you

going to tell her about tonight?"

"I don't want to."

I slapped him on the arm. "Of course you don't want to, you jackass. But don't you think you should?"

"Don't you think you should tell Erin how you feel?"

"You nearly cheated on your wife tonight. You and Susie need to talk about that—whether on your own or with a counselor."

"And you have feelings for your baby mama. Shouldn't you two discuss that?"

I stared at myself in the mirror behind the bar. Erin and I had promised each other brutal honesty, no matter what. And here I was hiding a gigantic secret from her—that it killed me every time she shot me down, that I missed seeing her, that she had ruined me for all other women. If I told her these things, she'd laugh and tell me I was being foolish. She'd claim I only had these feelings because she was playing hard to get and that they'd disappear once I had her.

And maybe she'd be right.

That was the risk, wasn't it?

Tommy, who was still pretty drunk at this point, pulled out his phone and dialed his wife's number. "Hi, honey. I almost cheated on you tonight but didn't… Mmm-hmm… Mmm-hmm. Okay." He hung up. "She says I have to come home immediately."

"That sounds about right."

He raised his eyebrows at me. "And now you're going to call Erin…"

"I'm not going to call a pregnant lady in the middle of the night."

"Fair enough." Tommy hugged me, grabbed his stuff, and beelined it for the door. I paid the tab and called a car.

On the drive home, I stared at my text conversation with Erin. *"Are you up?"* I typed and deleted that immediately. Of course she wasn't up. *"Can we talk sometime?"* I erased that, too. Her answer would be no. It was always no.

I couldn't handle another rejection. The only course of action was to keep my feelings to myself, until my desire for her finally ran its course, like she knew it would.

• • •

ERIN

"Congratulations, Meg!"

I handed an envelope containing a substantial Amazon gift card to our sixth grade teacher, who'd just gotten her master's degree. She took it from my hand and bowed slightly to the rest of the faculty and staff, who'd gathered in the school library for our end-of-year milestone party. Today we were celebrating weddings, anniversaries, babies, and graduations. Significant others had been invited—Nat and Chris had huddled together at one of the back tables. I focused on the task at hand, passing out gifts to my employees. I was Santa Claus without the beard. Though I did have the round belly.

"Tim Courtland, our seventh grade English teacher, and his wife, Gemma, are expecting their first child this summer. We have a lovely gift for you—a pack-and-play!"

Tim took his wife's elbow and helped her up to where I stood at the front of the room. Gemma and I were due on the same day—July 16th. But she had a partner to hold her hand. I had no one. Not that I needed anyone, but I'd never even had the option of anyone holding my elbow while I walked anywhere.

I blinked back tears.

"Congratulations, Tim and Gemma!"

I gazed out at the crowd, ready to announce the next gift, but a silhouette in the doorway caught my eye. It had to be a mirage. I turned my head and then turned back. He was still there. Ian.

I touched my chest where my heart now pumped double time. I hadn't invited him. How was he here? I tried to send an SOS to Natalie, but she was too busy licking frosting off Chris's fingers.

Katie pulled a chair behind me and gently pushed me into it. "My turn," she said into the microphone. "Our fearless leader, Erin, is pregnant with her first baby, in case you hadn't noticed."

The entire staff chuckled. Of course they'd noticed. I was a house.

I rolled my eyes, wrapping my arms around my stomach.

"We hemmed and hawed about what to get her, because she's not a woman who needs much. So." Katie handed me an envelope.

Staring at her, I ripped it open. They'd pitched in and made a donation in my name to the Glenfield Gala to support the fine arts programs at both Glenfield Academy and my old school. I touched my heart again. "This so sweet," I said.

"And I bought the cute espadrilles on your registry for myself...in your name." Katie leaned down and hugged me.

"Did you invite Ian?" I whispered in her ear.

"Oh, that was the other part of your present," she whispered. "Guess I forgot to mention it."

She handed the microphone back to me. Ian still lurked in the doorway, probably wondering what the hell he was doing here. Katie, who had been helping Maria Minnesota with Gala stuff, had run into Ian at a meeting. He'd asked about me, because, duh, of course he had. I was carrying his child, and she was my roommate/sister. It would've been weird if he hadn't asked about me. But she insisted there'd been more behind the inquiry, that he'd been—her words— pining for me.

I'd laughed and laughed and laughed.

But Katie'd won the match. She'd managed to get Ian and me in the same room.

I reached for the nearest box. "Our next gift goes to someone who needs no introduction—Glenfield Academy's own Natalie Carter." I winked. "Oh, and her fiancé, Chris."

Nat and Chris, hand-in-hand, danced through the crowd up to me, and I handed them a crystal vase they had wanted from Tiffany's.

Nat hugged me. "Did you see Ian's here?"

"Yes," I whispered.

"What's he doing?"

"Katie invited him."

Nat pulled away and looked me in the eye. "Maybe he's here to make some big, sweeping love proclamation."

I whispered in her ear, "You're not getting that SMARTboard. Not on my watch."

Besides, Ian Donovan did not have feelings for me beyond a general sense of curiosity.

Which was exactly how I felt about him.

He was hot and smart and funny, but he'd break my heart if I let him, and I'd gotten out of that business.

Ian grabbed a plate of food and sat with Nat and Chris while I finished handing out presents. After I'd dispensed the last gift, he lurked near the back, waiting for me, but I'd been bombarded by several staff members who wanted to chat. This was my life, Ian. I couldn't just drop everything when you decided to show up.

But damn it, I wanted to.

Though, at the same time, his presence scared me shitless. What had he come here to say? We hadn't spoken face-to-face in months. Tonight he'd come to…what? Tell me he'd met someone? That he'd changed his mind and decided he wanted nothing to do with me or our son?

After most of the crowd had cleared out, I started

cleaning up my own mess—my plate and napkin and cup of half-drunk decaf. Ian snatched the plate from my hands.

"I've got it," he said. "You should sit. Aren't your legs killing you?"

My face flushed. He remembered that my varicose veins hurt like hell. I sat in the armchair Katie'd procured for me earlier.

Ian scurried around, picking up the mic and a few other rogue Dixie cups. He'd come from work wearing a pair of khaki pants and a multicolored button-down. He looked great, honestly. The guy was in perfect shape. And I was sitting over here with a basketball under my dress and legs the size of an elephant's.

He wiped his hands together. "Anything else? You need me to move some tables?"

The place had cleared out, leaving the mess for me and the cleaning crew. Thanks, guys. Way to be cool. "Do you mind?" I said. "I'd do it myself…"

Ian waved me off. "You sit there and tell me where to put stuff. I've got this."

I had the best seat in the house, watching Ian in his perfectly fitted pants bend over and push library tables around. He'd even rolled up his sleeves, revealing muscular forearms. After he'd moved the last table, he ran a hand through his dark hair. "Anything else?"

Rising from my seat, I pointed to the food table. "We should take that to the kitchen, leave it for the cleaning crew."

"I can do it," he said.

"I'll help." I consolidated the veggie trays. "Walking is good for me."

He put the cake remnants back in the bakery box.

"It's good to see you." I stared hard at the broccoli in front of me.

"I've missed you," he said.

Our forearms brushed against each other, and he jumped away as if startled. "How have you been feeling?"

"Okay." I shrugged. "Fat, disgusting."

He turned to me. "You look beautiful."

I giggled. "You're full of shit."

Ian's eyes were dead serious. "I mean it."

He knocked the wind out of me.

Ian reached for a bag he'd apparently left behind the table and pulled out a long, thin box wrapped in silver and tied with a blue bow. "The wrapping reminds me of your Cinderella outfit the night we first met."

He placed the box in my hands and I stared at it. "What is this?"

"A little something," he said. "A push present. Isn't that what they're called?"

Staring warily at him, I opened the box. "Holy shit." My hand jumped to my mouth. This was not a little something. This was a massive topaz surrounded by diamonds.

Ian reached for the necklace, stepped toward me, and fastened it around my neck.

I touched the pendant. "Why?" I said.

"Because I wanted to do something nice for you. You work so hard, and you're always thinking about other people. I wanted to show you someone was thinking about you."

At that moment, I stopped thinking and lunged for him, wrapping my arms around his waist and touching my lips to his.

Chapter Eleven

Ian

I pulled away from Erin, which took all the strength in me. "What are we doing?"

Her blue eyes gazed up at me. "I don't know what *you're* doing, but I'm kissing you."

"Because I gave you a necklace?" The necklace had only meant to say, "I appreciate you." I hadn't bought it to get her back into bed. "That wasn't why I—"

"I know." Her fingers played with the middle button on my shirt, which she focused on like it held the darkest secrets of the universe. "You're right. This is a bad idea."

I took her hands in mine. "I never said it was a bad idea." Kissing her was the best idea. I couldn't come up with a better one—not renewable energy, not an unbreakable cell phone, not self-replenishing beer.

"But we promised each other we'd stay friends…"

"We also said we'd be brutally honest." I tilted her chin up. "The truth is, I haven't been able to stop thinking about you. Every time I invited you over and you shot me down, it agonized me. I tried going out with my friends, tried to recapture some of my old life, and all I could think about was you."

Erin stared at me, breathing harder. Her hard stomach tapped against mine. And then she was on her toes again, kissing me, but this time I went along with it. Until she finally pulled away.

"Damn it." She picked up a rogue plastic spoon on the buffet table. "We really can't do this. I'll lose the bet with Nat."

I chuckled. "If that's the only thing holding you back, I'll buy her the damn SMARTboard."

Erin grinned. She looked ready to pounce, ready to jump into my arms, but since she was eight months pregnant, she stepped gingerly toward me, and I met her halfway.

"We can go to my place," I said, as she dragged me by the hand down the desolate Academy corridor, lined by the first and second grade classrooms.

"No time," she said. "We'll go to my office."

"We're going to have sex in the principal's office?"

"Shhh!" She glanced around nervously, probably making sure no one was here. I laughed again, relishing the joy of being with Erin. My whole body lightened around her. My problems disappeared, and jokes and fun and happiness replaced them.

She shut the door behind us and locked it.

I eyed her desk. "Can I do the whole sweep everything onto the floor thing?"

Erin stepped over and plucked several items off the desktop—laptop, crystal award of some kind, a bulky manila folder. She looked over her stuff one more time. "Okay. Now you can."

I swiped everything to the floor. Paperclips rained down

to the carpet. Her nameplate clanked against the side of her metal desk. Then I lifted her onto the empty surface and kissed her hard, as if it were both the first and last time.

Afterward, we cuddled naked together in her swivel chair, my legs propped up on her desk, hers hanging over one of the arms. James moved under her skin.

"You look like a gremlin about to multiply," I said, touching the spot on her belly that had just jutted out. It looked like James was trying to kick his way out of there.

"And...we're done." She started to stand, but I held her tight against me.

"In a good way!" I laughed.

She scowled at me. "I look like a reproducing gremlin... in a good way?"

I hugged her around the waist and kissed her neck. "Yes."

"Well, okay then." She nuzzled her cheek against mine. "We should do this again."

"Now?" I glanced down at my lap. "I need a minute."

"Not now," she said. "We should probably GTFO before the cleaning crew wants to get in here." She nibbled my earlobe. "I mean, we should do this again tomorrow...and the day after that."

Fuck. Tomorrow.

"About that." A bitter taste rose to my throat, as I ran a finger down her smooth, milky upper arm. "I'm not going to be here tomorrow."

She pulled away slightly and glared at me in her no-nonsense principal way. "Metaphorically or physically?"

"Physically." I touched her sternum. "I'll definitely be here mentally, believe me. But I have to go to Tokyo"—I rolled my eyes—"again. The good news is that I'm only going there for Fumetsu to sign the papers. I'll be back in a few days."

Her face softened. "Okay, then. When you get back, we'll

do this again."

"And again and again and again." I kissed her cheek. "And in the meantime, we can text like teenagers in love."

"Maybe chat while watching a movie together like that one night?"

"Definitely," I said. "Then I'll be back by next weekend, and we can pick up exactly where we left off."

. . .

ERIN

"So, we're all set then, sponsor wise?" I rested my elbows on my desk. Maria Minnesota sat across from me. Katie had once again perched on the couch near the window, taking notes.

"I think we're on track," Maria said. Normally I didn't get all insecure around other women, but Maria the travel blogger was the exception. She was always super nice, but also incredibly put together, and I felt like Grimace the McDonald's character around her—all bloated and purple and shapeless.

"Fantastic." I closed my folder. Meeting adjourned. I needed her to leave so I could hop in my car and grab a burger at the nearest drive-thru. When I saw Dana earlier this week, on Monday, she told me my iron was low, so I took that as a license to stop at Wendy's every chance I got.

"I just wanted to say…" Maria, not taking the hint that her cue to leave had come and gone, remained in her seat. In fact, she'd uncrossed and re-crossed her legs, like she was prepared to spend another hour here, chatting. "Ian told me about the baby. I think it's great that you're doing the whole parenting thing on your own."

I smiled at the mention of Ian and instinctively checked my watch. Nope. Still no message from him. He'd sent me a quick one to let me know he'd arrived in Tokyo and that he'd call me later, but that was two days ago. "Thanks." I avoided Katie's gaze. I'd told her about Ian and me hooking up again, and she'd bombarded me with six hundred questions I had no answers to: "What does this mean? Are you *together* together? Are you moving out?" I'd said nothing had been decided, and that we'd talk when he was back in town this weekend.

Still, every time she caught me checking my phone, I noticed the look of pity on her face.

"You're smart to keep things with Ian platonic," Maria said. "He's god-awful at intimacy."

I nodded slowly. How was the gorgeous head of our school fund-raiser so well-acquainted with Ian's intimacy level?

She rolled her big brown eyes. "We used to date. Ish. For exactly one minute. Full disclosure."

I probably looked like a frog catching flies. Thankfully, Katie—my muscle—was there to speak for me. She got up, stepped over to the desk, folded her toned arms, and said, "Well, now Ian and Erin are dating." Katie narrowed her eyes at me in a question. "Ish?"

"You're actually together?" she asked.

"It's a work in progress," I said, my finger itching to touch my watch again, just to see if maybe, maybe I'd missed the pulse from a new text. "We haven't defined things yet."

Maria chuckled. "Don't worry." She leaned across the desk like we were coconspirators now, like we both had the exact same relationship-experience with Ian Donovan, like I wasn't the one sitting here all pregnant with his child. "He'll define things for you."

Her words landed like a thud in my bones. But I was the one who'd originally put the kibosh on the possibility of romance between us. I was the one who'd shot him down every time he wanted to get together. And, heck, I'd been the one to reinitiate physical contact at the Academy on Friday night.

But now here I was checking my phone every five seconds, waiting for him to call.

"Don't get me wrong," Maria said. "I'm happy for you." She widened her eyes, and I believed her. This wasn't a malicious conversation. It was a sisterhood chat. "It's just, I know what he was like during the time we were dating."

Katie cracked her knuckles. "You said you and Ian only dated for a second." She gestured toward me. "Things are different between him and Erin. There's a baby involved."

"I know," Maria said. "And I'm sure he's trying. He probably thinks he's putting in a real effort. But Ian sucks at letting people in. It goes 'job'"—she raised her hand above her head—"'buddies'"—she lowered her hand a fraction of an inch—"and 'everybody else'"—she bent over, dropping her hand to the floor.

"Erin's at buddy level." Katie winked at me in support. "At least."

I shook my head. I didn't need her defending me, not if she was going to start referring to me as Ian's "buddy." I felt like even less than that at this point. People texted their pals, at least. He'd gone radio silent on me.

But it had only been three days. A long weekend, basically. He was probably working hard in Tokyo, and we'd talk all about it when he came back on Saturday. I would not start reading more into this that I needed to.

"I'm sure you're right," Maria said. "Things are totally different. You're having a kid!" She shot me a gigantic, thousand-watt smile.

"We are!" I raised my arms in feigned enthusiasm. We *were* having a kid, which meant it wasn't just me Ian was ignoring right now. Before we hooked up on Friday night, Ian had texted me all the time. But now...nothing. It was hard not to draw the correlation. Especially since this situation couldn't be more clichéd if it tried. I stood, signaling the end of the meeting. I had to go home and curl up in a ball for a while.

"Thanks, Maria," I said. "We'll be in touch as the Gala gets closer."

After she left, Katie turned to me. "You about ready to get burgers?"

"I'm ready to go," I said. "But no food. I've lost my appetite."

Chapter Twelve

Ian

I saw the light at the end of the tunnel.

Fumetsu Enterprises was ready to sign with me on the dotted line, so all I had to do was bring them the contract to sign and talk logistics. I'd be back home to Erin in no time, as promised.

For the first time in months, I could imagine taking a break, putting in shorter hours, traveling less. We still had a month before James would make his debut. Maybe Erin and I could babymoon up in Wisconsin for a weekend or something.

But as soon as I saw Isamu, my friend and main contact at Fumetsu, waiting for me at the airport, I knew something was wrong.

Shoulders hunched, I made my way over to him. "Uh-oh," I said.

He held out his hand and I shook it, before making a cursory bow. "There's a problem," he told me.

"I'm a problem solver," I said.

"This problem flew in from Chicago six days ago."

"Who?" I asked. As far as I knew, Fumetsu was a well-kept secret. I'd been quietly courting them for months, waiting for the time they'd be ready to grow their business. I hadn't told anyone about the company, and Scott and Tommy hadn't, either.

"West Town Ventures?" Fumetsu said.

"Who the fuck?" I'd never heard of these people. They had to be new, out of their depths. I'd take care of them in short order.

"Hotel first?" Fumetsu said.

I desperately needed a shower, but it'd have to wait. "No time," I said. "Take me to the office."

Isamu gave me the skinny on the ride over from the airport. Another VC group had flown in from the states a week ago. They were a little hungrier and frankly, a little younger than my company. They were prepared to offer things my DOC Group couldn't handle.

I stared out the window blankly, watching buildings fly by in a blur as I synthesized the information. I hadn't come here prepared for a fight. I'd flown here with a golden novelty pen to sign some contracts. But I'd give Fumetsu whatever they wanted. I had invested too much time, money, and sweat into this to relinquish the deal to some new company that had decided to swoop in out of nowhere. I would turn on the charm and prove to Fumetsu that their first decision had been the correct one. They should and would sign with me, as planned.

Because I was Ian Fucking Donovan.

When Isamu and I stepped off the elevator and into the warehouse office of Fumetsu Enterprises, a trio of millennials in business suits greeted us. A young woman with a silver asymmetrical bob walked over to me, hand extended.

"Hi, Ian," she said. "I'm glad we could finally meet. I'm Liz Barton."

"Oh...hey..." That rang a bell. I racked my brain. Liz... Barton...

"Remember?" She fixed the cuff on her slate-gray power suit. "I went to Loyola Academy and wanted to talk shop with a fellow Rambler. You had your assistant blow me off the first time, and then you never returned my calls?" She smiled like the cat that had caught the canary. "I did some research to find out what you were working on, and my colleagues and I decided Fumetsu Enterprises was perfect for us." She grinned at Isamu and his colleagues. "And it appears Fumetsu thinks we might be for them, too."

"Yeah, we'll see about that," I said.

This Liz person pissed me the hell off, but game had to respect game. I'd done the same thing back when I was starting out. Tommy and I had found out about a solar energy start-up in Indiana, and we courted the shit out of them, pulling their business away from an older Chicago VC firm. It'd been our first major score.

But the old dudes I'd beaten out were past their prime. I was still young and hungry. I'd show Liz and her pals what real skill looked like.

Liz gestured toward her colleagues. "These are my partners, Luisa Roca and Ja Kimberly."

We shook hands, and honestly, maybe it was the jet lag, but I couldn't tell if Ja—tall, bald, and muscular in a long black skirt kind of situation—was a man or a woman, and then I beat myself up for thinking in such old-person binary terms. Ja was Ja, and I, in my polo shirt and khakis, was a relic. I adapted quickly. "Nice to meet you," I told them without missing a beat.

We all stood in the middle of the office in a sort of lopsided oval—Liz's people and the Fumetsu folks. No one moved. They were waiting for big, swinging dick, Ian Fucking Donovan, to show up and take the floor. Liz's group had already shown their hand to Fumetsu, and it was my turn now.

I straightened my shoulders, marched over to a desk, and set my briefcase on top. "This is cute," I said, "and I'm glad you've all had a chance to talk and get to know each other, and that Liz, Ja, and Luisa had a chance to practice their pitch, but I'm here with the contracts." I opened my bag and rummaged around for the papers Tommy had prepared for me. "DOC is prepared to offer you—"

I paused as something fell out of my bag and Liz started laughing.

"Wow, Ian," she said. "Rumor had it you were into some kinky stuff, but this...?"

Holding my breath, I looked to the floor. Lying there was a tube of nipple cream Tommy had given to me to celebrate my impending fatherhood (and because Susie had said it was a lifesaver). Written across the package in bright yellow letters were the words "BOOBIE BUTTER."

I snatched it off the floor and shoved it back into my bag.

Ja leaned over and whispered something in Liz's ear. Liz's eyes bugged out. "Really?" She turned to the rest of us. "Ja says that their sister used Boobie Butter when she nursed Ja's niece. Ian, do you have a kid?"

"No," I said.

"No." Liz folded her arms. "You don't have a kid, but you're carrying around balm for chapped nipples?"

"Well." The entire Fumetsu team watched me. I registered the disappointment on Isamu's face. He'd brought me here on the promise that I was a single-minded business person, that nothing—*nothing*—would get in the way of my dedication to his company. "No, I don't have a kid," I said. "Well, not yet. I have one on the way."

Grinning, Liz turned to Isamu. "He's on the daddy track. It was like I told you before he got here. The guys from DOC are past their prime. You need fresh, new blood to take you into the future. That's what we're prepared to offer you. We're young, hungry, and ready to dedicate our lives to the success of your business."

Well, so was I. Always had been, always would be. I shoved the contracts back into my bag. Liz would not beat me at my own game. "First of all, let's not underrate experience. You'd be taking a huge risk with Liz's company. My partners and I have been doing this for almost two decades. We are the past, present, and future. Second of all, nothing matters more to me than my job." A pang of guilt stabbed my gut, but I straightened my shoulders. I had been tasked with completing this deal for Tommy and Scott, and I would not let my best friends down. "Nothing. Isamu, you know that. You know me. If you sign with us and you need something, anything, I will drop whatever I'm doing in a heartbeat and be on the next plane to Tokyo."

Liz addressed Isamu directly. "We can station someone here permanently, or at least until we get things off the ground."

"We can do that, too," I said. Fuck if I knew how we'd manage that, but we would. I would. Whatever it took to sign this deal, I'd agree to it. We'd work out the details later. "We're prepared to give you whatever you need."

"Sure you are," Liz said, sarcastically, "as long as it doesn't interfere with nap time."

I spoke to the members of Fumetsu Enterprises. "I meant it when I said you're my number one priority. It's what I've told you all along, and it's the truth. Yes, I'm having a child. That changes nothing. I'm still the same guy who's shown you for months that I'm ready to turn your company into the powerhouse it deserves to be."

Isamu conferred with his partners. "We're going to have to think on this. We'll have our decision in the morning."

• • •

IAN

When I got back to the hotel, I texted Tommy right away. "Give me anything you have on Liz Barton's VC group in Chicago. They're here in Tokyo, trying to make a play for Fumetsu."

Shit. I hadn't yet talked to Erin. I sent her a quick message that said, *"I'm here. Talk later."* I couldn't even fathom what time it was in Chicago right now. She could be at work or asleep. And, anyway, I needed to decompress. I pulled off the clothes I'd been wearing since the plane, showered, changed, and headed down to the hotel bar for a quick drink before bed. I'd give Erin a call when I got back to the room.

The bar was nearly empty, save for Liz Barton sitting on a stool, staring at some baseball game on the screen in front of her. I could've just ignored her, booked it out of there; but, like it or not, she was my competition now. If we were going to operate in the same space in Chicago, it was important I keep her on my radar.

"Still awake?" she asked as I slid onto the stool next to her.

"For now," I said.

"No one would blame you if you bowed out."

"I'd blame me." I held up my drink in salute. "So, Loyola, huh? Where'd you go to grade school?"

"I.C."

I grinned. "City girl."

"Yeah, and you and your buddies are all trust-fund babies from Glenfield Academy."

"That's not quite the truth," I said, "but if it helps you

sleep at night." This woman could dish it out, and I respected her for it. It had to be the good old Jesuit education.

"I've put everything I have into this business," she said.

I raised an eyebrow. "You don't think I have? I'm forty. This has been my entire life since I graduated college."

"Mine, too."

"And you're what?" I leaned back, assessing her. The dyed gray hair made her look older, honestly. Why was this a trend, and when would it die? "Thirty?" I would've guessed thirty-five, but I decided to age her down, just in case.

"Twenty-seven."

I chuckled. "So, for five whole years you've been busting the pavement and breaking down doors." My phone buzzed, and I checked it. Tommy had returned my text. He said, *"Liz's portfolio is flimsy at best. They're short on capital, too. Honestly, I think they're bluffing about their ability to play ball here. Offer Isamu another two mil and see what happens."* I stared at my phone. Checkmate. Game over. She had no clue, but I was about to knock her out like Glass Joe in the first round of Mike Tyson's Punch Out.

A game she had probably never played because she hadn't been born yet.

I hesitated to land the final punch.

Why? This was an easy one. I'd been courting Fumetsu for months. The reward for all my hard work sat right in front of me.

But I'd just agreed to give Isamu everything he wanted. I'd promised one of us—Tommy, Scott, or I—would move to Tokyo to babysit the launch of the unbreakable cell phone. And, I had to be honest, the only one of us in any position at all to do that was me.

"Who's on the phone?" Liz asked. "Baby mama? You gotta go home and be a dad?" She made the universal sign for "whipped."

"Nah." I stared at Tommy's text. "My business partner."

"Is he doing the right thing and telling you to come home?" Liz downed her scotch. "You should listen to him. My partners and I have this deal by the balls. We can offer Fumetsu so much more than you can."

She was kind of right, wasn't she? We had the money, but Liz, Ja, and Luisa had the drive.

What was I fucking saying? I was going soft, that was what. The "Finish him" screen had come up on my *Mortal Kombat* game; all I had to do was deliver the final blow and be the Ian Fucking Donovan everyone expected to show up. Liz would have to learn the hard way—like I did—that this business wasn't for the faint of heart, that no one would hold her hand and tell her it'd all be okay. "Oh, really?" I said. "You can offer Fumetsu more than us? Can you offer them two million dollars more?"

"What?" Liz's face had gone white.

I showed her my phone. "Can you give them more money? Because I don't think you can."

I called Isamu and told him the new offer. We agreed we'd finalize everything in the morning. "Looks like I'm gonna need that golden pen tomorrow."

• • •

ERIN

"Hey," I texted Ian, *"I hope everything is going well! Here's your friendly reminder about our childbirth class tomorrow afternoon at the hospital."*

I placed the phone face up on the coffee table in front of me, between my flute of orange juice and Natalie's mimosa. We'd gone to a bridal shop for her fitting. She hid behind the pink and white curtain as a saleswoman zipped her into her dress. Katie was supposed to be here, too, but she was currently MIA.

I texted her, too. *"Where are you?"*

Another saleswoman, Karen, popped her head in from the other room. "How are you doing, sweetie?"

"Fine." I pointed to my glass of juice.

She leaned against the doorframe. "This probably brings back memories for you."

I narrowed my eyes, warily. What did this woman know about me and my memories? "Drinking OJ…?" I asked.

Karen shook her head. "No, silly. Wedding dress shopping." She nodded toward my ample gut. "How long have you been married?"

I touched my belly. "Oh, I'm not—"

Karen blushed. "I'm sorry. I assumed. I'm sure you'll meet the right guy someday!" She turned an ear toward the front of the store. "What was that? A phone call?" she yelled to absolutely no one. The only other employee working this morning was currently helping Nat into her dress. Karen quickly shut the door and disappeared.

I grabbed my phone again. The nerve of her, making assumptions about me. It reminded me of the time I'd gone to Home Depot for something in the dead of winter. I'd been wearing this huge, boxy parka, and the greeter woman informed me about a current deal on new construction projects. She pointed to my midsection and said, "You could build a nursery." I stood there speechless, but she doubled down. "You know," she said, "for the baby." I burst into tears, right there in the middle of Home Depot on a Saturday morning. Dirk and I had been trying, unsuccessfully, to get pregnant for almost a year at that point. I went home and immediately dumped the offending parka in the trash.

How dare that saleswoman assume I had a husband. How dare she assume I even wanted to get married. I always avoided asking these kinds of questions of other people. You never knew what was going on with someone else. Maybe there was no dad. Maybe we'd just broken up. Maybe he was dead.

Maybe fuck you, nosy person, because the dad was currently halfway around the world, ignoring my calls.

Tale as old as time.

I checked my phone again for good measure. I probably would've felt the pulse on my watch if a text had come in, but sometimes I didn't. Sometimes I missed it.

Nothing. No new messages.

Katie rushed in then, wearing her workout gear—skin-tight three-quarter leggings and a *barely there*, backless tank top. I'd never seen her dress like that before. She usually wore baggy sweats and too-large T-shirts. She skipped the champagne and poured herself a full glass of cucumber-flavored water. "Hey." She waved to me as she downed her beverage.

"Hi," I said. "New clothes?"

She spun around. "These are so much easier to lift weights in. Do I look okay?"

"You look amazing." She'd been wearing so much baggy clothing, it totally hid her new, toned bod. I pulled my capped sleeves down slightly to hide my flabby arms.

"My instructor today complimented my form. She says I'm an expert at Romanian deadlifts." She held her arms straight down in front of her, arched her shoulders, and leaned forward, sticking her butt back.

"Looks good to me," I said.

She leaned against the bar counter. "She even asked me to walk around the room, correcting other people's posture."

"Awesome!" I said. "But too bad for those other people." I avoided exercise classes altogether, because why should I pay money for other people to point out my faults?

Natalie emerged from her dressing room like a diva

taking the stage. Her outfit had transformed magically from a simple sundress to a full ball gown with a beaded halter top. She'd had her hair straightened recently into a sleek bob that looked so sophisticated paired with her dramatic eye makeup.

"Beautiful," I said. My girls were currently crushing it in the looks department. I was a tick about to pop.

Katie clapped. "I'd hug you," she said, "but I'm disgusting."

Yeah, sure. Katie was the disgusting one. She'd strutted in here, showing off her muscular back. I was the lumpy sack of potatoes whose boyfriend had stopped texting her and had decided to stay in Tokyo ten days longer than planned.

I had to get out of my head. Ian cared about me. He'd told me so the last time we were together…almost two weeks ago. He gave me this beautiful necklace. I touched the diamond and topaz teardrop pendant resting against my sternum. He hadn't texted because he was busy with work stuff. Full stop. He lived for his career. I'd known this going in.

Nat, regal like a queen, stepped onto the platform in front of the three-way mirror and rotated to see herself from all angles. "Chris has been texting me all morning." She giggled. "He wants to see pictures…right now." She beamed, winking at Katie and me in the mirror. "I told him he could wait a month."

I snuck another peek at my phone. Still no text from Ian. Chris had been texting Nat all morning, but my boyfriend couldn't be bothered to shoot me an *I'm busy, but I got it!* message. That I would've understood. I would've sent him a thumbs-up emoji, and all would've been well.

Dirk used to do this. He'd ignore my texts, and I'd let him get away with it, because I'd opted to play the part of the cool chick with a life of her own. And then he broke up with me for someone more emotionally demonstrative.

And now history was repeating itself.

"Chris is so smitten," Katie said.

Natalie smiled back at her in the mirror. "We both are. But it's also like, we've each been in bad relationships before. This time around, we're dedicated to making time for each other. That's really what it comes down to, priorities. He's mine. I'm his."

"It's good to have other priorities, though," I said. I hadn't just been playing the cool, busy chick with Dirk. I actually was that chick. I, too, had dedicated myself to my job. I had friends and a demanding schedule full of all kinds of fund-raising obligations.

"Of course." Nat frowned at me. "And we do, Chris and I."

What worked for one person didn't work for others. I was fine on my own, and so was Ian. "Just because two people live somewhat separate lives doesn't mean they're not dedicated to each other."

I stood and waddled over to a small rack of dresses along the back wall—the maternity section for knocked-up bridesmaids. "I need something spectacular for the Gala." Ian, no Ian, I'd crush it at the fund-raiser. I'd be Dr. Erin Sharpe, belle of the ball. He could decide to be a part of all that gloriousness or not.

Katie plucked a dress off the rack. "This is very you."

She wasn't wrong. She'd found a multicolored maxi dress that'd make me look like a circus tent. It was the ball gown equivalent of that boxy coat I'd worn to Home Depot.

"I'm not showing up at the Gala looking like a principal or like I'm trying to hide the fact that I'm one hundred weeks pregnant." I grabbed a slinky turquoise blue number with a slit up to there.

"You'll look hot in that," Nat said. "Ian will faint."

"If he does"—I held the dress up in the mirror—"that's

his problem."

...

ERIN

The next morning, I was the only person flying solo at my childbirth class for expectant mothers and their partners/ coaches, though not everyone there was in a couple. The woman next to me had brought her mom because her husband had been deployed overseas and wouldn't be back for six more months.

Now that was a good excuse.

Also on the good excuse list? Being dead or in a coma, which could've been where Ian was, for all I knew.

I'd stopped worrying about him, and I'd stopped checking my phone over it. I'd even turned it off and zipped it into my purse, which I shoved into the far corner of the room. Maybe he'd surprise me and show up. Or maybe he'd send an *"I'm sorry!"* text. In which case, I didn't want to know about it. He didn't need to know I'd been sitting around like a chump, waiting for his call. I was a strong, independent woman, who didn't need anyone.

"Do you have a friend you want to call?" asked the instructor, Missy.

I nearly bit her head off. I had to stop myself from unhinging my jaw and swallowing her whole. Instead I plastered on the most saccharine smile I could muster and said, "I'm fine on my own." It was my mantra.

The truth was, Nat was out with Chris's family, and I couldn't bother her. And Katie was at some all-day fitness showcase her cross-training instructor had asked her to attend. They were busy with their own lives, and I would be fine doing this by myself.

Just liked I'd planned in the first place.

I perched on the big bouncy exercise ball on my own. I breathed on my own—with the help of some righteous indignation. I survived the gory video on the miracle of birth all by myself.

I could only count on myself, and that went double for James. We were a pair, a team. I touched my belly and whispered, "You have me."

After the class, I bought myself a caramel shake at Oberweis and headed home, where I slipped into my comfy uniform of T-shirt and ratty old shorts, put on a movie, and fell asleep on the couch.

A few hours later, I woke to someone banging on my door.

I scratched my head, stood, and pulled open the door. There I found Ian, wearing a suit, pulling a suitcase behind him.

"You didn't answer my calls," he said. "I've been trying to get ahold of you for hours."

Rich.

So fucking rich.

"I tried to make it to the class." He followed me into the condo. I didn't invite him in. "My plane got in late, but I hopped into what looked like the fastest cab at O'Hare. We booked it to the hospital, but you were already gone. And then you weren't answering me. Erin, you have to answer me."

I cocked my jaw. Oh, really. Did I? "Noted," I said.

"You had me worried sick." He reached for me, trying to put his hand on my belly. I pulled away. "Is something wrong?" he asked.

Was something wrong? "No," I said. "It's all good." I bit my lip. The cool chick with a life of her own.

"No, it's not. Talk to me. Please."

"You're..." My eyes latched on his, and the anger bubbled

up. The cool chick disappeared, and the super-bitter pregnant lady who was sick of this shit took her place. "I can't believe you're actually harping on me for not calling you right now."

"I'm sorry," he said. "I figured you were probably fine, but I just get nervous when I don't hear from you. I don't mean to be so smothery."

"Oh, you're not smothery," I purred. Reaching into my purse, I pulled out my phone, turning it on for the first time since my childbirth class. There were several texts on the home page from Ian. I ignored those and opened up the rest of our text conversation. "Here's what you texted me while you were gone for the past ten days." I read the entirety of his side of our chat. "'Hi! I'm here! Talk later!' 'Things busy! Chat soon!' 'Going fine! You too?'" I looked up at him. "You know, you never did directly respond to my lengthy answer about my iron situation. And finally, 'I'll be back tomorrow for class.'" I glanced up at him, shutting off the screen. "Ten. Days."

"I legitimately was busy," he said. "And the time difference."

I moseyed to the kitchen and poured myself some water, and he followed me. "I get it," I said. "I totally, totally get it. Believe me." I casually held out my hand. "Let me see your phone."

"Why?" He, defiant, clutched his phone to his chest. "I wasn't cheating on you, if that's what you think." Oh, the panic on his face.

I left my hand where it was, waiting for his phone. "That's not at all what I think."

He rolled his eyes, unlocked his screen, and handed it to me.

I clicked on his texts and scrolled through his messages from the past two weeks. "Scott and Tommy," I said.

"That was about business."

"You texted them a whole screed about the condition of the golf course you were at one day."

He held up his hands in surrender. "Still business related."

"Someone named Nikki with the big portfolio?"

"She's a potential client, that's it. We were supposed to meet for lunch, and I had to cancel."

"Like how you were supposed to meet me at the childbirth class today, and you just didn't show."

He clamped his mouth shut.

"And Maria Minnesota." I raised an eyebrow at him. "Your ex."

He blushed slightly, but folded his arms in defiance. "You can barely call her that, and we were only texting about the fund-raiser. For *your* school. Which I'm involved in because of *my* business."

I shut off his screen and handed his phone back.

"I went to the bridal shop with Nat yesterday and she kept talking about how she and Chris prioritize each other. I'm not your priority."

"Erin, you are. James is. It's just…every time I went to call or text you, I knew it was going to be a lengthy thing, so I kept putting it off."

"For ten days. While you had plenty of time to text your ex about what we should serve for dessert at the Gala."

"Because that was an easy answer. It took two fucking seconds." He paced the floor, running his hands through his hair, making it stand on end. He looked like Beethoven. "Look, you and I went into this knowing the score. We both work. We're both busy. We live our own lives. I thought that meant we were going to be a little more casual about the BS relationship rules."

I touched my belly. "I think we're way past casual."

"You know what I meant. I thought we wouldn't play games and put unrealistic expectations on each other."

"The unrealistic expectation that you call me when you're out of town and that you show up when you say you're going to?"

"My plane was late!"

"And if you'd bothered to text me once in a while over the past week, that'd probably be less of a big deal. The truth is, you're never going to put me first." I started pacing. "Since I had a lot of time to think on my own this week, I realized that I used to let Dirk get away with this stuff. He'd ignore me, and I'd just wave it off. I'm done doing that. It bothered me that you didn't text me while you were gone. Maybe it shouldn't have, but it did. I get that your job is your life. You told me that up front, and I should've believed you." I repeated the gesture Maria Minnesota had shown me a few days ago. "It goes work…friends…everyone else."

He hesitated. I'd gotten to him. "That's not true, Erin. Not even a little bit." Lies. "But I'd been working on this deal for months. I had to focus on it. I had to see it through to its conclusion."

"So now it's concluded?" I said. "You're done. No more Tokyo."

He hesitated.

I laughed. "Of course more Tokyo," I said. "And probably Rio and Helsinki and Lima and —"

He cut me off. "Scott's calling." He hit the answer button.

"And now you're answering your phone in the middle of a fight. And my place in the ecosystem grows even clearer."

"Scott?" He placed his hand over his other ear to drown out my chatter.

I didn't let that stop me. "And I thought I was the one who avoided conflict. I thought I was the roly-poly bug who curled up in a ball when things got difficult."

"What?" Ian's jaw dropped. "Oh my God."

Arms still folded, I stopped ranting and stood still,

watching Ian. His face had gone green, then white. My stomach plummeted.

"Oh my God," he said again. "I'll be right there." He hung up the phone and stared at me wide-eyed, as if still trying to process the information. "Scott's mom died."

I reached for the counter to hold myself upright. And I'd just been ranting at him about answering his phone.

Ian rushed out of the kitchen and grabbed the handle of his rolling suitcase. "I have to go up to Winnetka."

"I'll go with you," I said, following him, grabbing my own phone to text Katie, to let her know where I'd be.

"No," he answered quickly, without a second thought. Then his face softened. "It's fine. You stay here."

"Because we had a fight?" I said.

"It's not that."

"Ian, I want to be there for you. I know you have to help Scott, but let me help you."

He shook his head. "This is, you know, family only."

My hand reached for my cheek, as if I'd been slapped. I'd been half-joking before when I'd put myself in the category of "everybody else," but Maria had been right. It didn't matter that I'd been carrying his kid for almost nine months. "I'm not family." I flopped down on the couch and looked up at him. He avoided my eyes. "Fuck, Ian."

He sat next to me. "It's not that." He reached for my hand, but I snatched it back. "Scott doesn't know about us yet. He doesn't know about the baby. I can't drop that bombshell on him today."

"Makes sense, but over the span of, oh"—I did the math—"seven months, the right time for you to tell your best friend you were going to be a dad never came up? Not one time?"

"He was going through a lot."

I'd never asked a guy to prioritize me before, but I deserved more than this. I deserved more than sporadic texting and zero presence in his "real" life. "Well." I turned away from him, facing the kitchen. I couldn't look at him. "Good thing we never defined what we were, because we're obviously nothing."

"You don't mean that."

"I'd tell you to tell your friend I'm sorry, but he doesn't know I exist."

I kept staring in the other direction until I heard the door close behind him.

Chapter Thirteen

Ian

Scott's mom had had a heart attack. She'd been through months of chemo and had been close to getting a clean bill of health. But then out of nowhere this morning, she got up, ate breakfast, and collapsed on the floor while doing the dishes.

Tommy and I sat with Scott in his mom's living room while we waited for the funeral parlor to come pick up the body. The paramedics had come in earlier, pronounced her dead thanks to her DNR, and covered her.

"I hadn't heard from her all morning, so I drove over and found her in the kitchen," Scott said. "I had no idea what to do, so I asked Alexa what to do when someone dies at home."

Tommy snorted. "Like when Ian was trying to figure out how to change a diaper."

Scott and I both burst out laughing. Gallows humor.

How many times had we sat like this over the years—Tommy in the arm chair, Scott and me on the couch—waiting for Scott's mom to either come in with cookies or to yell at us to go out for some fresh air?

My eyes stung. None of this felt real—Scott's mom, the fight with Erin. Exhaustion weighed down my limbs, and I had been walking through a fog since I deplaned today. Maybe I'd wake up an hour from now, in my own bed, and all of this will have been a bad dream.

"It doesn't look like she suffered." Scott let out a sob. "So that's good."

I wrapped an arm around him, pulling him close. I had to keep it together for Scott. His mom died, which so trumped my girl problems. I kept reminding myself to hold on to that perspective. Scott had lost the most important person in his life for good. All I'd lost was someone I'd slept with a few times, who happened to be carrying my child.

I let out a sob.

Now Scott wrapped his arms around me, and we cried together.

"We're all going to miss her." Tommy joined the hug fest on the couch.

I'd had everything figured out—job, friends, family. No sleepovers, no second dates, no strings. This was what attachments got you—grief. Nothing but tears and sadness and loss. The highs were nice, but the lows fucking sucked.

I'd lost my mom when she decided she could no longer be there for me. I'd been eleven then. I'd had more than a decade to get attached. I'd never give James that opportunity. He'd be fine without me.

And I'd be fine, too. Eventually.

"Guys." Scott lifted his head off our shoulders. "What do I do now?"

"Well," I said, straightening up, grateful for a bit of practicality, "you wait for the mortuary to come get her and then you plan the funeral, I guess."

"I don't mean now"—he pointed to the floor—"I mean

'now.'" He waved his arms around. "Existentially. I don't know what to do with myself. Taking care of her had been my main focus."

"Get through this week," Tommy said, "before you start worrying about the rest of your life."

"There's always work," I said. Work never died, and there was always more of it.

"I know this is kind of jumping the gun, and I shouldn't be thinking of me, me, me on the day my mom died, but"—Scott shook his head—"what *about* me? What happens to me now? I spent the past few months by her side watching her go through treatment. Who will be there for me when I'm sick?"

"You have us," Tommy said, squeezing Scott's arm.

"Tommy's Mr. Family Man," I said. "But you know you always have me—single, string-free Ian."

Scott chuckled. "That's for sure."

I ignored Tommy's eyes, which bored holes into me. My throat had closed up. Backing away from Erin and the baby was the right thing to do. I hadn't texted her more than platitudes for ten days, and honestly, I hadn't realized it. My job was number one, and it'd always have to be that way, if I wanted to stay on top.

Which I did.

"Can you picture Ian and me living down in Florida when we're seventy, like two Golden Girls?" Scott laughed through tears.

"We'll still be each other's wingmen." The thought sickened me. What did I need a wingman for? I'd had no interest in flings since I met Erin. But even before her, my flings had gotten messy. If I kept my focus on work, I'd end up disappointing no one.

"Ian's going to be a dad," Tommy blurted. He stared at Scott, though I knew he felt my laser eyes on him. "He knocked up Erin the principal, and she's going to have a baby in two weeks."

Scott's head slowly revolved toward me, like the possessed girl in *The Exorcist*. "Excuse me?"

After taking a breath to compose myself, I waved him off. "It's no big deal."

"You're going to be a dad," Scott said, "and that's no big deal?"

Needing to pace, I jumped up. I picked up one of Scott's mom's Lladro statues—a little boy dragging a mailbag full of fucking hearts. I replaced it on the shelf and flicked it angrily. "I'm not going to be 'a dad.'"

"Either you are or you aren't," Scott said. "Which is it?"

I spun toward him, biting the inside of my cheek. I would not cry over this. I would not fucking turn into a blubbering baby about some person I'd never even met, not on the day when my best friend's entire world had ended. "Not," I said. "I'm basically a sperm donor. Erin's fine on her own, and, well, so am I."

Tommy said, "But you said—"

I cut him off. "A moment of weakness. Erin and I thought about giving 'us' a try, and it didn't work."

"And now you're bowing out of your kid's life, just like that?"

I shrugged, running my finger along the edge of a picture frame—Tommy, Scott, me, and Scott's mom at Homer's eating ice cream. I remembered that day like it was yesterday. My mom had been gone about a week, and I'd been a wreck ever since she, Blake, and his Mazda Miata had pulled out of the driveway. But Scott's mom showed up at my door to take me out and fill me up with mint chocolate chip—sugar therapy. It had totally worked. I'd vowed to Scott's mom and the guys that this was how I'd parent—I'd give the kid ice cream whenever he felt sad.

Scott's mom had said it wasn't the ice cream that made

me feel better. It was the company.

I flipped the picture over. I couldn't look at it anymore. That kid had been naive. Heck, I'd been naive when I told Erin I'd be able to make time for her and the baby.

"When my mom left, it ripped me apart."

Tommy and Scott stared at me from the couch.

"You guys were there. You know it. I'm heading things off at the pass. I'm a lone wolf, dedicated to my work. I have to keep my head in the game if I'm going to compete with the folks coming up who are younger and hungrier."

"Or not," Scott said. "Why not take a break? Step back a bit." He glanced toward the kitchen. "Life's too short."

"Work is my life," I said, shrugging. Who would I be without it? I'd be no one. "I told Fumetsu I'd move to Tokyo for a bit."

"What?" Tommy said.

"To beat out Liz Bolton's group," I said. "It's what I had to promise them."

"You shouldn't have to do that," Scott said. "We can find someone else, some other way—"

I waved him off. "I want to do it," I said. "Work is my priority. Always has been and probably always should be."

. . .

ERIN

"Erin, put that down," Katie shouted at me from across the room.

"I'm fine!" I yelled back. "It's an empty vase for flowers, not a fifty pound barbell."

Nat snatched the vase from me and whispered. "You shouldn't even be here."

"Where else would I be?" I said, as she placed the crystal vessel on the round table nearest us. Classes had ended for the summer, Ian and I were no longer talking, and the only thing on my schedule was waiting for this baby to make his debut. Of course I'd be on hand for the Glenfield Gala setup in our school gym.

I glanced slyly at the open door leading to the hallway. Most of the volunteers had shown up to help before the event later this evening, but not the head of the finance committee. Ian was nowhere to be found. Not that I was looking for him.

"Kind of a low turnout." Katie set a box of party favors on the table next to us. Maria Minnesota stood on stage, barking orders to the moms and dads who had volunteered their morning to move tables. Most of these people were legit bosses in their professional and home lives. I relished watching an Instagram celebrity give them the business.

"The funeral is today." Nat tied a black ribbon around a white chair cover. The entire gym floor had been dotted with chairs wearing sheets. Ghost chairs surrounded us.

"I didn't know." Ian and I hadn't spoken in almost a week, not since our fight in my condo. He hadn't tried to get in touch, and fuck if I was going to make the first move.

"Have you spoken to him?" Nat asked.

I shook my head. Some dude put his arm around Maria Minnesota's waist and kissed her cheek. She smiled up at him—love. *Enjoy it now. It will all go to shit sooner or later.* "It's on him to get in touch with me."

"His friend's mom died," Katie said. "Hate to say it, but I think it might be on you."

I moved the vase to the exact center of the round table. "I spent ten days waiting for him to text or call while he was in Japan." That was the most alone I'd ever felt—ever. Even when things had been bad between Dirk and me, even after he'd already moved on to his nurse girlfriend, I'd been okay. I'd numbed myself with food and TV. But not hearing from Ian had turned me into a jealous, fretful goober, and

I'd promised myself I'd never be that person. "I'm Dr. Erin Sharpe," I said. "I deserve respect and consideration." It had become my motto.

"You do," Nat said. "But maybe text Ian to offer your condolences. He and Scott's mom were really close."

I smoothed out a wrinkle on the tablecloth. "Scott doesn't even know I exist." That hurt. My friends and family, my colleagues, heck, Maria Minnesota, knew about Ian and the baby. Had it been easy for me to put that info out there? No. I was a knocked-up, forty-year-old principal who'd had a one-night stand with Glenfield Academy's golden boy. It embarrassed me to even think about how I got to where I was right now, how I'd completely gone against every one of my guiding principles.

Still, I shared the news with everyone who asked—and even those who didn't.

"I'm sure Ian had a good reason—"

I cut Nat off. "You're sure Ian had a good reason?" I barked. "You? The person who told me to steer clear of him from the jump? Now you're making excuses for him simply because he's sad?"

Nat reached for my shoulder, and I shook her off. "I called Tommy to tell him I was sorry, and he told me Scott's mom had been sick for a while, which was probably why Ian had kept the news from him."

"Since December. That was how long he didn't tell his best friend that he was about to be a dad. It's now July, and I'm due any second." I shook my head. "But Scott not knowing is the icing on the cake. Ian only cares about his work. He will always put his career first. I've spent my entire life going after jerks who only cared about themselves. I'm done with that." I pulled out one of the chairs and sat. My legs had swelled to tree trunks.

"So, you're okay?" Katie asked.

"I'm fine."

Nat's eyes jumped to the door, and a big smile spread across her face. I followed her gaze, half expecting to find Ian there. But it was just Chris.

Nat ran to him and enveloped him in a massive hug, wrapping her legs around his waist.

I had to look away. That kind of all-encompassing passion no longer existed for me. Maybe it never had. I'd gotten three hot nights with Ian and a baby, and I had to stop expecting more.

Chapter Fourteen

Ian

Tommy and I rode with Scott in the procession from Faith, Hope, and Charity in Winnetka to St. Joseph's cemetery in Wilmette. Scott's mom had gotten a beautiful summer day for her services. The sun beat down from a cloudless sky and a faint breeze rustled the branches of the trees that flanked her gravesite.

I'd thought about my own funeral somewhat recently. The whole turning-forty thing had been a catalyst. I'd wondered who would show up. I was a guy whom everyone knew of, but not many people really knew. Probably the whole "work first" thing. Who'd take time out of their day to see me off?

Erin? Probably not. Not anymore.

Scott and his mom, however, had inspired the entire North Shore community to come out and pay their respects—fund-raising folks from their church and the Academy, heck, even the mayor had shown up. I spotted Liz, Ja, and Luisa hanging out near the back of the crowd, which actually choked me up, honestly. They really had no obligation to be here.

After Scott's mom had been laid to rest, my eyes scanned the crowd again—searching for something. An all-encompassing emptiness filled my gut, which made no sense. This was Scott's mom's funeral. He was the one who was supposed to feel loss, not me. I had to be the strong one.

But then I saw the blond hair poking out from behind a nearby oak.

No, not Erin.

My mother.

My own mother.

I stepped back, hiding a bit, and took a moment to examine her. We hadn't been in the same room since...I couldn't remember. Maybe it had been ten years?

She and my dad were talking, laughing, him in a suit, her in a long, flowing floral dress—sans a bra. She'd become one of those crunchy, braless ladies ever since she moved to Hawaii. She'd pulled her long, graying blond hair up in a bun, and she wore no makeup. This was not the mom from my childhood. That woman had worn business suits and had hair like a helmet. Now she looked like she reeked of patchouli.

I took another step back, ready to make a run for my car. She was here for what? To make amends? Too fucking late for that now.

This woman was a stranger to me, and I owed her nothing.

And the empty pit in my stomach grew. My life fast-forwarded twenty years in the future to some other funeral or wedding or whatever. I'd run into my own kid, and he'd think the same shit about me, that he owed me nothing. He'd look at me like I was a pathetic old man who was still trying to capture his youth with work and women.

And he'd be right.

Then I'd see Erin across the room, and I'd have to leave. I'd have to make up some excuse before ducking out and jumping on a plane to somewhere halfway around the world just to avoid feeling any way at all about it.

With a deep breath, I approached my parents. "Hi," I said.

My dad gave me one of those one-armed man hugs, which was hardly more than a pat on the back. Then he headed off to chat with one of his golf buddies.

My mom held back. Her eyes watered, and I tried to ignore them. Just seeing her emotion—heck, seeing her, period—had drummed up all kinds of nonsense inside me.

"You're here," I said, stating the obvious.

"Scott's mom and I were good friends...back in the day. And...I wanted to be here for him...and you."

I stared at the ground, digging a divot in the dirt with the toe of my Sperry loafer.

"Your dad told me about the baby. Congratulations."

"Thanks," I said. "It's, well...thanks." I had planned for years what I'd say to her if I saw her again. I'd yell and scream and blame her for every mistake I'd ever made. But today, at my best friend's mom's funeral, I could only feel sad. Sad that this stranger was my mom. Sad that I was about to take on that outsider parent's role in my own life.

My mom smiled sadly. There were new wrinkles next to her eyes. "You look more and more like my dad."

These were the kinds of things she always said to me when we talked, the things I used to do as a baby, the absolute truths she'd known about me when I was five—that I looked like her dad, that I loved math, that Ryne Sandberg had been my favorite baseball player. These were all still true facts to her, the only facts. She knew me, her son, at the surface level only. She had no concept of my day-to-day life. Our relationship went no deeper than faded memories and banal trivia.

And this was how I'd know my son, too. I'd see him on occasion, weekends, maybe the odd week here and there, and

I'd only know the little things, the inconsequential things that anyone who'd been in a room with him five minutes would know.

"Hey, Mom." My mind catalogued all the things I could say to her, the accusations and guilt trips. Instead I said, "Thanks for coming." I reached for her, and she hugged me. It was the first time we'd touched like that in years. I hadn't hugged my mother in maybe a decade, not because she was dead or in prison or separated from me in some legitimate way, but because I'd chosen long ago to shut her out on account of her life choices. She'd tried to make amends many times over the years and I'd thwarted her every attempt.

Like James would probably thwart mine.

She squeezed me tight. "Thank *you*." She let me go and tucked a stray strand of hair behind her ear. "I want to know more about this baby." She smiled at me under a heavy gaze.

"There's not much to say," I said. "The mother and I aren't together." I glanced around absentmindedly, always keeping half an eye out for Erin, just in case.

My mom looked so sad, I added, "It's okay."

"Can we grab dinner tonight before I take off?" she asked.

I shook my head. "I'm leaving."

She cocked her head.

"I'm moving. To Tokyo. For work." My plane left later this evening. After the funeral, I'd head home to finish packing.

"But the baby...?"

"He'll be fine." My voice faltered, but I covered with a cough.

"Ian." She put a hand on my forearm, and I let her. "I know I'm not the one you want to get advice from, but look at your cautionary tale of a mother. Don't make the same mistakes I did. Don't work yourself until you implode." She nodded toward my dad. "Don't push your love away until it's so far gone it'll never come back."

I nodded, and I kept nodding. It was the only thing keeping me from crying. I had to get out of there, away from her, at least for the moment, before I totally lost it here, in this public place. "Good to see you." I turned and walked away. I had to. My chest was going to burst with emotion all over Scott's mom's grave.

Wiping my eyes while walking back to the car procession, which was about to leave for the post-funeral banquet, I ran into Liz and her partners. We shook hands all around, and I choked down a sob or two. "Thank you so much for coming," I said.

"Of course," Liz said. "We're so sorry."

I pulled out a handkerchief, blew my nose, and nodded. "So…how's business?" Enough death, dying, and existential crises for one day. It was time to get back to brass tacks, to my comfort zone.

Liz shrugged. "Could be better."

It had been bothering me for days how I'd taken down their company in Tokyo. I wasn't sure why. Maybe it had been because she was a fellow Rambler. Whatever it was, I had regrets. "Look. I'm sorry about how everything went down. I didn't mean to be that big a dick."

"Yes, you did." She chuckled.

"Okay, yes, I did." I glanced over at Scott, who was now talking to Tommy and Susie, who was holding Maeve. My mom had gone back to talking to my dad like he was a stranger she just met. It was the same way she'd just talked to me. It was how the entire world would talk to me if I moved to Tokyo for a few months, if I kept traveling and moving and working at the pace I'd been. "I think you guys are great, though," I told Liz. "You're young, you need more capital and connections, but you're great." I drew in a deep breath.

Liz laughed. "If only you old guys could throw us a bone

once in a while."

"Where'd be the fun in that?" I waved my phone at her. I had to get out of here, to go home and pack before my flight, before I took off for Tokyo for three months—the first three months of my son's life.

Almost at my car, I paused.

Maybe I owed it to myself—and Erin and James—to give this one more shot, to give her one more chance to let me back in. No regrets. Nothing left unsaid.

I pulled out my phone typed two simple sentences: *"I'm sorry. Please give me one more chance. Please, Erin."*

And…crickets.

· · ·

ERIN

"Has anyone seen my phone?" I yelled over the roaring sound of the hair dryers. Nat, Katie, and I were getting our hair and makeup done before the Gala tonight.

Katie, in the seat next to me, rummaged through my purse. "I don't see it. Is it in your pocket?"

I patted my hips. I was wearing a cotton dress. "I don't have any pockets. Shit." My eyes scanned the floor around my chair. No phone, just hair clippings.

"Have you seen my charger?" came Nat's voice behind me.

My eyes met Nat's in the mirror. "Crap."

"You left it in the gym," she said.

I nodded. "Sorry." I hit the side of my head. "Pregnancy brain." I'd left my phone charging in the Glenfield Academy gym, where I'd plugged it in while setting up for the Gala this morning.

"No problem," Nat said. "I'll get it tonight."

I examined my face now. Yvette, my stylist, was currently

playing around with my pixie cut, preparing to add little crystal butterflies to my hair. I'd already had my makeup done—an iridescent eye shadow paired with a smoky eyeliner. Super dramatic. Paired with my slinky blue dress, I'd look like a whole new Erin tonight.

Aside from the whole swollen legs/stomach like a beach ball thing, I was a fox. A catch.

Too bad I had no one to impress.

Maria bombarded Nat, Katie, and me as soon as we stepped foot in the gym later that evening after we'd gotten all gussied up. "The cake!" she screeched. "The cake is ruined." She apparently hadn't left the gym all afternoon and had planned to get dressed at school. Her hair was up in curlers, and she wore only a robe.

"What's wrong with the cake?" I asked, dessert being the most important part of any fund-raising event.

"Come see." She dragged us toward the dessert table on the far side of the gym, next to the stage. The place looked great, honestly. The Glenfield Academy gym had been transformed into a luxury ballroom, complete with twinkling lights and candles. The black, white, and silver theme made the whole thing *très chic*.

"Look." Maria pointed at the cake.

The two-tiered confection had been covered in white roses and piped with silver ribbons. "It's gorgeous," I said.

"Yeah." Maria's nostrils flared. "Now taste it."

"Taste it?" Nat asked.

"Try a bit of the frosting."

I glanced at my friends. Maria had lost her mind. She was now asking me to behave like a three-year-old at his birthday party, dunking my finger into the icing before the cake had been cut.

Maria dove right in. She plunked her index finger directly into the bottom tier and scooped out a glop of frosting.

"You ruined the cake," I said.

"Try it." Her eyebrows narrowed to a V.

I leaned over and licked a bit of frosting from her finger. "What the?" I spit it out immediately and wiped my mouth with my forearm. "That's disgusting." Katie handed me a cocktail napkin from the nearby bar and I used it to clean my tongue.

Maria pointed accusingly at the cake. "The bakery used flour instead of powdered sugar. The whole thing's inedible."

My shoulders dropped. "Dang."

"Exactly."

"What are we going to do?" The rollers bobbed against Maria's head.

I almost asked her what *she* was going to do—seeing as she was the fund-raising chair. But she also appeared to be in a very fragile state right now, and she was currently still in her dressing gown, while the other ladies and I had come completely glammed up.

Also, I was the boss.

"Katie." I pointed to my sister. "Go to Mariano's. They have delicious desserts—pick up some cupcakes. People love cupcakes."

"They do," Katie agreed.

"Nat, call the bakery and tell them what happened. We expect a full refund."

"Aye-aye." She glanced around the room. "But I need my charger."

I pointed to the other end of the gym, near the door. "You'll find it over there, with my phone."

Maria looked at me expectantly.

"And you," I said, "go get beautiful."

All the girls took off on their various tasks, and I spun around to survey the scene. We were still about a half hour away from when we'd open the doors. The decorating committee was currently lighting candles and setting up place cards. I stepped over to the bar and grabbed a bottle of Dasani.

"Erin!"

Mouth full of water, I glanced up to see Nat sprinting toward me.

"Erin." She waved my phone in my face. "Ian texted."

I covered my mouth to keep the water from dribbling onto my dress.

She handed me the phone and waited while I read the messages. "I'm sorry. Please give me another chance," then "I'm getting on a plane to Tokyo tonight, but I don't want to. Tell me you want to try to work things out," then "I miss you so much."

Nat, hand on hip, said, "He texted you." She raised a perfectly plucked eyebrow. "He. Texted. *You*."

I stared at the phone. That's what I'd said I wanted, right? That I'd been waiting for him to get in touch with me. And now he had.

My fingers grazed the screen as if ready to give him everything he wanted.

I pushed the phone away from my body. "No. What's changed? Is he just going to hurt me again?"

"You won't know unless you text him back." Nat shoved the phone toward my chest.

"But I said I'd be fine on my own." Texting Ian back would amount to failure on my part. "And I am. Totally, utterly fine. I—"

Something pinged in my gut.

"It's not that you're not 'fine' on your own," Nat said. "It's just that maybe you'd be more fine with Ian, and he with you. You've been miserable without each other. Maybe try being happy for once."

I grabbed my midsection. "What the…heck?" I caught

myself before the very un-principal-like "fuck" slipped out. I was at work, after all. A trickle of wetness had started running down my leg. My underwear was wet.

Did I just pee in my goddamn pants? I glanced down at my gorgeous blue dress. A circle of wetness grew just below my groin on my ice-blue dress.

"Erin?" Nat draped an arm around my shoulders. "You okay?"

I was still peeing. More and more liquid kept dribbling down my leg. But no. I wasn't peeing. I was actively stopping the flow of urine, at least I thought I was.

My skin chilled as the realization hit me. "I think my water broke." My knees buckled, but Nat helped keep me upright.

"Oh my God. We have to get you to the hospital. I'll call Katie to come back." She was on her phone in a split second.

I held my own phone with shaking fingers. "And I'll text Ian."

Chapter Fifteen

IAN

I chuckled as the credits rolled on *One Day at a Time*. Erin had suggested I watch this show, and I'd "whatevered" her about it until today.

I stood and stretched my legs in the business class lounge, downed the remainder of my scotch, and checked the departure board. My flight to Tokyo was still delayed, as we were waiting on a plane from Denver or something. I didn't care about the logistics.

After buying a second drink, I flopped back in my chair and turned on another episode of *One Day at a Time*.

"Great show," said the woman next to me.

My knee-jerk reaction was to counter with a "not interested," but instead I looked over. She wore a wedding ring and her hands cradled a definitely pregnant belly. Like, so pregnant, I wouldn't feel weird commenting on it. "Congrats," I said.

She rubbed her stomach. "Thanks."

I turned back to my show, which no longer tamped down my loneliness. This sadness would go away, eventually. It happened when my mom left, and it happened when my childhood dog died. At some point, probably weeks or months from now, I'd be totally fine.

About halfway through the episode, my ears registered the word "Tokyo" through my headphones. I pressed pause and listened. My flight was now boarding.

I packed my tablet and picked up my bag, nodding goodbye to the pregnant lady next to me. I stepped toward the door and hesitated a moment before reaching into my briefcase.

I'd turned off my phone as a defense mechanism, so that I wouldn't have to endure the silence of not hearing from Erin. At least with the power off, I could pretend that maybe she was texting me back.

But now, just before boarding a thirteen-hour flight, I had to give us one more shot. I turned my phone on and waited for the inevitable nothing.

My phone buzzed.

And it buzzed again.

I had a text. From Erin.

Right there on my home screen.

"Ian, my water broke. Meet me at the hospital."

I dropped the phone, spinning around as if looking for confirmation that this was really happening.

"You okay?" the pregnant lady asked.

"My..." What even was Erin to me now? Shit. "The woman I love is in labor," I announced.

My new pregnant friend clapped with joy. "Congratulations. Are you flying to see her?" She nodded toward the departure board.

Was I flying to...? I shook my head. "No." I picked up my

phone. "No. I'm flying away from her. I have to go to her."

"Where is she?"

"Downtown," I said.

She wrinkled her nose.

"What?"

"Good luck getting there."

She pointed to the TV broadcasting the local news. A large protest currently marched its way up and down both sides of the Kennedy, the expressway I needed to get me into the city.

"Shit."

"Good luck." She returned to her book.

There was more than one way to get downtown. The blue line connected right to the airport. I hadn't taken the El in years, but desperate times.

Before leaving the safety of the business class lounge, I called Erin, because texting wasn't good enough. Yanking at my hair, I waited as her phone rang.

• • •

ERIN

None of this matched up with my birthing plan. It was all wrong. This was not how my child was supposed to enter the world.

When I had gone to the birthing class, I'd been all, like, "Yes, I'm going *au natural*, no drugs, no nothing." I'd planned on walking this baby out of my uterus, as nature intended.

But when I got to the hospital, Dana put me in a bed with an IV, pumping me full of antibiotics because of this dumb strep positive something or other—I didn't understand the full scope of the situation. And then she strapped a fetal monitor to my gut. And then there was the whole thing where I was leaking fluid everywhere I went, which seemed to make

Katie and Nat pretty uncomfortable, so I stayed in bed, like a patient, like a chump. I was no longer in charge. I loathed not being in charge.

I checked my phone again. Still nothing from Ian.

"He's not answering me," I said. "Still."

"He's probably away from his phone," Nat said. "Like you were all afternoon, remember?"

"Maybe he's being all unresponsive out of spite. Maybe he's playing games."

"With a woman in labor?" Katie said. "Ian'd never be that callous. Right, Nat?"

Nat looked lost in thought. "Not with Erin," she decided.

Oh, good. So I had to play Nat's hunch that I was the exception to the rule.

I breathed through every contraction, envisioning the pain as it radiated from my midsection down through my legs to my toes. These were truly the worst period cramps known to womanhood. I tried to focus on *The Office*, which Katie had started streaming for me on the TV, but most of the jokes barely registered in my brain. I was on edge, waiting for the next wave of pain, never quite knowing when it was going to come or how bad it was going to get. That was the worst part, the not knowing. If things stayed the way they were, I could handle it. But where was my current pain on the scale? I had no frame of reference. If this was an eight, I could handle a ten. But, Holy Mother of God, if this was a four, I was fucked.

"I can't do this," I said.

"Sure you can." Katie, texting away, mindlessly patted my hand.

"You're doing great." Nat fluffed my pillow, which only made me more uncomfortable. She was the opposite of Katie, hovering, cooing. It stressed me out. I felt like I had to acknowledge her every move, when really I just wanted to be left to my own devices. It was like when I had the flu or something. Just leave me alone with my TV. Let me handle this on my own. I was the boss, after all. At least, I used to be the boss. Today I felt more like a zoo animal whose entire nether regions were on display for all to see.

"When my sister had her baby, you could hear her screams for miles." Nat squeezed my shoulder. "You're doing way better, comparably."

"Not helping." I gritted my teeth, forcing my eyes to focus on Michael Scott. The last thing I wanted to do today was entertain people, to constantly reassure everyone else that I was doing fine, that I was super excited about this day and the fact that I was about to push a fully formed child through my vagina. The truth was, I was freaked the fuck out, constantly teetering on the edge between tears and anger.

Where was Ian?

"Can I get you more ice chips?" Natalie's eyes were still on the door.

"No!" I barked. My next contraction was starting. And fuck the ice chips. Fuck all of this motherfucking, cocksucking bullshit!

Nat bent down next to me and started panting right in my goddamn ear, but it was the wrong rhythm, the wrong depth. I tried to push her away, but she took it to mean that I wanted to hold her hand. She clutched mine, and it was all wrong. Her hands weren't strong enough. They were too smooth, too small.

"Stop watching the door!" I cried as the pain reached my toes. "He's not coming!"

"He might be," Natalie said.

"He also might not be." Damn it. I'd been doing just fine on my own without Ian. I gestured toward *The Office* on the TV, tears streaming down both cheeks. "Maybe I don't need a guy like Ian. If anything, I need Jim, someone safe who will go all-in on me, who won't bail, who will prioritize me over everything. That is not Ian Donovan."

Katie's phone made a noise like she'd just sent a text. I'd been hearing that stupid sound all afternoon. "It took Jim, like, one hundred years to get up the nerve to tell Pam how he felt."

Curse Katie and her TV trivia knowledge. What did she actually know about anything? Jim was perfect. Jim was the ideal. "But he did tell her eventually," I said. "And he stuck by her."

"And then they had marriage trouble in the later years."

"What the fuck, Katie?" I said. "Why are you arguing with a woman in labor? Jim is perfect, full stop. Leave it alone!"

"Maybe you should face facts that you're not a Jim girl," Nat said softly. She was still next to me, cradling her own hand like a wounded bird. I'd crushed it during the last contraction. Not my problem. Not today. Sorry, Natalie.

"What's that supposed to mean?"

"Jim's too sweet for you, too romantic. He'd be all up in your business all the time, being too nice, and you'd lose it. Like you said when I was telling you about how Chris and I are in touch constantly. You're not that kind of girl. You like your space. Ian can give you space."

"You're so right!" Katie said. "Erin would eat a guy like that alive."

"That's why you and Ian kind of made sense." Nat kept bringing up Ian, like her crushed hand had taught her nothing about the force of my rage.

"There's such a thing as too much space," I said. "He basically ignored me while he was in Tokyo, and now he's avoiding my texts while I'm in labor."

Nat reached down and stroked my hair. "I guarantee he's not avoiding your texts. I'm sure there's a good explanation, and we'll hear from him as soon as he gets the messages.

Don't jump to conclusions. Not yet."

"And if he doesn't call me?"

"Then fuck him. You don't need his ass."

I squeezed her hand, much gentler this time. "Thank you."

The three of us stared at my phone, waiting.

Then it buzzed. Ian's name popped up on screen.

"He's calling!" I squealed.

"So answer it." Nat covered my hand with hers. "And be nice. Remember: innocent until proven guilty."

I nodded and answered the phone.

"Erin?"

My heart almost dissolved into a pool of mush when I heard his voice.

"I'm on my way," he said.

"Okay." Those were the only two syllables I could choke out at the moment.

"I'm sorry I didn't respond before. My phone was off. It's the only reason why. I'm at the airport now, but I'm getting on the blue line and coming for you. Wait for me, please. I…" He paused. "I prioritize you."

And I said, "Good. Because, Ian, I need you."

Chapter Sixteen

IAN

I texted Natalie as I ran to the blue line. *"I'm hopping on the train now. The Kennedy is shut down. Text me with any news. ANY NEWS."*

She wrote back, *"Will do."*

I skidded to a stop in the blue line vestibule. These weren't the machines I remembered from back in my twenties. These loomed in front of me—shiny, new, and intimidating. I pressed the touch screen. Nothing. I tried the next machine. Still nothing.

A young guy with red hair scanned his phone on the turnstile and went through. I glanced around. No one in sight. There wasn't even anyone working the booth.

I took a deep breath and jumped the turnstile.

And a cop stopped me immediately.

"Sir," she admonished me, one hand on her billy club.

I held up my hands in surrender. "I'm sorry," I said. "I have to get downtown. My...my girlfriend"—white lie, sure, but hopefully about to come true—"is in labor."

"Still doesn't mean it's okay to break the law."

"I know." I showed her my phone, because the redheaded guy had somehow used his to get past the gate. "I haven't ridden the El in years. I admit it. I'm a total old fart when it comes to using those machines."

She raised an eyebrow. "You can get the Ventra app."

I nodded. "Good to know." I mentally added, "For next time."

She put her hands on her hips.

Oh, for this time. She would not free me from this hell. I tapped on my phone screen as my train pulled away.

I groaned.

"Another one will leave in ten minutes."

"I guess now I have time to…" I waved the phone.

She nodded.

I created a Ventra account, entered my credit card info, and paid the whole, whopping $2.25 to ride the train.

"And next time," the officer said, "you'll know what to do."

I hopped on the waiting blue line train and found a seat across from two musicians carrying guitar cases. I nodded at them, my feet tapping at a rate of four times per second.

I finally exhaled when the train pulled out of the station. *"Train on the move,"* I texted Nat. My battery was low, less than 10 percent, but I had to keep it on, in case Erin needed me.

The battery percentage ticked down as the train moved, and I did turn it off once we went down in the tunnels. *Please don't need me right now*, I mentally begged Erin. *I'm on my way.*

At the Washington station, the train stopped, the doors opened, and then they never closed. The musicians and I sat there staring at each other for a full minute. "What's going on?" I asked.

They shook their heads. I glanced out the door. No commotion. Then a mechanical, disembodied voice boomed through the speaker: "This train will no longer run due to a service delay."

"Someone jumped on the track," one of the guitarists said.

"How do you know?" I asked.

He shrugged. "I don't, but isn't that always the case?"

"Shit." If that was, in fact, the case, we'd sit here for hours. I grabbed my suitcase and briefcase and dashed off the train, turning my phone on as I booked it up the stairs. No texts from either Erin or Nat. I had 2 percent left on my battery life. I used it to open my Lyft app. Surge pricing, plus a good fifteen-minute wait.

"What the fuck?"

My eyes scanned my surroundings. There was something going on, a protest. Whatever had been happening on the Kennedy had made its way down here.

I was only a mile from the hospital. I had a suit on and was transporting a heavy suitcase, but I'd have to run—in July, in Chicago, when the humidity was nearly corporeal. My shirt dampened almost immediately as I took off on foot toward Randolph. I booked it left on State, flipping off anyone who tried to hit me or head me off.

When I finally made it to the hospital, I left my suitcase at the front desk, and hopped on the elevator. When the doors opened on the labor and delivery floor, the receptionists stared at me. I'm sure they saw my sweaty clothes and disheveled appearance and figured they should keep their fingers on the panic button under the counter. "Can we help you?"

"Erin..." I panted, clutching the cramp in my side, while leaning against the desk. "...Sharpe."

"Are you a relat—"

"I'm the father," I cut her off. "The father of the baby."

"Room 1402," she said, shaking her head. I heard her mutter to her coworker, "Took that guy long enough to get here," but I ignored it. I had no time to deal with other people's nonsense. It *had* taken me long enough to get here, but the only person whose opinion of me mattered right now was Erin's.

I skidded around the corner and halted right outside room 1402. The door was shut. I knocked. Erin's sister, Katie, opened the door a crack. She wore a blue hospital gown and a hairnet. "Hey," she said.

"Tell me I didn't miss it." I couldn't have missed it. I couldn't let Erin down again. I was here for her from this point on, whatever she needed.

"Ian?" Erin called from inside the room.

Katie let me in, and the nurse handed me my own blue gown and cap, plus slipper thingies for my shoes. I threw them on as fast as I could, hoping they at least somewhat masked my damp, sweaty clothes, and darted to Erin's side. She hadn't delivered the baby yet. I'd made it in time. A nurse sat on a stool at the foot of Erin's bed, rubbing her shins while her feet hung in stirrups. "Just hold on," the nurse was saying. "The doctor is finishing up a C-section. You're about ready to go, but she'll be here any minute."

I grabbed Erin's hand and patted it, kissing her fingers. She squeezed back.

"You made it," she said.

"Just in time, apparently." I was choked up already. The room was full of machines and towels and all the stuff they'd need to help the baby once he arrived. It was cold and sterile, dark and frightening. And I'd almost let Erin do this on her own. I'd never leave her side again.

"I can do this now," Erin said, arching up to see the nurse at her feet. "I'm ready," she said. "Ian's here."

Panic drained color from the nurse's face. "But the doctor—"

The nurse didn't even get the sentence out before Erin started pushing. About two seconds later, a baby's cry filled the room. Just like that, we were parents.

Holy shit.

I gazed down at Erin next to me. I'd soaked through my clothes getting to her, but she'd barely broken a sweat. She grinned at me. Emotion radiated through my entire body—joy and fear and relief and a bursting, all-encompassing love. I brushed a lock of hair out of Erin's eyes, leaned down, and kissed her forehead. "Good job, Mom," I said.

• • •

ERIN

Ian and I finally had a chance to be alone about an hour after the baby was born.

The word "alone" had taken on a new meaning now that we were a trio…if that was, in fact, what we were.

"So." I'd actually gotten the kid to latch for breastfeeding, and now he was hungrily taking in food.

"So." Ian had pulled the armchair next to the bed in my new, private hospital room. I had changed into my own pajamas, which Katie had fetched for me from home—along with the rest of the hospital bag I'd painstakingly prepared weeks ago, when I'd assumed I'd be safely at home when I went into labor.

"What's up?" I laughed.

"We're parents." He tickled the kid's feet.

"No going back now. Right, James?" I had a hard time saying his name for some reason, even though it was a perfectly reasonable name, my father's name, the name Ian and I had both agreed upon. It felt strange on my tongue, though, like it weighed more than one syllable. This was our kid's name. Did it suit him? Would it suit him? "Is this weird?"

"Is what weird?" Ian pulled his eyes away from our son's adorable baby foot.

I shrugged. "Everything."

He moved to sit next to me on the bed and wrapped his arm around my shoulders. He kissed the top of my head. "Yeah, it's weird," he said. "But it's also pretty amazing."

James had fallen asleep eating. I unlatched him, fixed my shirt, and let him rest against my chest. God, that was nice. "So…Tokyo."

"What about it?" His eyes were on James's sweet face.

"Are you going back?"

He cupped my chin and turned my face toward him. "Never."

I raised an eyebrow. "You're never going back to Tokyo? Ever?"

"Not unless you're with me."

"But the business—"

He touched James's little foot. "The business can suck it."

"Ian." He had no idea what he was saying. The baby haze had consumed him, siphoned away his reason. This was a man who lived to work.

"I mean it." Now his eyes were on me.

"Where did this come from?" I asked.

"My mom, of all people. She showed up at the funeral, and I realized I don't want to make the same mistakes she did." He laced his fingers between mine. The heat of his skin melted me. Here we were, sitting in my hospital bed, our weird little family. "I've always avoided attachments, because I figured work would always be there for me. But that's not even true. There are hungrier, less-jaded young people out there waiting to take my place. And when they finally do, what will I be left with?"

"James and me," I said.

He touched my nose. "Exactly. Scott said he can start picking up some of the slack, and I think we might want to start bringing in some fresh blood, giving ourselves a little break. We are the bosses after all. What's the good of being the boss, if you can't take time off?"

I felt something in my face shift as he mentioned Scott.

Ian noticed. "I told Scott, by the way," he said. "It was actually his idea for me to step back, be with my family—I'm talking about you, by the way." He raised his hand above his head. "It now goes 'you and James'"—he lowered his hand a tiny bit—"'my friends and family'"—he pointed to the floor—"'work and everybody else.' If you think you can handle that."

"I know I can."

Ian leaned down to kiss me, just as the door to my room opened up and in streamed Katie, my mom and dad, and two other Baby Boomers, whom I guessed were Ian's parents.

While everyone else huddled near the door, my mom ran to James and cooed, tracing a line down her grandson's forearm. He rested his head on my T-shirt, gazing up at her with slate-gray eyes under a tangle of black hair, just like his dad's. "Hi, James," my mom said. "I'm Grandma."

Those words choked me up.

"Mom and Dad, this is Ian."

"And"—Ian smiled down at me—"Mom and Dad, this is Erin."

"So, Ian…" My dad sized up Ian, the man who had knocked up his daughter—after a night of drunken debauchery, but my dad didn't know about that. "Tell us about yourself."

I could've sunk into the mattress from the embarrassment and the weight of it all—introducing my parents to my man friend, whose baby I'd just pushed out of my birth canal. And being introduced to his parents, whom I was meeting for the first time while wearing no makeup and old pajamas.

"What are your intentions?" my dad asked.

"Dad," I admonished him, finger on the call button. I needed a nurse to bounce these people out of here.

"I'm going to be a personal trainer," Katie blurted out of nowhere, shifting the heat to herself. Thank God for siblings.

My parents stared at her like she'd grown a second head. "You're what?"

"Good for you," Ian's dad said.

"I'm going to get certified and help people get fit."

My mom straightened up. "Did we not just pay for four years of college for you, not to mention a wedding for a marriage that lasted two years? Now you're going to take more classes? And who's going to pay for it?"

"Erin's friend Nat owes me some money," Katie said. "Or she will…"

My mom's jaw dropped. "Someone owes you—"

"I'll pay for her classes," I said, coming to Katie's rescue, because of the sibling code. "I'm gonna…pay for her personal trainer classes, and she's going to…"

"Help with the baby." Katie turned to face my parents. "I've been floundering, frankly, working as a substitute and a glorified assistant. I didn't know who I was or who I wanted to be until I started working out. I want to help other people realize their potential, too."

My mom blinked at me. "You two had this all planned out?"

"All planned out," I lied.

Now Mom focused on Ian. "And you're okay with all this, the Bobbsey twins doing their little daycare thing?"

He widened his eyes at me, and I shook my head. My parents were the absolute biggest dorks. He straightened his shoulders and looked at my mom, probably regretting everything he'd just gotten himself into. "I'm totally cool with it," he said. "I'm taking some time off to be with Erin and the baby, but after that Katie will be a huge help."

"And you're getting married?" My mom folded her arms.

"Mom," I said, "why do we need a ring when we already have a baby?"

"Katie, did you know about this?" My mom glared at her second daughter.

"Hey, Mrs. Sharpe." Ian directed her attention to the other side of the room. "Maybe you can help us with the car seat, since you're probably an expert. It's our final exam. They won't let us leave the hospital until we pass this last test. Feed the kid? Check. Change a diaper? Check. Once we figure out how to buckle a car seat, we apparently have all the tools we need to raise James for the next eighteen years."

Katie sat next to me on the bed and tickled James's toes. "I think we're gonna make a great team." She nodded toward Ian. "All of us."

I smiled as he grinned back at me. He managed to distract my mom with flattery, which Katie and I had never been able to do. "I think we will," I said.

Chapter Seventeen

ERIN

"I haven't cried this much since he was born!" I stood in front of the bathroom mirror, wiping my eye makeup off again. I kept ruining my mascara. This was my third attempt at a smoky eye.

I glanced down at James, who stared up at me from his bouncy seat on the tile floor next to the tub. He pulled his mouth into this huge, toothless grin, and my tears started flowing again.

"I can't do this!" I cried.

"You can and you will." Ian, in nothing but a pair of plaid pajama pants, walked in carrying two steaming mugs. Here was yet another reason to stay home—my hot, half-naked man friend, who knew just how I liked my coffee and who'd be available for an Afternoon Delight while James napped. "Your school needs you, and you need your school." He nodded toward James on the floor. "Little Dude and I are going to be just fine."

My lip started to quiver at the thought of my tiny baby being just fine without me.

Ian held up a hand to staunch my tears. "I mean, we'd be more fine with you here, obviously, but the two of us will survive the day, when we're not counting down the minutes until your return." He grinned as he sipped his coffee.

I knew he was messing with me, and I giggled. I was being foolish. Everything would be fine. I'd head back to work and James would spend the day with his dad. Easy peasy. It was just that James and I hadn't spent much time apart since he was born, save for the one night in August when Nat and her new husband, Third-Base Chris, had basically hijacked the baby and ordered Ian and me to go out for a grown-ups-only dinner. I'd kept my phone on the table the entire time, ringer volume jacked all the way up, just in case.

And so had Ian.

"This is good." Ian rested his hands on my shoulders. "For you and the kid. You love your job, don't you?"

I nodded. I did love my job. And, after three months of taking care of an infant all day, every day, I did long for other problems to solve beyond "Does this poop look weird?" or "How do I get rid of cradle cap?"

Ian massaged my neck, which almost put me in a trance. "Then go back to work today and be brilliant. You'll be home before five."

"I'll be home before five," I repeated absentmindedly.

"And when you get home, there will be an amazing dinner waiting for you."

I focused on his milk-chocolate eyes. "What kind of dinner?"

"James and I were thinking…roasted chicken with root vegetables. And I have a bottle of champagne chilling in the fridge for you, for us, to celebrate your first day back at work."

I kissed his cheek. "You're the best," I said.

"I am."

I turned back toward the mirror and picked up my mascara wand again. Ian believed I could do this, and I believed him. He'd been through this himself, after all. He'd stayed home with me for two weeks after James was born, before heading back to work to train their new junior partners. His VC group had absorbed the one owned by Liz, Ja, and Luisa, and they would handle—exclusively—the Fumetsu rollout.

Ian hadn't cried when he returned to work, because he'd known our kid would be well taken care of. And now it was my turn. Now that the millennials were taking over most of the day-to-day stuff at work, Ian had decided to stay home with our three-month-old for another two weeks, to fill in the gap between the end of my maternity leave and my sister being able to nanny for us full time while pursuing her new career as a personal trainer.

"What are your plans for today?" I asked.

"Well, we're going to walk to the grocery store first, then maybe hit up story time at the library. You know, or he'll just nap all day and I'll watch the talk shows."

"All good options," I said.

"And we'll miss you all day long and wish you were here."

"Sure, you'll miss me terribly while you're out at the park with all the hot, young moms." I raised an eyebrow at him. We could joke about this. We were partners, and I trusted him. If something between us stopped working, we'd discuss it and we'd fix it.

"Those young moms have nothing on your old ass," he said with a wink. "And you know it."

"I do know it." I waved a hand down my body to indicate my dress, which was bright blue and covered in ducks. "Honestly, this dress," I said. "What do you think?"

"Honestly, it's ridiculous." He leaned in and kissed my cheek. "But it's totally, utterly you, so I love it."

I punched him in the arm, kissed the baby goodbye, and headed out for my first day back at work, ready to conquer the world.

. . .

IAN

"Okay, buddy." I mimed covering my eyes and James mimicked me. I glanced over at my mom, who was perched on her couch next to her boyfriend, the infamous Blake. My dad sat across from them in the armchair. The three of them sipped coffee while watching their eighteen-month-old grandson play his favorite game—hide and seek.

This was truly the definition of paradise—spending time with my family in Hawaii during January, AKA the dead of winter back in Chicago. Though, if this were truly the perfect Norman Rockwell painting, I probably would've been sharing this with my dad and mom, who were still married and madly and love. But that wasn't my life. This was my life. And Blake wasn't all that bad, now that I'd given him a chance. Sure, he was kind of dramatic about recycling and solar power and liked to walk around barefoot everywhere, but that was part of his charm. And he made my mom deliriously happy, which wasn't nothing.

Plus, my dad seemed to like him, too, so who was I to hold a grudge?

I crouched down next to James on the floor. "Let's count to ten."

James said each number with me in his adorable toddler voice—pronouncing "three" like "free" and singing the word "ten" like it was the most important syllable in the English language.

"Now it's time to find Mommy," I said.

James's chubby hand wrapped around my index finger

and the two of us waddled out of the family room and into the kitchen. "Where Mommy?" James asked.

"I don't know..." I scanned the floor, hunting for Erin's long blue floral dress. "Mommy's a good hider."

"Mommy?" James yelled, and his voice echoed through the halls.

We turned toward the lanai, and that's when I spotted Erin's six-months pregnant belly sticking out from behind a potted palm tree. I chuckled. This was how we met—the night of the bachelorette auction. She'd ducked behind a tree to scratch her butt, and...the rest was history.

I beckoned James around the corner and into the living room and whispered in his ear. "Mommy's behind the tree." Then I handed him a small velvet box. "Give this to her."

I stood back as James toddled toward his mom, holding the four-carat ruby and diamond ring I'd been carrying around for weeks—ruby for James's birthstone, and diamond for our baby girl, Lois, who was due in April. I'd planned on giving it to Erin tonight at dinner, when we had reservations for two at the fanciest restaurant on the island, but this was better. This was perfect. This was us.

James waddled up to the tree and handed the box to his mom.

"James, what is this?" Erin's voice pivoted to her no-nonsense, boss-lady tone. "Where did you find this? Is this Nana Jeanne's?"

I stepped into the room, pausing for a second to admire my family—my kid in his diaper and a Thor T-shirt, my girlfriend, swollen with our daughter, leaning down to talk to him. How could I have ever believed I didn't want this? "It's not Nana Jeanne's," I said. "It's yours."

With a skeptical principal look on her face, she opened the box. Her hand flew to her mouth immediately. I knew why. The ring was that spectacular. "Ian. What? What is this?"

I strolled over, plucked the box from her hand, and got down on one knee. James did the same, kneeling right next to me, gazing up at his beautiful mom.

"Will you marry me?" I asked.

Her eyes kept darting from me to the ring.

I winked. "I know you're not about 'defining' things, but I think it may be about time that we admitted this thing between us is permanent." I took her hand and slid the ring onto her finger. The sunlight through the window glinted off the rock. Scott and his new boyfriend, a famous silver-fox news guy he'd always had a crush on, had helped me pick it out. They'd done well. Really well. This was an oval ruby surrounded by tiny round diamonds. According to Scott, it was similar to the ring Prince Andrew gave Sarah Ferguson, but he was sure our marriage would meet a better fate.

I'd told him I didn't believe in fate or bad omens. I believed in Erin and me.

"So?" I said. "What's your answer?"

"Yes!" she squealed. "Of course yes!"

"Then why do you look so pained?"

She rubbed her belly. "Because I want to get down on the ground to kiss you, but I don't know if I'll be able to get up."

I hoisted James into my arms, and our happy little family shared hugs and kisses behind the tree where we'd found Mom.

Acknowledgments

Many, many thanks to everyone who helped get this book off the ground—Beth Phelan for getting the ball rolling and Louise Fury for kicking it in the goal. Last cheesy sports metaphor, I promise. (Read: no, I don't.)

To everyone at Entangled Publishing for making this book awesome. To Kate Brauning and her team—especially Bethany Robison and Hoda Agharazi. I've loved working with you ladies over the past five(!) books. Bethany, I feel like I really do need to insert a sports SOMETHING here for you, so here it goes: you are all as lovely and wonderful as Christian Laettner in his prime. I can bestow no higher praise upon you.

Thank you to Liz Pelletier, Stacy Abrams, Curtis Svehlak, Holly Simpson, Riki Cleveland, Alethea Spiridon, Heather Riccio, and everyone else who saw this book to completion. Winky-face.

Thank you to my home team, especially John for getting everyone out of the house when I needed to work and the kids for being okay with watching way too much *Gravity Falls* this summer when I was on deadline.

Thanks to my mom and dad and John's mom and dad for helping me out by watching their grandkids so they didn't have to watch TV *every* afternoon.

And thank you—yes, *you!*—for reading.

About the Author

Julie Hammerle writes romance novels that focus on nerds, geeks, and basket cases falling in love. On the YA side, she is the author of *The Sound of Us* (Entangled TEEN, 2016) and the North Pole romance series (Entangled Crush, 2017). A graduate of Butler University with degrees in secondary education and Latin with a minor in music, Julie lives in Chicago with her family and enjoys reading, cooking, and watching all the television.

Young adult novels by Julie Hammerle...

THE SOUND OF US

ANY BOY BUT YOU

ARTIFICIAL SWEETHEARTS

APPROXIMATELY YOURS

Discover more August titles…

THE JULY GUY
a Men of Lakeside novel by Natasha Moore

A summer fling might be the only thing that gets art professor Anita Delgado through the next few weeks. When she meets sexy salvage specialist Noah Colburn, he's tempted by her offer of a no-strings fling for the four weeks she's in town. But he's running for major of his hometown of Lakeside, New York, and the gossip mill is notorious for ruining even the most upstanding reputations.

WHAT WERE YOU THINKING, PAIGE TAYLOR?
a Belles of St. Clair novel by Amanda Ashby

After her carefully ordered world imploded, Paige Taylor cracks up. It seemed like a good idea at the time to reinvent herself—move from Manhattan to the tiny beachside town of St. Clair—and take over the local bookstore. Soon Paige discovers that reinventing herself takes more than just a change of address and a pithy quote on Instagram. She needs to face the truth about her life, and that's something she can't do alone.

ADVENTURES IN ONLINE DATING
a novel by Julie Particka

For Alexa McIntyre, the answer to everything comes down to numbers. Three sons. One divorce. One great life…except her boys are getting older and they really need a man around. Enter the number twenty, as in after twenty minutes with someone she knows whether or not she wants them in her life. So, she hatches a plan to meet any man who remotely strikes her interest—for a twenty-minute date at her favorite coffee shop. It's the perfect way to find her perfect match in the most efficient way possible.

CPSIA information can be obtained
at www.ICGtesting.com
Printed in the USA
LVHW032309260319
611967LV00001B/8

9 781730 897177